Stephen Tud

THE VISITORS BOOK

Stag & Arrow Books

Copyright © 2009 by Stephen Tudsbery-Turner
The moral right of the author has been asserted
First published in Great Britain in 2009 by Stag & Arrow Books

The characters and situations in this book are entirely imaginary and bear no relation to any real person or actual happening.

This book is sold subject to the condition that it shall not, by way of trade or otherwise, be lent, re-sold, hired out or otherwise circulated without the publisher's prior consent in any form of binding or cover other than that in which this is published and without a similar condition including this condition being imposed on the subsequent purchaser.

Printed and bound in Great Britain by the Lancing Press. Photograph on the front cover courtesy of The Frith Collection

ISBN   978-0-9561788-0-0

For Hilary

Stephen Tudsbery was born in the Wirral and educated at Repton and at the Universities of Durham, Newcastle upon Tyne and Cambridge. For many years he was Senior Lecturer in History and the History of Art at the North East Surrey College of Technology. He is the author of three books on picture postcards and various articles on historical, artistic and heraldic subjects. He spent his early years in Surrey, the setting for **The Visitors Book**, *but now lives in Somerset. He lists his interests as dog walking and collecting livery buttons.*

CHAPTER ONE

1.

Tuesday 8th February 2000

After about twenty minutes Tim reappeared with a solitary policeman, who gingerly made his way to the edge of the well and directed his flashlight down the aperture. It was a far more powerful beam than had been produced by the Colleymore torch and it clearly picked out the bones at the foot of the shaft. The skull, which the torch had barely located, was now perfectly visible.

The policeman stared down the well and sighed deeply. 'Right,' he said. 'I'll get somebody to have a look at it, but I think it's the museum service and not the police you'll be needing.' He paused for a moment. 'Now that's interesting,' he went on. 'Take a look at that.'

I walked around the side of the well to stand beside him and looked along the shaft of light that was directed to a point slightly to the left of the skull. There, amidst a jumble of stones and bits of bone, lay a small silver pistol.

2.

Saturday 27th June 1964

Nicholas Markham turned his rather battered Ford Anglia off the Barcombe Road and drove slowly down Woodland Avenue. He stopped outside number 16 then reversed the car into the drive, braked and turned off the engine. He walked over to the front door and pressed the bell. Moments later the door was opened and Nicholas found himself face to face with a small girl.

'Hullo,' he said. 'My name is Nicholas Markham. Is your mother in?'

The girl stared at him. 'My name is Bobbie,' she announced, then she turned and shouted, 'Mummy, there's a man here to see you.'

There was a sound of dishes being put on a draining board and then a woman who could not have been much older than Nicolas himself appeared in the hall. She wiped her hands on an apron and then ran her fingers through her hair in a slightly distraught fashion.

'Thank you dear,' she said to the girl, who promptly vanished. 'Mr Markham,' she went on. 'This is really very kind of you. David said that you would look in. Come in and have a cup of tea and then I will show you the book. I'm Jane Emburey, by the way.'

Nicholas followed her into the hall and then on into what was clearly a sitting room. 'A dishy red-head,' that was how David Walton had described her, and he was certainly right about that. Nicholas stared at her appreciatively then pulled himself together.

'I'm Nick,' he said.

"Victor,' said Jane to a large man with dark hair and heavy horn rimmed glasses, who was sitting by the window engrossed in the sports pages of the daily paper. 'This is Nick Markham, who is going to help me with the heraldry.'

'If I can,' put in Nicholas, modestly.

Victor Emburey raised a hand in greeting. 'Good luck to you,' he said. 'Jane, if you are making some tea I will be in the garden with Sam,' and he heaved himself out of his chair and disappeared through the French windows.

Nicholas remembered the words of David Walton. 'He's not exactly my cup of tea, but he is the captain of the cricket club. I'm his vice, so I have to keep in with him. He's not someone I would choose to have a drink with, unless of course it was just after the match, but he's a great leg-spinner and an excellent organiser. I sometimes wonder what Jane saw in him. I think they met at university.'

'Have a seat while I get the tea,' said Jane.

She walked back into the hall and Nicholas walked over to the window. Victor was in the garden playing French cricket with two small children, a boy and the girl who had answered the door. Nicholas watched them for a moment.

'There's a crest on a book that she's discovered,' David had said, 'and there are several more in Drayfield Hall itself. She'd be terribly grateful if you could explain them to her.'

Nicholas smiled. He could certainly do that without any trouble and it would be an excellent excuse to get inside the house. Last time they had been rather shirty about the whole thing. Maybe they thought he was after the family silver, though as far as he knew the place was all but derelict. As he gazed out over the lawn Jane Emburey appeared out of a side door with a tray of drinks, which she placed on a garden table. She then returned to the house and moments later appeared through the sitting room door with a second tray.

'Tea and ginger nuts,' she announced. 'Now, I'll find you exhibit A,' and she walked over to the bookcase. She picked up a rather battered brownish book and handed it over to him.

Nicholas carefully put his tea on a side table, put a ginger nut into his mouth, and turned the book over curiously. It had discoloured over the years but quite clearly what had once been probably bright red had now faded do a dull beige. The words *Drayfield Hall* were just distinguishable on the front and beneath them one could just make out a coat of arms, a chevron between three birds of rather indiscriminate appearance.

Nicholas smiled, 'Well, that is certainly heraldry,' he admitted somewhat indistinctly through his ginger nut.

He opened the front cover of the book and there in bold italic script was the date 1860 followed by a list of names, all written in the same hand. It was a visitors' book, the entries in which commenced in 1860 and finished in 1914. At first they were simply lists of names in the same handwriting but as he turned the pages the lists were replaced by actual signatures. On some pages faded sepia photographs commemorated long forgotten house-parties, but sadly more of these had been torn out than had survived. Race meetings were clearly the occasions for visitations, and Derby Weeks almost always resulted in a large turnout at Drayfield Hall. Members of the Sedgley family were regular guests at these gatherings – twelve seemed to be the favoured number of visitors – and it was obviously a common occurrence for three or four members of any one family to attend a house party.

'Quite a find,' said Nicholas, a pensive look crossing his features. 'The Sedgleys of course were the family who lived at Drayfield Hall.'

Jane nodded. 'And the coat of arms belongs to the Sedgleys, that at least I do know.' She looked at him as if for confirmation.

Nicholas looked at a line of writing on a page inserted inside the front cover. *Argent a chevron between three sedge-warblers azure*, he read.

'I looked that up in *Burke's General Armory*,' said Jane. 'But I am afraid that that represents the be-all and the end-all of my heraldic studies. I am doing a dissertation on upper class entertaining in the late Victorian and Edwardian periods and I am using Drayfield Hall as my local example. My other chief example is Bearwood in Berkshire. It was once the home of the Walters, who were the proprietors of *The Times*, but it is now a school. The architect was Robert Kerr, who wrote a book about Victorian house planning. He was the subject of my BA dissertation.'

Nicholas nodded. 'Who lives at Drayfield Hall now?' he asked.

'No one,' replied Jane. 'The park is open to the public and is administered by a joint-committee set up by the two neighbouring parishes. The house itself is deserted. Well, not quite. The servants' wing has been turned into flats and some of the upstairs rooms are used occasionally by the local technical college, but basically it is empty. Except for what was once the library? That is furnished as a board room and it is used every now and again for meetings of the joint-committee. There are three family portraits hanging there and I hope to use at least one of them to illustrate my work.'

'Then how did you get hold of the Visitors Book?'

'I got permission to go round the house. I wrote to the committee and was told to contact the park superintendent. He took me round one day. We found this there with one or two other bits and pieces.'

She stood up and walked across the room to a cupboard. Nicholas watched as she rummaged around inside then produced a cardboard box and a pile of books. 'My treasures from Drayfield Hall,' she said.

She handed them to Nicholas, who gingerly opened the box. Inside were some broken china labels bearing the legends *Port, Malmsey and Sherry*, a twisted silver desert spoon, and a penny with the head of King Edward VII and the date 1909. The books were five bound copies of *Punch*, not dissimilar in appearance to the Visitors Book. He looked up at Jane, who coloured slightly.

'Yes,' she admitted. Mr Innes thought he was giving me six *Punches*. He didn't realise that one was something else. Never mind. I will take great care of it and hand it over to the committee when I have finished. I am concentrating on a house party that took place in the summer of 1897,' she went on. 'I am researching the various people who were at the party and the reasons why they were there, and I am also working out the logistics of the place. You know, how food got from the kitchen to the dining room, how the staff went around the house without colliding with the gentry, all that sort of thing. At Bearwood, for example, there were six separate staircases. One was the principal staircase. One was called the Men's Staircase and one the Women's. Then there were the Back Stairs for the servants, a staircase for bachelors and another for young ladies. Can you believe it? And as for nurseries, there was a Day Nursery, a Night Nursery and one for strangers. Talk about apartheid! Drayfield unfortunately only had two staircases and one nursery.'

'Why 1897?' asked Nicholas.

'A good photograph to go with the list of guests,' replied Jane promptly. 'Plus the fact that it was the party when the then Miss Sedgley met her future husband for the first time. Finally, but this is a bit of a long shot, I have been told that there is a letter in existence that mentions the house party of 1897. I haven't set eyes on it yet, but it is in a collection in Shropshire. It was written by Lady Violet Sedgley to her sister, the Countess of St Boswells. My tutor told me about it. He had been doing some work in the National Register of Archives and came across the reference.'

'Is Jane boring you with her house party?' said Victor as he walked in from the garden. 'I warn you, she will go on and on about it until the cows come home.' He spun the cricket ball he was carrying and flicked it from one hand to the other. 'Do you play?' he asked.

'I am afraid not,' said Nicholas, 'though I do follow the game and help out with the school team. And there's no need to worry about the house party. I find the whole thing quite intriguing. No, I mean it, I really do.' He turned to Jane. 'So, where are you up to now and what is going to happen next?'

'You'll be getting the Jameson Raid next, that's what'll be happening unless you keep your wits about you,' said Victor, as he carefully balanced the cricket ball on the top of an empty candlestick on the mantelpiece. 'Charles Sedgley and the Jameson Raid. It normally takes about fifteen minutes, and then you'll be into the American connection and the Marlborough House Set. Still, you are welcome to stay on here for as long as you like.' He selected a pipe from the rack next to the candlestick and tapped it noisily against the side of a strategically placed and very heavy glass ashtray.

'Charles Sedgley,' said Nicholas thoughtfully, 'What do you make of him? He wasn't the owner of Drayfield Hall, was he? I vaguely remember the Jameson Raid.' He blushed then hastily went on, 'I'm more at home with the Tudors and Stuarts. Wasn't it something to do with the Boer War?'

'No,' said Jane. 'Charles Sedgley was a nephew who was a guest at the party, but you are almost right about the Jameson Raid. It was an unauthorised invasion of Boer territory by a British force in 1896, four years earlier than the war. I have discovered that Charles Sedgley was involved. It is all quite exciting. I think that I'll apply to be a lecturer when I get my degree. Research becomes quite addictive, you know.'

'Grubbing around in the cellars of derelict houses,' said Victor scornfully, 'and you'd be no use as a lecturer. You hate talking in public. And how many more months have you got before your course finishes?'

But his wife was not listening. She was rummaging through some papers on the desk by the door. She retrieved a single typed sheet from a pile of manuscripts and brought it over to Nicholas. 'Here you are,' she said, 'the 1897 house party. Plus,' and she picked up the Visitors Book from the floor beside her and opened it, 'the signatures and a photograph. What more could you ask? Oh and there are books on local history and architecture in the bookcase. I am very well set up, you see.'

Nicholas ran his eyes over the typed list and then at the row of signatures in the book. It was the Derby Party of the early summer of 1897. The list ran to eleven names including one obvious family group. There seemed to be a fair sprinkling of officers and aristocrats and the photograph was an excellent one. Ladies reclined elegantly upon garden furniture; a young man disported himself languidly on a bentwood chair on the left hand side of the picture, while other gentlemen stood importantly in the background. The sun appeared to be shining brightly upon the scene.

'And you say that one of these men had just been involved in something dubious in South Africa,' said Nicholas. I wonder what everybody thought about it at the time. Now that would be a nice tit-bit for your research,' and he placed the Visitors Book and the typed sheet on the coffee table in front of him.

Victor snorted derisively and strode out of the room. Jane watched him go, a look of annoyance on her face. Then she shrugged her shoulders.

'There's nothing like a little encouragement from the home,' she said with a note of resignation in her voice.

A sudden noise erupted in the garden and she walked over to the window. 'Oh dear, Bobbie appears to have been hit with a tennis ball, she sighed. 'Have a look at the exhibits while I pop outside and repair the damage.' She looked at him and smiled. 'Who'd be a mother, or a wife for that matter. Still, I don't think it's serious,' she went on in a more cheerful tone of voice, and she disappeared into the garden.

Nicholas picked up the book and stared at the front cover, a far away look in his eyes. He then opened it where a picture postcard of Drayfield Hall acted as a convenient bookmark and stared once again at the guest list for the party of June 1897. There were eleven signatures in all, the most flamboyant by far being an Elizabeth Howard, whose name appeared about half way down the sheet. At the top were the names Rossdale and Sybil Rossdale, and under them Archie Rossdale and then Matilda Rossdale. Then something at first quite indecipherable, which after a while metamorphosed into George M. Johnstone, or it could have been George N. Johnstone or even George H. Johnstone. Presumably the typed sheet would reveal all. The obviously extrovert Elizabeth came next, followed by a much neater Millicent Howard. Two sisters, perhaps, he mused, or even a mother and daughter. In which case, where was Mr Howard? At number seven appeared the rather crabbed name of Robert somebody, whose surname appeared to start with either a C or a G. When he moved on to number eight Nicholas realised that it was a C and that the mysterious Robert was in fact a Robert Carey, for the signature beneath his was in immaculate copperplate and was clearly that of Charlotte, presumably Mrs Carey. Finally, and rounding off the party, appeared the signatures of Lancelot Rutherford and the infamous Charles Sedgley.

Nicholas studied the last signature carefully then turned his attention to the typed sheet, which clarified the Johnstone doubt. It was an M. There were also dates besides some but not all of the names. Charles Sedgley, for example, was born in 1875 but there was no date of death.

Mr George M. Johnstone, on the other hand, had no dates at all. 'Poor old Johnstone had no dates at all,' hummed Nicholas to the tune of *Colonel Bogey* as he stood up and walked across to the bookcase.

A search through several shelves of books finally unearthed the new Pevsner's *Surrey* in the *Buildings of England* series, and next to it was the much earlier *The Little Guide* to Surrey. Nicholas looked up Drayfield Hall in the Pevsner.

Asymmetrical, two storeyed, neo-Tudor house built in the early c19 to the designs of Sir Jeffry Wyatville. Stuccoed and castellated. Its most prominent piece is a three-storeyed central tower with angle buttresses and pinnacles. The kitchen wing belongs to an earlier c18 house.

He far preferred the more lyrical description in *The Little Guide*. *Drayfield Hall, the seat of the Sedgley family, is a rambling and picturesque early nineteenth century mansion with an imposing tower and crenellated skyline. The main entrance is flanked by a charming loggia, and the interior contains some interesting heraldic decoration. Remains of a former building have been incorporated into the present house. Local legend has it that Lord Nelson visited Drayfield in 1805, shortly before the battle of Trafalgar, with Lady Hamilton, whose portrait still hangs in the drawing room.*

Nicholas replaced the books and walked over to the desk. He picked up a sheet of paper that lay on the top of the pile there. It was clearly work in progress. *The Victorian Country House – a machine for entertaining in – apologies to Le Corbusier,* Jane had written. Underneath she had listed below the heading *Drayfield*, (a) Offices, including kitchen and laundry, (b) Storage, including cellars, (c) Accommodation and (d) Thoroughfares. She had ticked the first three and had ringed the fourth, 'thoroughfares', in red. Nicholas smiled and returned the sheet to the pile.

When Jane returned from the garden she found Nicholas still studying the Visitors Book.

'All well with the wounded,' she said. 'Sorry to have left you to your own devices for so long.'

'No problem,' replied Nicholas, honestly. 'I found it quite fascinating. Now, tell me all about these Sedgleys. I notice that you haven't got the date of Charles's death nor for that matter any dates at all for George M. Johnstone?'

'The Sedgleys arrived at Drayfield in the last years of the eighteenth century,' said Jane. The first Sedgley, a Charles, seems to have made his fortune dealing in horses during the Napoleonic Wars. His son, a Frederick, predeceased him but his grandson, another Charles became a pillar of county society. He was High Sheriff in 1856, I think. I've got the exact date in my notes. It was really the classic example of three generations make a gentleman. His son, a second Frederick this time, inherited when number two Charles died unexpectedly four years later. He was then a serving officer in the Grenadier Guards. He was the Frederick Sedgley who was living at Drayfield at the time of the party. I got all this from a local history written in 1909 and of course there is a mass of detail in *Burke's Landed Gentry.*' I had to get both those from the library. I got horribly confused by all the Charles's and Fredericks, but I drew up a family tree and it all became a little clearer.'

'And Mr Johnstone?' said Nicholas.

'Not much, I am afraid,' said Jane thoughtfully. 'He was another soldier, but apart from that, nil. He's the only member of the house party who is a virtual blank. I have even got something on the Howards, who were American. Johnstone doesn't feature anywhere, except some brief details about his military career from the Army Lists. It's very annoying. All I have discovered is that he seems to have resigned his commission in 1896 and certainly doesn't seem to have served in the Boer War.'

'What about the Howards?' asked Nicholas.

'Mrs Howard was a Miss Tritton. Her father, Andrew Tritton, was a dollar millionaire who made his fortune building railways in the Middle West. Millicent Howard must have been immensely wealthy and she went on to marry the future Lord Rossdale, who was Archie Rossdale at the house party. It was probably all set up. Archie Rossdale to marry Millicent Howard, Lancelot Rutherford to marry Victoria Sedgley. The other youngsters were Charles Sedgley,'

'Of Jameson Raid fame,' put in Nicholas.

'Of Jameson Raid fame,' agreed Jane, 'and Matilda Rossdale. And that's the end of the matchmaking. They certainly didn't marry each other and it doesn't look as if they married anybody else either. At least if they did Burke's doesn't mention it. I wrote to the present Lord Rossdale, but he was very vague and said that he understood that she went out to Africa as a missionary, but he couldn't be certain. Apparently all the family papers were lost during the war when a bomb destroyed their London house in Knightsbridge. Still we have two happy couples at any rate.'

'Oh I don't know,' said Nicholas. 'If they were arranged marriages they probably all hated each other.'

He stared at her as she walked across to the desk and shuffled through some of her notes. A dishy red-head certainly, but it wasn't just the striking hair or the fact that she was nicely curved in all the right places, it was the eyes, yes that was it, the eyes. They were almost green in colour and possessed a liquid luminosity that he found quite mesmerising.

Jane looked up. 'Are you concentrating?' she asked severely.

Nicholas pulled himself together. 'Of course,' he replied. 'Go on.'

'My theory is,' said Jane, as she rejoined him on the sofa 'that Charles Sedgley and George Johnstone were best friends and served together in South Africa. When they were forced to resign their commissions after the Jameson Raid they went off together to be mercenaries somewhere.'

'And were never seen again,' said Nicholas with a smile. Anyway, I gather you want me to look round Drayfield Hall? David said that you were told that some of the shields commemorated family marriages.'

'I would be enormously grateful if you would,' replied Jane earnestly.

'Well, one of your books says that the heraldic decoration is well worth a glance so I am sure I will enjoy myself,' said Nicholas easily. 'Count me in and I shall be only too pleased to do some blazoning for you. That means describe the coats of arms in heraldic language, and of course I will translate and explain,' he added hastily.

'Can you manage a day next week?' said Jane. 'David said something about you being a teacher in Sussex. I mean do you get a half day or anything?'

'I could manage Thursday afternoon, if that is any good for you,' replied Nicholas. 'I am finished by mid-day all being well.'

'That would be perfect,' said Jane. 'I'll have to be back by four o'clock to collect Bobbie, but if Mr Innes will open up for us at two that will give us the best part of two hours. If we finish the heraldry early we could hunt for more treasures in the housekeeper's room. That's where I found the books. The drinks labels and the other things were in the cellars.'

'There's one thing I don't understand,' said Nicholas. 'How come you are doing a degree at all? I hope I am not prying but you are, how shall I put it?'

Jane stared. 'Rather long in the tooth?' She smiled. 'Well, I had the option to convert my BA dissertation into an M.Litt. thesis but marriage rather got in the way. Now the children are both at school and Sam is a weekly boarder I thought I might take the plunge. My tutor, who was at Durham and is now at Newcastle, was happy with the idea, so here am I, a student at thirty.'

She picked up the phone and dialled a number. 'Mrs Innes,' she said, 'it's Jane Emburey here. Could I speak to your husband?'

All appeared to be in order. Nicholas's credentials were established, the heraldic decorations were to be the reason for the visit, and they were expected at Drayfield the following Thursday at two. Nicholas stood up to go.

'By the way,' said Jane suddenly. 'How did David discover you?'

Nicholas thought quickly. 'Barcombe Library,' he answered.

'Barcombe Library?' said Jane in surprise. 'That's a long way from Steyning.'

'It's a bit of a coincidence,' said Nicholas slowly, 'and I don't know why I didn't mention it earlier, but …'

'Hang on a second,' interrupted Jane as the noise of children quarrelling drifted in through the French windows. 'That's Bobbie in trouble again,' and she turned and ran into the garden.

Victor, who clearly felt that the cries of small children were women's business, strolled in from the hall. 'What a din,' he remarked. He walked over to the sofa, sat down and kicked off his shoes. 'If you ask me this whole thing is a total waste of time. What on earth does she want with a degree anyway? It's not as if she needs a job.' He puffed vigorously on his pipe. 'There's absolutely no need for all this gallivanting around,' he said definitively. 'It's a good thing she has an understanding husband.'

Nicholas made up his mind.

'What's a coincidence?' asked Jane as she re-entered the room.

'I was actually doing some heraldry when David met me,' said Nicholas. 'I knew Barcombe had a better reference section than Steyning and I was on my way back from a match. Now,' he went on quickly, 'I must be on my way. Goodbye, Victor. I'm sure we'll meet again.' He walked into the hall and turned to Jane who had followed him.

'Until Thursday,' he said.

'Until Thursday,' she replied, and watched with a quizzical expression on her face until his car turned out into the road.

3.

Thursday 27th May 1897

Edward Lord Rossdale, a tall silver-haired and distinguished looking man, glanced at his friend then stared out of the window of the Savile Club at the traffic making its way down Piccadilly.

'It may be very kind of them,' he said, 'but it is quite out of the question. Lady Sarah is a married woman and what she does is her husband's affair. Matilda is my daughter and until she is married she is my responsibility. There is no question of her going to South Africa. Apart from anything else the political situation out there is immensely volatile, what with the raid and its aftermath. No, it would be dangerous as well as most unsuitable.'

His companion nodded. 'Brenton was talking of the British South African Company and the possibility of a secondment, but I think I have dissuaded him. At the present time it could jeopardise his future in the regiment.

Look at what's happened to young Sedgley,' and the Earl of Eversleigh shook his head sadly as he made his way back to his favourite armchair.

'He will be with us at Drayfield,' said Lord Rossdale, following him. 'There will also be a couple of other officers. Rutherford from the Blues and Johnstone from the Royal Welch. Johnstone's the son of a neighbour of mine in Norfolk. Frederick Sedgley's other nephews are not able to be there this year and Lady Violet was short of eligible bachelors. Johnstone has also been in hot water in Africa, but that seems to be no handicap when it comes to invitations, so I felt safe in suggesting to Archie that he should fix things up with all parties.'

'Brenton still has hopes for Matilda, or so Lady Eversleigh tells me. He will be anxious to have his name on her card,' said the Earl of Eversleigh, and he signalled to a passing servant. 'Cigars if you will, Wilkins,' he said.

'It would be an excellent match, not to mention a great weight off my mind,' said Lord Rossdale. He thought for a moment. 'According to my wife, Matilda still thinks in terms of Sedgley. He spent a lot of time with us as a youngster, but has absolutely no prospects and now that he has resigned his commission goodness only knows what the future will hold in store. No, tell Brenton to put his best foot forward, Faint heart never won fair lady, as my father used to say.'

Lord Eversleigh smiled and selected a cigar from the box that the club servant offered him. 'And what of your birds this year,' he asked. 'Are we to expect good shooting? McNaught is very optimistic about our prospects and by the time you join us the heather should be positively stuffed with them;' and he eased himself back into his chair and sipped his whisky appreciatively.

4.

Monday 31st May 1897

Shortly after three o'clock on a warm summer's afternoon two young ladies were engaged in serious conversation by the lily pond in the gardens of Drayfield Hall. The sun was high in the sky and both were making full use of their parasols. Matilda Rossdale, Tilly to her friends, the taller of the two, was dressed in green and her auburn hair was pinned up beneath a wide brimmed hat. Victoria Sedgley's hat, although not quite as striking as her companion's, was still equally fashionable, as were the pronounced leg-of-mutton sleeves of her blue silk blouse. As they spoke Victoria produced a small pair of gold rimmed spectacles from the tiny handbag she carried and strained unsuccessfully to see the letter from which her friend was quoting.

'Eligible and available, that's what he says,' said Tilly Rossdale to her companion, and she perched herself carefully on the stone wall that surrounded the lily pond. She turned her attention once again to the letter in her hand. 'Apparently Mr Rutherford is one of Archie's fellow officers in the Blues and Mr Johnstone is in the Royal Welch Regiment. It's Mr Johnstone who is our neighbour in Norfolk,' she went on. 'Mama and Papa were talking about it in the train. His father is the man who has taken Nuttall Priory, and he asked Papa as a favour if he could get his son invited here for the Derby Party.'

'He will probably be quite dreadful,' said Victoria Sedgley firmly. 'Otherwise why would he have to be angling for an invitation?'

'No, listen,' said Tilly. '"Very dark and handsome with wavy hair and flashing black eyes. Quite a dish for you young ladies." That's what Archie says. He's been away in Africa with the forces of the Chartered Company.

Presumably that's why he needs some introductions.' She studied the letter once again. 'Where was I? "You are sure to like him as he has quite a reputation for daring-do and he was well in with Rhodes and Jameson." Well, I think that is most encouraging, don't you?' she asked.

'If he was in Africa he must have met Charles,' said Victoria. 'I wonder if he left under a cloud as well?'

Tilly coloured. 'Archie says that he took no part in the Raid, so perhaps they never came across one another,' she replied. 'Anyway, we'll find out when they all turn up. Archie says he will be here first thing tomorrow. When are the others due to arrive?'

'Mr Rutherford and Mr Johnstone are coming down from London this afternoon and Charles will get here this evening,' replied Victoria. 'Now, what does your brother say about Mr Rutherford?'

Tilly glanced at the letter once again. 'He's the third son of Lord Rutherford of Achnasheen, so that's all right. He goes on to say, "Lance Rutherford is quite a different kettle of fish and he still has his commission. He hasn't been to South Africa and wouldn't know the difference between a Boer and a Kaffir. On the other hand he is a thoroughly decent fellow and is sure to be a great favourite with Lady Violet."'

She frowned. 'Why do you think he says "he still has his commission"?' she asked. 'Does that mean that Mr Johnstone no longer has his? But earlier he says that Mr Johnstone took no part in the Raid.'

'I think Mr Rutherford sounds rather boring,' said Victoria. 'Especially if Archie thinks he will go down well with Mother.' She seized the letter from Tilly and adjusted the tiny gold rimmed spectacles. 'Look,' she went on, 'you missed this bit. "I did hear that there had been a problem regarding a card game in Cape Town and that Johnstone was not in good odour with the High Commissioner's circle."

How exciting! Perhaps he is a professional gambler and that's why he no longer has his commission.'

Tilly stared into the lily pond and watched as various goldfish flitted in and out of the shadows. 'Tell me about the others,' she said.

'Sir Robert Carey is a friend of father's. Dry as dust. He's a lawyer and a Liberal. Mother didn't want him to be invited but father insisted. To make matters worse he doesn't approve of gambling, so I doubt whether he will enjoy the sweepstake. I have no idea about his wife but I doubt whether liberal lawyers make particularly exciting matches. If you want to impress him talk about Gladstone.' Victoria giggled, folded up the letter and returned it to her friend.

'Go on,' said Tilly.

'The famous Mrs Howard and her daughter Millicent.' Victoria paused and thought for a moment. 'She's the one who's going to marry the Duke of Westerdale. Mother wanted them so that she could worm her way into the Prince of Wales's circle. Mrs Howard is a great friend of the Countess of Dudley. Mother thinks that if Mrs Howard has a good time then we will all be invited to parties at Marlborough House. Mother still has hankerings after the high life. It all comes from being an earl's daughter, I suppose. Father hates the idea. In fact I believe that Mother's insistence on Mrs Howard gave him the necessary leverage to introduce the dreadful Sir Robert Carey into the family circle. And what of Lord Brenton?' she asked suddenly.

'What about Lord Brenton?' said Tilly suspiciously.

Victoria glanced at her companion over the rim of her spectacles. 'He will be at Lady Clonkerry's ball,' she said.

'It is a matter of supreme indifference to me whether or not Lord Brenton will be at Lady Clonkerry's ball,' replied Tilly with acerbity.

'But your parents . . .' began Victoria.

'My parents will of course be delighted,' said Tilly, 'and I daresay Mama will dance with Lord Brenton. I will not, if I have any say in the matter, which of course I won't,' she added despondently. She looked up and along the Rose Walk that led to the house. 'Aha!' she said suddenly. 'Things appear to be happening. Put away your spectacles and we will perambulate slowly and with great state towards the terrace. It could be the glamorous Mr Johnstone, but then again it could be the unspeakable Sir Robert Carey.'

The two young ladies gathered themselves together and walked slowly down the Rose Walk. Their skirts dragged slightly on the gravel but then, as Tilly had remarked earlier, at a Sedgley Derby Party fashion was absolutely everything.

'Girls,' said Lady Violet Sedgley, as they reached the terrace. 'Come and meet Mrs Howard and Miss Millicent Howard. Mrs Howard,' she went on, 'allow me to introduce my daughter Victoria and her great friend Matilda Rossdale.'

'Miss Sedgley, your mother has told me a great deal about you,' said Elizabeth Howard as she held Victoria's hand in the manner approved of in royal circles. 'Miss Rossdale,' I have just had the pleasure of speaking to your parents in the small drawing room.' She held out her hand to Tilly Rossdale and gave a rather husky laugh. 'Where I come from, of course, your small drawing room would be our very large drawing room.' She paused. 'Do forgive me,' she went on. 'That is a joke I have cracked before on several occasions. It is one of my favourite ice-breakers.'

'Do you *crack* jokes in America?' asked Tilly curiously.

'Indeed we do my dear,' replied Elizabeth Howard. 'Here, I suppose, you exchange pleasantries? Now ladies, may I present to you my daughter Millicent?' and she motioned towards the girl standing beside her.

Tilly noticed with slight annoyance that Millicent Howard was almost as tall as she was herself and strikingly good-looking into the bargain. Her blonde hair, and there seemed to be plenty of it, was piled up under her hat and her eyes were a brilliant corn-flower blue. Tilly recalled only too well that Charles was particularly susceptible when it came to young ladies matching that particular description. She pulled herself together and put a brave face on it.

'Good afternoon, Miss Howard,' she said politely. 'Will you take a turn with us in the garden? My aunt, I am sure, will be monopolising your mother, and Victoria will be able to show you a fine selection of flowers, trees and goldfish.'

'I am not really her aunt,' put in Lady Violet, hastily, 'but I have known her since she was so high. She is a very outspoken young lady,' she went on, 'but quite delightful.' She turned somewhat uneasily towards Mrs Howard, who gave another of her husky laughs.

'Quite charming,' she said. 'Millie, dear, do join the young ladies and go and see the goldfish. I need to be primed by Lady Violet about Derby Party protocol and our fellow guests. It is crucial that we Americans to not commit any faux pas on these occasions,' she continued, smiling at Lady Violet as she did so. 'Why, only last month I addressed Lady Jane Crashawe as Lady Crashawe, and the dook, I mean duke, who was taking me in to dinner almost had apoplexy.'

Lady Violet and the three young ladies all laughed politely.

'I should love to see the goldfish,' said Millicent Howard. 'Lead me to him, or perhaps it should be them.' She twirled her parasol with a certain panache and stepped forward to join Tilly and Victoria.

'Forgive my mentioning it,' said Victoria as they set off down the Rose Walk, 'but your accent is by no means as pronounced as your mother's.'

Millicent glanced at her and laughed. 'The benefits of a French education,' she said. 'I spent two years in Paris and have lost the Midwest and all but forgotten New York. Mother did not have my advantages. But tell me, where are the young officers. There must be some, or is this another of those mysteries of English society that we Americans have to learn?'

'Two are travelling down as we speak,' said Tilly, 'one arrives this evening and the fourth, my brother, will be with us first thing tomorrow morning. But surely you have no need of young officers?'

'Your reputation goes before you,' said Victoria mischievously.

'Reputation?' queried Millicent.

'A certain duke,' went on Victoria. 'We read all about it in *The Lady's Realm*.'

'Don't believe everything you read in *The Lady's Realm*, Miss Sedgley,' responded Millicent sharply, and then continued, "Oh I'm sorry, that was very rude of me. It's just that I am so sick of reading about myself in the society pages and it's all so wrong. I hate it when I am married off to all and sundry. I am an independent human being, not a piece of merchandise to be bought and sold.'

'I know exactly how you feel,' said Tilly quietly.

'It's just the same in Paris,' went on Millicent, 'and we Americans are worse than anybody. You would not credit how many so called heiresses have crossed the Atlantic because their social climbing mothers have ideas of hitching them to some impoverished English aristocrat.'

'Oh I know,' said Victoria excitedly. 'The Duke of Marlborough and two Dukes of Manchester; they've all married rich Americans.'

'Well here's one rich American who is not about to join that particular club,' said Millicent firmly. 'Now this I take it is your famous goldfish pond, so all I have to do now is spot my goldfish,' and so saying she leant over the edge of the lily pond and gently agitated the water with the tip of her parasol.

5.

Barcombe News. Thursday 4th October 1998.
It is with considerable regret that we report the death of Brigadier Sir Denzil Beckingsale at his house Barcombe Lodge last Monday at the great age of 97. Sir Denzil, who was a pillar of the local community for the whole of his adult life, had been in declining health for several months. It is understood that the bulk of his estate, including Barcombe Lodge itself, will pass to his only surviving daughter, Mrs Rosemary Fitter, but that the famed Beckingsale Collection of seventeenth century Dutch paintings has been left to the borough. "We have known of Sir Denzil's most generous bequest for several years," said a spokesman, "and plans are in place to set aside a suite of rooms in the Town Hall to form the Beckingsale Gallery, which will display these fine paintings for the benefit of the general public as a whole." (Full Obituary page 17.)

CHAPTER TWO

1.

Drayfield Hall lies about a mile outside the village of the same Barcombe. The road from Barcombe to Southwater leads directly towards the lodge gates before turning sharply left, while the drive, after leaving a small entrance lodge on the left hand side, continues in the same direction for another half a mile. The traveller then has the option of turning right towards the hall itself, or of proceeding straight ahead for another half mile before another right hand turn leads to a second lodge on the main London to Southwater road. (Tourist's Guide to Surrey: Rail and Road by R.N.Worth, F.G.S., with Map and Plan. 1881)

****

Monday 31st May 1897

The fly that conveyed Charles Sedgley from Barcombe station to the hall smelt strongly of oil and old leather. It was also hot and very stuffy. While relieved that Albert Chesney of the Station Hotel at Barcombe was a licensed fly proprietor, and that it was thus possible for him to reach his destination without too much trouble, Charles was still only too aware of the fact that he was going to be at least two hours late in arriving, and that his aunt would be far from happy at this state of affairs. He glanced for the third time in as many minutes at his half hunter.

'A quarter past eight,' he said to himself. 'Dinner will have started at seven o'clock sharp and I am sure to be in the doghouse from the word go. Not a good start to the week.'

The fly jolted as it hit a stone in the road and Charles hastily grabbed his suitcase, which was on the seat beside him. It then lurched off to the right as it reached the lodge gates. The horse was obviously doing the thinking for its owner, and Charles leant out of the window in desperation.

'Easy does it, Albert,' he shouted. 'I would rather arrive late than dead.'

'Very good, Mr Charles, Sir,' came back the reply, and the fly continued at precisely the same pace until it reached the right hand turning that heralded the sight of the Tudor garden wall. Two minutes later the front of Drayfield Hall loomed up before them, and Charles made out the statuesque figure of Anderson, the butler, waiting by the open front door. Charles groaned inwardly. If Anderson had been standing there ever since the family brougham had brought the rest of the younger guests, then he could expect an even frostier reception from his aunt.

'Good evening, Anderson,' he said, 'I do hope that you have not been waiting here for long.'

'Good evening Mr Charles,' replied the butler. 'Welcome to Drayfield, Sir. No, I realised that you were likely to arrive by the later train and so have only been here for a matter of minutes. I would have sent William to the station to meet you but,' and here he coughed discreetly, 'Lady Violet required his presence in the dining room.'

'I quite understand, Anderson,' said Charles hastily. 'I expect everyone is in the middle of dinner now?'

'Indeed, Sir,' came the reply. 'Perhaps you would care to join the rest of the party for coffee and brandy in the small drawing room? In the meantime would you care for some sandwiches and cold meat in the library?'

'An excellent idea, Anderson,' said Charles. 'If you would inform my uncle and aunt that I have arrived, I will go upstairs and change,' and as the butler stood to one side he entered the vestibule with a purposeful step.

A few minutes later Charles left his bedroom and made his way down the red pile carpeted staircase. At the foot of the stairs he hesitated. After a moment's thought he turned left and entered the small lobby that separated the dining room from the library. A buzz of conversation from the former assured him that the meal was still in progress, so he quickly opened the library door and slipped inside.

Anderson had been as good as his word, plates of sandwiches and cold chicken had been left on the table in the centre of the room and beside them stood a decanter of whisky, a bottle of soda water, and a box of Havana cigars.

As he settled himself into a deep leather armchair and contemplated the rows of *The Gentleman's Magazines* that faced him in the bookcase next to the fireplace, Charles raised his glass in homage to the portrait that hung above the fire. It was his grandfather and namesake, and the two men were extremely similar in appearance, a coincidence that had often been remarked upon by other members of the family. Both were tall and spare and the possessors of a shock of hair that fell over their foreheads in a pronounced quiff. Indeed the only significant feature that separated the two was that the younger man sported a smart, clipped moustache while his forbear had been clean-shaven.

'Your good health, grandfather,' said Charles, for although he had never known his ancestor, he had always felt a close affinity to him. It had been his grandfather who had amassed the contents of the library now graced by his portrait, and Charles himself was an avid reader. At least a dozen volumes had accompanied him to the Cape two years earlier, a fact that triggered a train of thought that caused him to grimace involuntarily. As he munched his way through the sandwiches he gently massaged the shoulder that still bore the scars from his African adventure. It was very much to be hoped that his uncle and aunt had not been studying the papers too closely over the past few days. But still, if they had, they had. Charles was determined to enjoy his weekend, come what may, and as if to emphasise the point he selected a cigar from the box on the tray. Soon a pleasant aroma of rich Havana pervaded the atmosphere.

The biggest problem was of course the presence at the house party of Sir Robert Clayton, whom Charles had last spoken to in court, and the exchange had not been a friendly one. Rapidly relegating Sir Robert and his wife, who was also a guest at Drayfield, to the recesses of his mind, Charles mentally ran through the list of other members of the house party. The Rossdales, Lord and Lady and their offspring, Archie and Tilly, were very well known to him. Indeed he had spent much of his childhood at Felton Park, the Rossdale's home in Norfolk, by virtue of the fact that Archie Rossdale was his oldest friend and that his own parents were abroad. Tilly Rossdale was certainly his oldest female friend and if he had his way she would be far more than that. Unfortunately the world, including so it seemed Tilly herself, seemed to regard him as a surrogate brother to the young Rossdales, and he was also well aware of Lord and Lady Rossdale's hopes and plans for their daughter. These did not include an alliance with the younger son of a younger son.

As far as the other guests were concerned, Charles looked forward with anticipation to meeting the Howards. Elizabeth was the talk of society through her friendship with the Prince of Wales and Millicent through her good looks and her presumed relationship with the young and eligible Duke of Westerdale.

'We are all agog to be introduced to the famous Miss Howard,' Archie had written to him a few days earlier. 'She is greatly sought after here in Town and is rumoured to have the Duke of Westerdale quite under her thumb. It is commonly known that the duke is utterly penniless and the story goes that the dowager duchess and Mrs H have done a deal. Tritton dollars in exchange for the coronet of a duchess. From what you tell me the same sort of thing goes on around the Limpopo river, but there cattle rather than American currency form the bargaining chips. Did you know that old man Tritton, Mrs H's father, gave his daughter and her husband $1,500,000 when they married? They must have inherited a good bit more when he died. It does not bear thinking about.'

Lancelot Rutherford was a friend of Archie and a fellow officer in the Blues and Charles had met him before on various occasions. George Johnstone had served with the Royal Welch Regiment and was known to him by reputation. The two men had also been introduced at a race meeting some months earlier but Charles had not warmed to a man whose behaviour and reputation marked him out as a person to be treated with extreme caution. Johnstone, like Charles himself, had been seconded to the British South Africa Company, but they had never actually met in Africa, although rumour had it that Johnstone was there at the time of the raid. Again, like Charles, he had surrendered his commission, but the exact circumstances that led to George Johnstone leaving his regiment were shrouded in mystery. Johnstone, like Sir Robert Carey, was a guest with whom Charles Sedgley hoped he would have the minimum of contact.

Charles watched as a section of ash dropped from the end of his cigar and landed in the centre of the ashtray. He then stood up, stretched, and walked over to the bookcase opposite the fireplace. Above it hung a large picture of a party of horsemen and women outside what Charles imagined was a wayside inn. There were three riders on horseback, an assortment of rustics and a gypsy woman with her small infant. He remembered as a child staring up at the picture and imagining himself as the dashing cavalier with the red cloak in the centre of the composition. Archie was the male to the right of the cavalier, who was carrying a hawk or a falcon on his outstretched arm, and Tilly was the beautifully attired young lady riding side-saddle on a magnificent white horse. She was dressed in a yellow gown with silver-grey edging around the neck and cuffs, and she wore a hat totally dominated by two swirling feathers. Tilly, he felt sure, would look divine in a yellow gown with silver-grey edging, but then as far as he was concerned Tilly would look divine in anything.

Charles fingered his moustache and smiled ruefully as he stared at the picture. After a minute or two had elapsed he returned to his chair and *The Gentleman's Magazines*. He had not long to wait for at precisely a quarter past ten the library door opened and Anderson reappeared.

'The ladies have adjourned to the saloon, Sir,' he said, 'and Mr Sedgley has suggested that you join the other gentlemen in the dining room.'

Charles placed the remaining half of his cigar in the ashtray on the centre table and rose to his feet. He returned a copy of *The Gentleman's Magazine* to its correct position on the bookshelves.

'Thank you Anderson,' he said. 'Lead me to the fray,' and giving his grandfather a surreptitious wink as he passed him he followed the butler into the lobby. Anderson opened the door into the dining room.

'Mr Charles Sedgley,' he announced in stentorian tones.

Charles entered the dining room. 'Uncle Frederick, good evening. Good evening gentlemen. A thousand apologies for my late arrival.' And with his hand outstretched he walked over to where his uncle was seated at the head of the table.

Despite appearances and the fears of her nephew, Lady Violet was not totally displeased by Charles's failure to catch the appropriate train from London. Although she would have denied it vehemently, the mistress of Drayfield was intensely superstitious and had Charles arrived on time

Lady Violet would have had to face the unpalatable truth that she was entertaining a party of thirteen for dinner.

The news that Archie Rossdale was unlikely to be able to join the house party before Derby Day itself had caused far more annoyance when it came to numbers than it had to her plans for the smooth running of the week ahead of her. Five years had elapsed since Victoria had come out, and Lady Violet had long since given up any hopes of anything developing out of her daughter's long standing friendship with Archie Rossdale. Like Charles Sedgley, Archie was a useful makeweight at Drayfield gatherings and anyway, with both Tilly Rossdale and Millicent Howard on the guest list, the need for eligible young men was as keen as ever. As for Charles himself, both Frederick and Lady Violet Sedgley had always entertained hopes that a marriage between the cousins would mean the name and the estate would remain united, but there again the older generation seemed doomed to disappointment.

Fourteen was an excellent number, and with four young men and three young ladies the extra male could partner Elizabeth Howard. It was vital that Mrs Howard should enjoy her first visit to Drayfield, and that any reports that might filter back to Marlborough House would be favourable ones. Lady Violet was well aware that the Prince of Wales had a firmly established routine when it came to country house visits, but there was always the possibility that a new house could be added to the list. It was common knowledge that Elizabeth Howard was a particular friend of Georgiana Countess of Dudley, and rumour had it that the previous year, when the Prince's horse *Persimmon* won the Derby, HRH had spent that evening in celebration with Lady Dudley. With those two ladies on her side a royal visit to Drayfield would be almost a certainty, or so Lady Violet hoped.

'I am prepared to forgive your disgracefully late arrival, Charles,' Lady Violet announced in the saloon after dinner, 'only because, given Archie's absence, and in deference to those who mind about such things, it would have been necessary for me to introduce Lady Palmerston into our little gathering.'

'Lady Palmerston?' said Elizabeth Howard. 'Who, Lady Violet, is Lady Palmerston, and why would it have been necessary for her to join us?'

'I didn't know that there was a Lady Palmerston now,' interrupted Lord Rossdale. 'What happened to the title after Lord Palmerston died? The only Lady Palmerston I ever heard of was the Prime Minister's wife. She passed on about four years after her husband, and that's over thirty years ago.'

Violet Sedgley laughed. 'No,' she said. 'Lady Palmerston is a doll. She was given to my sister-in-law by the real Lady Palmerston when she visited Drayfield in my father-in-law's day. Fanny never really cared for her and so I adopted her when I married Frederick. She really belongs to Victoria now, but she comes into her own when we have to seat thirteen at dinner. Lady Palmerston makes up the numbers to fourteen, and so those that are of a superstitious bent need have no fears. Lady Palmerston always saves the day.'

'I say, what a capital scheme,' said Lancelot Rutherford, a short and rather stocky officer from the Royal Horse Guards, who was perched precariously upon a carved wooden chair to the right of the fire-place. These had been his first words since the gentlemen had joined the ladies after the meal and, having made his contribution to the conversation, a look of terror passed across his face and he relapsed into silence.

'My father was a great favourite of Lord Palmerston,' mused Frederick Sedgley, 'but he died within a year of the

Prime Minister's visit. We will never know whether a great political future lay ahead of him. I somewhat doubt it though. The Sedgleys have always been more interested in books than in politics.'

'Do show us Lady Palmerston, Victoria,' said Matilda Rossdale. 'It is most unfair. Think of all the times that I have visited you here and I have never seen her. Mama,' she said loudly, turning to her mother, 'have you ever seen Lady Palmerston?'

Lady Rossdale, who was rather hard of hearing, leant forward.

'Yes, I believe I have,' she answered, 'and I can claim to have seen the original. It was at a reception at her house in Park Lane shortly before she died. She seemed quite a small lady but had obviously been extremely beautiful in her day. I am afraid that I rather towered over her when I was presented. She was sitting bolt upright and was wearing a black-ribboned cap. She said that my hair was very similar to her own, although hers of course had then gone very grey.' Lady Rossdale preened herself ever so slightly. She was particularly proud of her thick auburn hair, which her daughter had also inherited, and she was well aware that it possessed no trace of grey.

'Perhaps you have never been a member of a party numbering thirteen, Miss Rossdale,' remarked George Johnstone somewhat dryly.

Lady Violet glanced at him apprehensively. Johnstone, like Lancelot Rutherford, was one of her wild cards and both had been invited at the suggestion of the Rossdales. The unknown was always potentially dangerous and Lady Violet had yet to make up her mind about them.

Rutherford, the second son of Lord Rutherford, struck her as being rather boring and extremely nervous. Johnstone on the other hand was quite the reverse. He was certainly a fine figure of a man but his remarks were also rather too familiar for her liking, although on reflection she presumed that he was well known to the Rossdales and that his flippancy towards Matilda was acceptable for that reason. She was less happy with his attitude towards Millicent Howard and her own daughter, Victoria. On the other hand she was well aware that it was the 1890s. Times were changing, thanks to the example set by the Prince and his friends, and she considered that perhaps she should not be so censorious.

'You are perfectly correct, Mr Johnstone,' she said. Very rarely are we faced with our present predicament, and so Lady Palmerston's appearances have been few and far between.'

In some ways Lady Violet felt that George Johnstone reminded her of her nephew. There was an air of devilry about them. Both wore moustaches and both were serving officers, although not in the same regiment, for Charles had followed in the family tradition and had joined the Grenadiers. Thinking of Charles caused her a slight twinge of conscience. Her nephew had been unusually subdued from the moment she had set eyes upon him. The banter, which was normally a feature of his conversation, had been missing, and he was now sitting in the window gazing out into the darkness. She hoped that her initial tones of reproof had not had too detrimental an effect upon him.

'Charles,' she called out, 'you remember your aunt Fanny's Lady Palmerston, don't you?'

Charles awoke from his reverie and turned to face a row of enquiring faces.

'Indeed I do Aunt,' he replied. 'A singularly lovely young lady,' he went on,' although not nearly as striking as the present company, it has to be said.' He smiled politely, but Lady Violet could still detect the note of unease in his voice. She glanced around the rest of the room before stopping short with a feeling of disquiet that must have matched the younger man's expression.

Sir Robert Carey was staring at her nephew with a face that was as black as thunder.

2.

Thursday 2nd July 1964

'That fountain was placed there, and I quote, "by the sons and daughters of Charles and Adelaide Sedgley",' announced Jane as Nicholas obeyed her instructions and turned right into the grounds of Drayfield Park. 'There is another one at the other end of the drive that commemorates Lady Violet Sedgley. Apparently she was a teetotaller.'

They continued along the drive and Nicholas parked the car in front of the house itself.

'Early nineteenth century section straight ahead of us. Late eighteenth century servants wing to the left, plus a rather spectacular Strawberry Hill gothic window at first floor level,' Jane informed him.

They had arrived with about ten minutes to spare. There was a slight drizzle, so they sheltered inside the large gothic porch. Jane pointed out the more important features. A small archway to the left led to the 'charming loggia' referred to by *The Little Guide.* Nicholas walked along it and peered through the four barred windows that he passed, but could see little through the grime. At the end of the loggia a locked door led to the servants' wing to the left of the main block. As the rain was now fading away they strolled across the gravel forecourt and looked back at the building. On the right hand side of the porch was a much larger three light window with some interesting stained glass in an arched section at the top of each of the lights.

'That's the small drawing room,' said Jane.

Each light contained a figure in Tudor costume, and Nicholas suspected that the one in the centre was King Henry VIII, but as he was viewing them from the wrong side it was difficult to be certain. He was about to ask Jane whether or not he was correct when Mr Innes came round the side of the house brandishing a large key in his right hand. Jane made the necessary introductions and Mr Innes shook hands. He stared hard at Nick.

'We've met before, haven't we?' he asked.

'Last year,' admitted Nick. I visited Drayfield in the summer and wandered round the grounds. I've never been inside though.'

'You never told me that you had been here before,' said Jane in surprise. 'Why on earth didn't you mention it?'

Nick looked slightly guilty. 'It was only the gardens,' he said quickly. 'I had no idea that the house had so much else to offer.'

'I hope you find it worth your while,' said Mr Innes as he opened the door. He presented Jane with the key, and with the parting request, 'Drop it into the Garden Lodge when you have finished,' he disappeared round the side of the house.

The front door opened into a large and quite empty hall. There was an ornate fireplace on the right hand side and directly ahead of them were huge double oak doors. Jane walked up the doors and tried them. They were unlocked. She turned and faced Nicholas.

'Down there,' she said, gesturing with her right hand, 'is the corridor. It leads to the staircase and the door to the servants' wing. Over here,' and she motioned with her left hand, 'is the door to the small drawing room. I suggest we start in there and then work our way round to the other rooms.'

Nicholas nodded.

'It's really rather clever,' Jane went on. 'Not quite up to Bearwood's standards, but the corridor runs parallel to all the important rooms on the ground floor. They all link up and so a servant could nip along the corridor from the drawing room at one end of the house and get to the smoking room at the other before anyone important who was going from room to room. Now, come and have a look at your heraldry,' and she led the way into the small drawing room.

'The fireplace is quite impressive, and apparently someone from London came down two years ago and told them that the mirror was worth something, but of course all the furniture and fittings went before the war when Mrs Rutherford died.'

'Mrs Rutherford?' Nicholas said. 'Oh yes, the last owner.' He remembered the Rutherford entry in the Visitors Book. 'Daughter of Frederick and Lady Violet.'

'Yes,' said Jane. 'Victoria Sedgley.'

'Presumably named after the Queen?' asked Nicholas.

Jane nodded. 'I think so. She was born in 1872. Her husband was a colonel in the army, but he died about ten years before she did. I'll show you their tomb in the churchyard if you like. I told you, didn't I, that one of the reasons why I chose the 1897 party was that her future husband was a guest? As far as I can make out that was his first visit. As we said before, he was probably invited as a possible groom for the daughter of the household. At twenty-five she must have been regarded as shelf material so they were bound to be getting desperate. Now, what about those?' and she pointed to a rather attractive frieze of shields, crests and roses that ran round the cornice.

Nicholas recognised the Sedgley shield and crest amongst a selection of others whose relevance was not immediately obvious.

'Very nice,' he said. His eyes then fell upon the window. It was King Henry VIII in all his glory flanked by two of his wives. Nicholas recognised them as Queen Catherine of Aragon and Queen Anne Boleyn.

'Why is King Henry VIII here?' he asked, pointing to the window.

'When King Henry was courting Anne Boleyn he used to come here, or so they say,' answered Jane. 'We are half way between her home at Hever Castle and his palace in London. Richmond, wasn't it? They met at the house that was here before the one that had the cellars we cleared.' She thought for a moment. 'They used to say that Anne Boleyn came back to haunt the place, but as this part of the house wasn't here when she was I don't think it is very likely. I suppose she could haunt the servants' wing, but that doesn't seem a very royal thing to do. Now, if we go through this door here,' and she unlocked the door which faced the windows, 'we will see the large drawing room or saloon.'

Nicholas followed his guide through the reception rooms that faced the gardens on the south side of the house. As Jane had said, they were all connected and above the doors were rather delightful rococo coats of arms. Only one room was furnished and this was the library. It contained the usual huge fireplace and overmantel, but it had also been equipped with a large table surrounded by a great many chairs, and the walls, which were lined with empty bookshelves, were also graced with three impressive portraits.

Jane stopped beneath one of them and ran her fingers through her hair. Nicholas watched her in fascination as she collected her thoughts.

'This is now called the committee room,' she said. 'The joint-committee meets here four times a year and that's why we have the table and chairs. They bought two of the portraits when the house was sold, and the third was presented to them about ten years ago.'

Nicholas walked over to the picture she was indicating. A small gold label underneath it bore the legend 'Lady Violet Sedgley by Ellis Roberts. Presented by Richard Sedgley. 1954'. The portrait was of a lady standing in a landscape. She was wearing a flowing white off the shoulder dress with a gold belt, and around her was draped a voluminous cerise train. She had a mass of dark hair, which cascaded over her right shoulder, and she stared out of the picture with an air of confidence and well-being.

'It's a beautiful painting,' said Jane. 'She was a very lovely lady, wasn't she?'

'Very lovely,' Nicholas agreed.

'That's her husband over there,' and Jane, pointed at one of the other portraits. 'The large one over there is the second Charles, her father-in-law. They had them valued some years ago and Lady Violet is worth something but the other two don't quite match her when it comes to hard cash. Still, I think that it is great that they are all still here.'

Nicholas nodded. 'Money shouldn't come into it,' he said. 'That is just such a fantastic painting.'

Jane stared at it closely. 'I wonder where it was painted? The landscape reminds me of the peak district. What do you think?' She looked at him inquiringly.

'It could be,' Nicholas replied. 'Or he could have made it all up. Perhaps she was standing in his studio with an immense backdrop behind her. Tell me,' he went on, 'who was Richard Sedgley, the man who presented that picture?' and he pointed to the portrait of Lady Violet.

'A cousin of Mrs Rutherford,' replied Jane, 'but he didn't inherit. The house was left to another cousin, a Mrs Woodhead, and she sold up. Now,' she said firmly, 'I've told you about the pictures, you tell me about the heraldry.'

Nicholas thought for a moment. 'Well,' he said, 'they're all impaled coats of arms. The Sedgley arms are on the left hand side as we look at them and the wives arms are on the right hand side. None of the wives were heiresses, because if they had been their arms would have been on little shields in the centre of the Sedgley shields. At a guess I should think that the arms are those of Charles the first, Frederick the first, Charles the second and Frederick the second. This last one,' and he ushered her out of the committee room into the ante-room that separated it from the dining room, 'is the Frederick of your house party,' and he pointed up to a flamboyant coat of arms that featured the Sedgley sedge-warblers flanking a shield itself divided into four quarters. 'That looks sufficiently aristocratic,' he said, 'and Lady Violet was an earl's daughter, wasn't she?'

'The Earl of Storeton,' said Jane. 'I am very impressed. Now, follow me. This way to the smoking room.'

She opened up the door opposite to that which had led from the ante-room and ushered him in to a small panelled room. As had been the case with all the others except the library it was totally devoid of furniture but the fireplace, which was considerably smaller than the ones they had seen so far, and a pastel portrait of three boys that hung above it. Jane shivered and thought for a moment.

'This house is haunted,' she said, 'but it's not by Anne Boleyn.'

3.

Monday 31st May 1897

Frederick Sedgley ran his fingers through his beard and uneasily settled himself back into a deep leather armchair. He stared pensively at the portrait of his father that hung over the mantelpiece in the library. He was beginning to think that his judgement had been seriously at fault when it had come to working out the guest list for the Derby house party.

It was he who had decided that the Careys should be invited. 'Surely, my dear,' he had remarked mildly to his wife, 'if you and Sybil insist upon filling the house with young friends of Victoria and Archie,' then I might be allowed one man with whom I will be able to converse upon topics other than horse racing and the army.'

'Sir Robert is a Liberal,' responded Lady Violet, 'and although I shall never allow politics to dominate the dinner table at Drayfield, it is very likely that with Rossdale present, not to mention four young officers, the subject of Africa will be touched upon. It is not as if the Careys have a son or daughter either. All that we shall gain will be a man to whom you will be able to talk genealogy– and you have ample opportunity to do that at the Athenaeum – and a lady of whom none of us know anything. We should be on much safer ground if we invited the King-Montagus. There are four of them and we could accommodate the extra couple by utilising the Red Dressing Room, and the addition of two more young people will certainly please Victoria.'

The fact that on this rare occasion Frederick Sedgley had gained the day – it turned out that Victoria harboured an intense dislike for one of the young King-Montagus, Sedgley rather thought it was the girl – now seemed something of a pyrrhic victory. The subject of Africa had indeed dominated the dinner table. The differences of opinion voiced by Sir Robert and Edward Rossdale became quite heated, although both seemed equally suspicious of the activities of the new Colonial Secretary, and that at least gave them something upon which they could agree. Equally unfortunate was the contribution of George Johnstone to the conversation, although his baiting, yes there could be no better way of describing it, of Sir Robert seemed to amuse Elizabeth Howard.

Frederick Sedgley had gained the distinct impression that Elizabeth Howard and George Johnstone were known to one another. Exactly why he felt this was so eluded him, but there was something about the way they occasionally exchanged glances. At the same time he was perfectly sure that Mrs Howard was not overly pleased to see the young officer. The whole thing was something of a mystery and Sedgley decided that it would be as well not to dig too deeply. All the same it was not a good omen. Elizabeth Howard was a well known member of the Marlborough House set and although her own daughter was about the same age as George Johnstone, Frederick Sedgley was well aware that differences in age did not mean much within the Prince of Wales's circle. Still, at least it had been Lady Violet who had been responsible for inviting her.

'It will probably mean an invitation to join the Royal party,' she had explained to her husband, 'and that is not something to be sneezed at. But, my dear,' she continued, I do feel that the Rossdales are treating us as if we were some sort of coaching inn. They are off to Gatton Park on Thursday and then to the Deepdene on Sunday. And it is not as if the rest of us have been invited as well.'

What with the differences between Lord Rossdale and Sir Robert, the behaviour of Elizabeth Howard and George Johnstone, and the absence both of his nephew Charles and Archie Rossdale from the table – they were young men whose sparkle usually enlivened parties at Drayfield – Frederick Sedgley felt that the evening had not been the success he had anticipated.

'What exactly do you mean by "infernal filibustering",' George Johnstone had said in all innocence to Sir Robert Carey when at long last the subject of Africa appeared to have dried up with the arrival of the strawberries and cream. Then no sooner than Sir Robert responded to Lord

Rossdale's instant and angry interjection the young man was adding further fuel to the flames.

'I suppose you would argue that there is little to choose between Kruger and Rhodes except nationality?' he observed as he carefully pushed a strawberry to the edge of his plate before leaning back to watch as once again Sir Robert attempted to define his opinions in the face of the splutterings of Lord Rossdale.

To give him his due, thought Frederick Sedgley, Robert Carey had tried very hard not to exacerbate the situation, and Edward Rossdale was not the easiest of men with whom to talk politics. He had determined to express his appreciation of that fact to his friend after the meal but, to cap it all, Sir Robert had retired early and deprived his host both of that opportunity and of the genealogical discussion to which had had been so looking forward. Frederick Sedgley sighed deeply. He rose and selected a cigar from the box that Anderson had thoughtfully, though unusually as it was the library, left upon the table. He then strolled over to the door into the smoking room. Old habits died hard. Although smoking was now permitted in the library, Lady Violet was tolerably liberal in her own fashion, in his father's day this had never been the case.

Once within the smoking room Sedgley opened the door that led into the hall and listened. Sounds of activity emanated from the butler's pantry, a fact that caused him to smile with satisfaction. The master of Drayfield was a kindly man who disliked the idea of keeping his butler up after midnight if he was the only member of the family still around at that hour. As it was, however, Anderson was clearly still at work. The butler had very strict rules when it came to the silver, which nobody, but nobody was ever allowed to handle beside himself. As a result he was inevitably faced with a late night whenever the Sedgleys gave a dinner party, but Anderson was not a man to compromise. There was obviously no need to worry about keeping the man up unnecessarily and, reaching into his waistcoat pocket for his vesta case, Frederick Sedgley walked over to the window and stared out into the cloudless night.

'We should be in for a fair day's racing,' he said to himself as he lit his cigar.

4.

Thursday 2nd July 1964

The rooms upstairs were with one exception devoid of interest. They had once been the main bedrooms but were now used on occasion by the local technical college, which had left rather primitive desks and chairs stacked on the landing. Nicholas noticed that there was some rather nice stained glass in what was obviously the master bedroom, a room that had a superb view over the gardens, but for the most part he kept his eyes on his companion. Victor, he felt, was a lucky man who did not deserve and, he felt sure, did not appreciate the delightful creature beside him.

'Yes,' said Jane with a smile, 'that glass contain the monogram *FVS*. It commemorates Frederick's marriage to Lady Violet. That squiggly bit must be the "and". Ampersand, that's the word I want. What do you think?'

Nicholas pulled himself together and nodded. 'Absolutely,' he said, and followed his guide back to the staircase. Half way down where the stairs doubled back on themselves there was a rather heavy oak door with an ornate round brass handle. Jane paused and opened it slowly as if half expecting to find something on the other side. Nicholas thought it was probably another bedroom but in fact it was a corridor with a door on either side then a blank and very modern brick wall.

'This was the housekeeper's room,' said Jane, as she opened the door. 'As you can see, you can't go any further down the corridor because they have sealed it off.'

'What about that one?' asked Nick, and he pointed to the other door on the opposite side of the truncated corridor.

'That was originally a guest room,' replied Jane. 'The corridor went on through to the servants' wing which has now been totally gutted and turned into flats. I believe that door simply masks a wall behind which is a bit of one of the flats. The corridor above this one does exactly the same thing. It's a pity because I could have done with seeing it as it was.'

The housekeeper's room was full of broken furniture, old picture frames, piles of yellowing newspapers and assorted junk. Presumably rubbish that had been cleared out of the bedrooms when the college had taken them over. It was from here, Jane informed Nicholas, that she had salvaged the bound volumes of *Punch* and the Visitors Book, and it was in the housekeeper's room that she was to make yet another discovery.

'Look what I've found,' she said, and she pointed to a broken basin, clearly once part of a washstand set. In it lay the arm of a china doll.

Nicholas reached forward to pick it up and as he did so his fingers brushed against Jane's as she too stretched out for the relic. For a split second their eyes made contact and Nicholas felt that they were linked as if by an electric charge. Then a deep blush suffused Jane's face. She pulled back her hand and turned away.

'Oh my gosh,' she said. 'That's the last thing I need.'

'Jane,' said Nicholas slowly. 'I don't know about you but . . .'

'No!' interrupted Jane. 'Don't say another word. Just give me the arm and we will return the key to Mr Innes. And please don't look at me like that,' and without waiting for his reply she turned and walked quickly back to the staircase.

CHAPTER THREE

1.

Tuesday 27th April 1999

I first made contact with the name of Jane Emburey shortly before the Millennium celebrations when the borough of Barcombe took possession of the famed Beckingsale Collection.

Brigadier Sir Denzil Beckingsale had bequeathed his collection of Dutch art and artefacts to the borough on condition that it should be displayed in a suitable location and open to the general public, free of charge, on at least two days a week. His daughter, Mrs Rosemary Fitter, was one of three trustees appointed to vet the suitable location, the others being Councillor Lathom, his oldest friend and the man widely credited with having engineered the bequest, and his solicitor, Roger Collet, senior partner in the firm of Collet, Jordan and Jeremy.

The council argued long and hard over the question of a location for the Beckingsale Collection and for several months the odds were on a suite of rooms being made available in the Town Hall. In the end, however, it was decided that the main ground floor rooms at Drayfield Hall should be renovated and opened up as an art gallery. The servants' wing would be restored and existing staff flats would be refurbished.

When I started work at the Town Hall in the summer of 1998 work had begun on the flats but the collection itself still remained in the brigadier's old home on the other side of the town. On the other hand, the lease held by a catering firm that had been using the ground floor for wedding receptions had expired, and the local technical college that had used the main upstairs rooms as overflow classrooms for adult learners had built a new teaching block and no longer needed their Drayfield facilities.

'We have seen the last of the cake makers,' as my colleague Tim Lewis put it.

I rather liked Tim Lewis. He was a youngish man, not much older than me, although he had recently married and was losing his hair fairly rapidly. When I got to know him better I appreciated that the two circumstances were not related. He lived in a converted mill in Barcombe but patronised *The Green Man*, a rather pleasant pub about three minutes' walk from the main gates of Drayfield Hall. He was one of the Barcombe representatives on the Fine Arts Committee and provided much needed light relief when the agendas were particularly tedious.

Drayfield Park was the property of the borough of Barcombe and the adjoining town of Southwater and had been administered by a joint-committee created by the two councils since before the Second World War. The councillors in their wisdom now set up a second committee, the Fine Arts Committee, to be responsible for the fledgling gallery. The new committee had already met twice before I joined it in the spring of 1999 – seconded by the legal department at the Town Hall. Meetings were held, as was the case with the other joint-committee, in Drayfield Hall itself, where one of the ground floor rooms had, from time immemorial, been set aside for that purpose.

'Highly convenient for a swift one after the meetings,' Tim Lewis informed me, 'and to give him his due Walter Barnes does not hang around when he chairs a meeting.'

'We will need a new secretary,' said Councillor Barnes, 'as your predecessor has been given leave of absence to have a baby. This will probably be a permanent situation as I gather that on her return it will be on a part-time basis.'

My first meeting was on a wet Tuesday evening in late April and as it was my introduction to the committee I can remember the details quite clearly. Councillor Barnes, a tall, sandy haired man, was in the chair. He opened proceedings by introducing me to my new colleagues. He then cleared his throat and there was immediate silence. As Tim Lewis had earlier hinted, he turned out to be a ruthlessly efficient individual, whose main task appeared to be informing the others what was going on, and what was going to be happening in the near future. There were two representatives from Barcombe, two from Southwater, the three Beckingsale trustees, the Barcombe Borough Librarian, and myself as secretary. The place allocated for the Art Gallery Curator had yet to be filled. A grand total of ten members and we met in what was known as the Committee Room; an impressive neo-gothic chamber dominated by three immense oil portraits – I later discovered them to be members of the Sedgley family, former owners of Drayfield Hall.

The first few items on the agenda were taken with extreme rapidity. The restoration work on the flats was well underway, and one of them had been earmarked for the individual – yet to be appointed – who would be responsible for the gallery's security. There was access from this particular flat to the main staircase of the house, while the upstairs bedrooms, formerly occupied by the gentry were being turned into an apartment for the future curator, and a room halfway down the main staircase was being turned into his or her office. The security of the art works occupied the bulk of the meeting, and almost as much time was discussing the matter of insurance, despite Councillor Barnes's assurance that everything in that respect was well under control.

'You are all of course aware,' he announced, staring at the Southwater representatives who had raised the matter, 'that we are talking about a collection of Dutch paintings that are second only to the Dulwich Art Gallery, when it comes to non-national collections in the south-east, and a gallery that will rival Ranger's House in concept ?'

Mrs McGinty, a small mousey creature from Southwater, looked suitably abashed, while Desmond Davies, her associate from that neck of the woods, avoided Councillor Barnes's stare and nervously shuffled his papers. His name sticks in my mind because shortly before the meeting commenced he came up to me and in a conspiratorial fashion muttered, 'my name is Davies with an ie, not Davis, I do hope you don't mind me mentioning it.'

'And now,' said Councillor Barnes, 'Item seven on the agenda, the Sedgley Room. You will have two separate sheets in your files.' There was a hush as members of the committee found the correct sheets of paper. 'It has been suggested that as the Beckingsale Collection will take up no more than three of the staterooms plus the entrance hall itself, one of the two rooms to the left of the Lobby B, which you will see quite clearly marked on your plans, will be re-named the Sedgley Room and will contain items relevant to the past history of the house.' He paused for a moment and then went on, 'you will appreciate that we are sitting in the Sedgley Room at this very moment.'

His audience stared around in bemused fashion, as if expecting to see the words *Sedgley Room* to appear in neon lights along one of the walls.

'The room already contains three Sedgley portraits,' he went on. Committee members nodded wisely and Mr Davies, who was seated with his back to the pictures in question, turned round and stared at them. 'Now we have been advised that two of these portraits, although of not outstanding worth, are excellent examples of late-Victorian shall we say country house representational painting. The third, by an artist named Ellis Roberts, is almost though not quite of the standard of the works in the Beckingsale Collection.' He paused, and inclined his head in the direction of Mrs Fitter.

'If I may continue,' he went on, 'we have been further advised that Sotheby's will shortly be selling a portrait by Margaret Carpenter of the Charles Sedgley who bought Drayfield in the first place. An anonymous benefactor – he stared at Councillor Lathom – has offered to match any sum that the borough might care to offer for this work, on condition that it is hung here at Drayfield alongside the other three portraits. I need hardly add,' he announced grandly, 'that were we able to acquire the Carpenter, the Sedgley Room would make an excellent and well stocked adjunct to the rooms housing the Beckingsale Collection. Next door,' he said, pointing to the doorway in the corner of the room, 'we have the one-time Smoking Room, and our Borough Librarian has ideas for housing appropriate volumes and papers there that relate to the history of the Drayfield estate.' He gazed expectantly around the room. 'Are there any questions,' he asked abruptly.

There was a buzz of conversation and then Edwin Hooper, one of the Barcombe representatives, a rather pompous little man with a whispy moustache, asked, 'Mr Chairman, is there much material to hand about the Sedgleys? I mean,' he tapped his teeth with his pen, 'if we are to have a room devoted to them, not to mention three possibly four pictures, we really ought to have some written material available for visitors. Perhaps we could even sell something on the door?'

Councillor Barnes looked across the table to Mrs Vanstone, the borough librarian. 'Mrs Vanstone,' he said, 'perhaps you would like to comment?'

'Thank you, Mr Chairman,' replied the librarian, a slight lady with spectacles and attired in a rather threadbare cardigan. 'We have in the local collection a University of

Newcastle master's dissertation written in the 1960s by a,' she paused and consulted her notepad, 'Jane Emburey.' She stared in an owl-like fashion around the table. 'It is entitled *Behind the Green Baize Door: the Mechanics of Victorian Country House Entertaining.* It deals with workings of the house but has quite a lot on the family as well. There is a chapter entitled *Drayfield Hall and the Sedgley Family.*' She coughed in a self-deprecatory fashion. 'It could be worth our while getting in touch with this lady, if indeed she is still around, to see whether we could make use of her work. We could always produce a pamphlet along the lines suggested by Mr Hooper. She might of course be happy to supply such a work herself.'

Councillor Barnes tapped his papers thoughtfully. 'An excellent suggestion, Mrs Vanstone,' he said. 'Mr Tregaskes,' and he turned to me, 'would you look into it for our next meeting? See if you can track down this Jane whatshername and see what she says. Now,' he said, 'can we turn our attention to item eight on the agenda, the matter of car parking.'

Next day at the Town Hall it was made clear to me that my work for the foreseeable future would revolve around Councillor Barnes and the Fine Arts Committee. During the morning I attended a meeting in the Borough Architect's office, where alterations to the ground floor of Drayfield Hall were discussed, and after lunch I made my way to the local library to meet Mrs Vanstone.

'Walter Barnes is quite determined to make a success of this art gallery,' she said as she rummaged through a filing cabinet and produced a black book with gold lettering on the front. 'He has his eye on the Mayor's job, of that I am quite certain, and if the gallery works the publicity and the kudos he will gain will put him well and truly up with the front runners. Yes, here is that thesis I mentioned yesterday evening.' She handed over the book, which was typewritten and ran to some two hundred pages. 'Mrs Emburey apparently made use of a visitors' book,' she said. 'Now, we have no record of such a book in the library, and so it is possible that she still possesses it, or at the very least knows of its present location. I would dearly love to have it for my display in the Smoking Room. That's the room at the end, next door to the one in which we held our meeting. The old library,' she added kindly.

She thought for a moment. 'There was an envelope with about a dozen photographs that came with the book,' she said. 'The pictures were of bits and pieces that Mrs Emburey had collected or had sight of during the course of her researches. One of these items was what she described as *The Drayfield Tray*. It appears to have been a silver salver with an armorial escutcheon in the centre. It was clearly a very handsome piece and it too would be a welcome addition to our display.'

'Where do I find this Mrs Emburey?' I asked.

'I really have no idea,' replied Mrs Vanstone. She no longer lives here, or certainly not as Mrs Emburey. There is a Barcombe address at the start of her thesis, but the present occupants have no idea who she is or where she lives. It might be an idea to try the names she has listed in her acknowledgements, and of course it is possible that Newcastle University could help. I would have done it myself some weeks ago if I had the time,' she added, 'but we are short staffed as it is, and if Councillor Barnes wants these extra jobs taken care of he will just have to produce the wherewithal. Well of course he has now, otherwise you wouldn't be here, would you?'

I smiled and nodded.

'I suggest that you make full use of our photocopier, as I can't let you take the book away with you,' she went on. 'If you would like a cup of tea, have a word with Mrs Appleby on the front desk. There is a machine in the entrance hall but really the tea is not very nice at all. I will be in my office if you need me.' With that Mrs Vanstone favoured me with a brief smile and then disappeared into an inner sanctum.

The next few weeks were taken up with the appointment of a curator for the fledgling gallery. We advertised in the quality dailies, two Sundays and three or four leading art journals. There were fifty-seven applicants, of whom ten were selected for interview, three were short-listed and the result was Mark Paddon-Browne.

My new responsibilities included the job of framing the advertisements and sorting out the legal side of things. Then followed my appointment as secretary to the interviewing panel, a body made up of Councillor Barnes, Mrs Fitter on behalf of the trustees, with Desmond Davies and Tim Lewis, nominated for Southwater and Barcombe respectively.

The interviews - there were four sessions in all - were not without interest. I had noticed at my first joint-committee meeting that other members had tended to shuffle away from Desmond Davies. The panel's first meeting made it clear why this was so. A strong personal odour, to put it mildly, pervaded his presence. It dominated that first session, when I sat next to him, and I made it my business to sit as far away as possible on all future occasions.

In the end Mark Paddon-Browne emerged as the clear favourite. He was well qualified, had written papers on various aspects of seventeenth and eighteenth century paintings, and although his expertise lay chiefly in the field of French rococo, it was clear that Dutch seventeenth century art was well within his scope. 'I think Denzil would have approved of that very tall young man,' said Mrs Fitter, when the board members discussed the final three candidates prior to the final session. Indeed, the only problems to emerge did so when Mark was actually offered the job and they involved the practicalities of life rather than anything to do with curatorial work.

'I am afraid I don't drive,' he said. 'I wonder how I would cope out here?'

'Out here,' said Mrs Fitter in some amazement. 'This is an outer London borough, you know.'

'Oh yes,' replied Mark in some confusion. 'It's just that where I am at the moment . . .' He paused. 'Well, the gallery is in the centre of the city and my flat is only ten minutes walk away. Then there are the shops and so on. It's all very much to hand.'

'Ten minutes walk across the park will take you to the lodge gates,' said Mrs Fitter briskly. 'Two minutes down the road is a bus stop. Another ten minutes will take you to the station, and it's a main line to London, as you know. Tescos will actually deliver as well. No, I don't think you will have any problems at all.'

'The apartment sounds magnificent,' said Mark, 'but won't I be a little cut off? I mean all by myself. And how do I get in and out when the gallery is closed?'

Councillor Barnes, who quite clearly had convinced himself that Mark Paddon-Browne was the man for the job, began to look uneasy. Apart from anything else the two unsuccessful interviewees had left the building. I had been instructed to give them their marching orders before the position had actually been offered to Mark, so convinced the chairman had been that the post would be accepted instantly. He looked around for inspiration and then his eyes fell upon me.

'I don't think you have any need to worry,' he said. 'Perhaps our secretary could spell out one or two practical details to put your mind at rest.'

I pulled myself together rapidly. This was the first occasion upon which I had been asked to contribute anything to the interviews, and it took me a moment or two to collect my thoughts.

'You won't actually be as isolated as all that, Mr Paddon-Browne,' I began. 'There are six flats in the old servants wing of the house and one of those will be occupied by the security man.'

'Who has yet to be appointed,' put in Desmond Davies.

'His so-called back door actually opens on to the main staircase and in a sense he will be your next door neighbour,' I went on.

'There is a separate door to the front of the house at the end of the loggia, the arcaded bit to the left of the main entrance,' I explained. 'To all intents and purposes it would be your own personal entrance.'

'The fact that you are living above the gallery is an added bonus when it comes to the security aspect,' said Tim Lewis, 'but it in no way anchors you to the gallery out of hours. We would probably ask you to liaise with the security man, and he would need to keep you informed as to his movements, but these are all details that can be ironed out when you are both in post.'

'Why don't we ask our secretary to take Mr Paddon-Browne on a brief tour of the upstairs once again,' put in Mrs Fitter. 'He will then be able to visualise more clearly how he will exist at Drayfield when he is not hard at work in the gallery.' She flashed a toothy smile in Mark's direction, and then began to stack up her papers.

'Excellent idea,' said Councillor Barnes. 'I suggest the rest of us have a cup of tea – if there is any left – and we will resume in twenty minutes times, hopefully to get the paperwork in order.' He stood up. 'How does that sound, Richard?' he asked.

'Fine, Mr Chairman,' I replied, and I ushered Mark in the direction of the door.

'I do want this job, you know,' Mark said as we reached the bend in the staircase and I indicated the future office. 'I can't explain what came over me, asking all those stupid questions. You must all think I need my head examined.'

'Not at all,' I replied. 'There's no point in taking a job if you are not going to be happy living in a new environment.' I shook the door but it was locked. 'If we went in there we'd be in what was once a corridor with the office door on the right. The rest of the corridor is sealed off but it used to lead into the servants' wing. It was blocked up shortly after the war.'

At the top of the staircase was a small landing with another door on the right and a gothic arch in the centre. A rather elaborate wrought iron gas lamp holder was built in to the balustrade at the corner where the stairs ended and the landing began.

'Your very own outside light,' I said. 'It's electric now of course. There's a switch here and one at the foot of the staircase.'

'What happens through that door,' asked Mark Paddon-Browne, pointing to the door we had just passed.

'That's the door to the security man's flat,' I said. 'I believe it originally led to more bedrooms. As you can see we have filled in the arch that leads to the main landing and given you your own front door. It took a long time for the permission to be granted because this is a listed building. The work was only completed last week. It all had to be done in such a way that it could easily be removed and the opening reinstated.'

I produced a yale key from my pocket and unlocked the apartment.

'There you have it,' I said. 'On the right a kitchen, a dining room, a bedroom and a bathroom. On the left through the arch is a short corridor leading to a bathroom, a bedroom room and a sitting room. The three rooms are all inter-connected. It's really very cunning. You have en suite facilities, and the sitting room can be accessed from your own bedroom and from that door down there.'

I pointed to the single door on the left hand side of the hall. Mark walked down to it and opened it, instinctively stooping as he did so.

'Good grief,' he exclaimed. 'my furniture would only fill a quarter of this.' He moved to the window. 'What a fantastic view. Are these gardens open to the public. I suppose they must be.'

I nodded. 'They have been ever since the two councils took over the hall just before the war. It's just that up until now no one has dreamt up any use for the house as a whole. Bits of it have been used for an assortment of purposes, but now with a little luck it will come into its own again. I think this was the main bedroom in the good old days. You see that monogram above the top light in that window?'

Mark craned his neck. '*F&VS?*' he asked.

'That's right,' I said. 'Frederick and Violet Sedgley, former owners. Violet was the daughter of a wealthy aristocrat, and her father decorated the house for them as a wedding present.'

We completed our tour of the apartment and then returned to the Committee Room. Councillor Barnes was back at his seat in the centre of the long table flanked by Mrs Fitton and Tim Lewis.

'Mr Davies has had to leave us,' he said. 'Now, Mr Paddon-Browne,' he went on, 'how do you feel about things?'

'Quite reassured, thank you,' responded Mark.

'Then you accept the position?' said Councillor Barnes.

'With much pleasure,' replied Mark. He leant forward and shook the proffered hands. I passed over several sheets of paper to Councillor Barnes, who passed them back across the table. He then turned to his two colleagues.

'I think that just about rounds things off,' he said. 'I will sort out the legalities with Mr Paddon-Browne and our secretary and then we can pass on the good news to our colleagues in the morning. Thank you both for giving up so much of your time. Tim,' he went on. 'I believe you offered to give Mrs Fitter a lift back to the Town Hall?'

'Certainly,' said Tim Lewis, and stood up. 'Congratulations again, Mark,' he said. 'I look forward to a long and fruitful association.' With that he and Mrs Fitter left the room, leaving the rest of us to, as Councillor Barnes put it, deal with the legalities.

2.

Tuesday 1st June 1897

Lady Violet stood by the window of the large drawing room and gazed out over the terrace towards the Rose Walk and the lily pond where her daughter was talking to Lancelot Rutherford. She was always happy to see Victoria in conversation with a young man. Now in her early twenties it was high time she found the right man and settled down, but Lady Violet rather doubted that Mr Rutherford was the right man. His conversation the previous evening had hardly been scintillating and as a personality he could under no stretch of the imagination be called exciting.

Behind her an air of calm and contentment pervaded the room. Sir Robert and Lady Carey were chatting to her husband, Edward Rossdale was engrossed in *The Times*, his wife was engaged upon her embroidery and Millicent Howard was reading a copy of *Punch*. That was all as it should be. When she planned the week's events Lady Violet had set aside Tuesday for a quiet time *at home*, sandwiched between the activity generated by Monday's arrivals and the excitement of the Wednesday Derby. The only discordant notes were the raised voices in the small drawing room, where her nephew Charles was playing chess with Tilly Rossdale, and the expressions on the faces of Elizabeth Howard and George Johnstone, who appeared to be arguing on the terrace in front of her. Lady Violet had been unaware that these last two guests had met before, but clearly that had been the case. Equally clearly all was not well between them. Lady Violet had noted the slightly barbed comments both had exchanged at each other's expense over the previous evening's dinner. She was no fool when it came to relationships, and she suspected that they were somewhat more closely connected than either chose to make clear to the assembled company. Now they were pacing the terrace and although she could not hear what was being said, Lady Violet could see quite easily the taut expressions on their faces.

As for Charles and Tilly, well they always seemed to be arguing. They had been brought up together at the Rossdale's home in Norfolk, and Lady Violet knew from personal experience that brothers and sisters always argued.

She sighed in exasperation. Raised voices and angry expressions were not what were required at a Drayfield Derby Party. She turned away from the window and gave her full attention to the scene behind her.

'Hardly an article,' Sir Robert was saying, 'more a short piece.'

'And your subject, Sir Robert?' asked Sybil Rossdale, laying aside her embroidery and looking enquiringly at him.

Sir Robert Carey smiled at her. '*Punning Mottoes of the Peerage and Baronetage,*' he replied. 'It purports to be an amusing essay but will probably appeal only to a very limited audience.'

'Punning mottoes,' said Sybil Rossdale thoughtfully. She inclined her head in his direction. 'Could you give us an example?'

'Certainly,' answered Sir Robert. 'Our host's and hostess's near neighbour, the Earl of Onslow at Clandon Park. His motto is *festina lente*.'

'*Festina* loosely translated as *go on, lente* meaning *slow*,' put in Frederick Sedgley. Go on slow. Onslow, do you see?'

'I think that is absolutely fascinating,' said Millicent Howard, putting down her *Punch*. 'Do give us another example, Sir Robert.'

'Well, the Earl of March's motto is simply *Forward*,' said Sir Robert, then there is Sir Alex Dixie, his motto is *Quod dixi, dixi*. The translation is *What I have said, I have said.* Another favourite of mine is Sir Anthony Weldon's. *Bene factum*, meaning literally *well done*.'

'I think your essay should appeal to far more than a limited audience, Sir Robert,' said Millicent firmly. 'Have you any other favourites?' She stopped suddenly and blushed. 'Oh I do beg your pardon,' she said. 'How very impudent of me. I am monopolising the conversation. It is a very particularly American habit, and Mother would be most annoyed.'

A ripple of laughter greeted her remark, and Sir Robert went on good naturedly, 'I am delighted that my efforts are going down so well, particularly among the younger generation. I think, my dear Miss Howard, that the prize for the most impudent motto should go to the Temple family who later became Dukes of Buckingham and Chandos. Their motto was *Templa quam dilecta*, that is to say . . .'

'*How beloved are the temples*,' put in Lady Violet, delightedly.

'Exactly,' said Sir Robert.

'And look what happened to them,' said Frederick Sedgley, giving a short laugh. 'Bankrupt in the 40's, extinct in the 80s. How are the mighty fallen. The first dukedom to become extinct since, since when, Robert?'

Sir Robert Carey thought for a moment. 'Oh they go very regularly,' he said. 'The last Duke of Cleveland eight years ago, and in the present century we've lost Bridgewater of canal fame, Ancaster of no particular fame whatsoever, then there's always …'

'Stop, my dear Sir Robert, do stop. It's too terrible,' interrupted Lady Violet. 'Dukes are clearly an endangered species and they must be protected. I am sure you agree, Miss Howard?' she said archly, and she looked across towards Millicent.

A flicker of annoyance passed across Millicent's face but it was gone in an instance. 'Indeed,' she said, 'and your own motto, Lady Violet, what is that?'

Lady Violet walked over to a chair beside Millicent and sat down. 'My own family motto is *Praemium virtutis honor*,' she replied, 'which means *Honour is the reward of virtue*, but the Sedgley's is *Prato et pelago* meaning *By sea and land*. I am not sure of its origins but my husband will tell you.'

'The Rossdales have *Et marte et arte*,' said Lord Rossdale suddenly, setting down his paper and joining in the conversation. *Both by strength and art*. Dashed fine motto it is too.'

'Various Scottish families have that motto, Lord Rossdale,' said Sir Robert Carey with interest. 'Do the Rossdales come from north of the border?'

'We do as a matter of fact,' said Lord Rossdale. 'Came down with King James I in 1603 and settled in Norfolk. Been there ever since. I have a shooting box in Wester Ross but that's a fairly recent acquisition.'

'The Sedgleys . . . ' started Frederick Sedgley, but he was interrupted by the discreet entrance of Anderson, who coughed politely.

'Mr Archibald Rossdale,' he announced.

3.

Barely minutes before Albert Chesney's dilapidated fly deposited Archie Rossdale at the front door, George Johnstone had entered the house. He walked rapidly up the main staircase and along the so-called Bachelors' Corridor at the top until he reached his bedroom. Once he was inside he sat on the edge of his bed and considered his position. He had not bargained for the more than frosty reception that had greeted him from Elizabeth Howard.

'London is London,' she had said, 'but here at Drayfield we are no more than slight acquaintances. I trust that we will both enjoy a pleasant week but there must be nothing more. It will be Mrs Howard and Mr Johnstone as it was at Carlton House Terrace, and dear George,' she had continued ominously. 'You are well aware of my feelings about Millicent.'

Johnstone stared morosely out of his window and watched as Archie Rossdale clambered out of the carriage and was ushered into the house by Anderson. He had hoped that his relationship with Elizabeth Howard would develop along more profitable lines in every sense of the word, but clearly this was not to be the case. As it happened Millicent Howard was not in his sights, or had not been, but he disliked being put down, as he saw it. The stupid woman will deserve everything that she gets, he thought to himself. There were various possibilities open to him at Drayfield and one, perhaps even two, would not be at all to Elizabeth Howard's liking. He opened his pocket book and slid out the piece of paper that had been carefully placed inside it. One never knew when ammunition might be required. He read it through once again and then replaced it. Feeling rather more satisfied with himself than he had when he entered the room, he stood up and adjusted his tie in the mirror.

Minutes later Johnstone emerged from the Bachelors' Corridor and moved across to the gothic archway that marked the start of the main landing. He turned and looked over the balustrade. All seemed quiet. The rest of the party was obviously still in the saloon where Archie Rossdale was probably regaling them with the story of the exploits in town that had led to his arrival a day later than the others. As he listened the sound of muffled laughter rose up the stairwell. Rossdale was a popular member of the house-party and clearly had been able to explain away his tardiness to Lady Violet's satisfaction.

Johnstone walked through the arch and looked about him. An arch to his left led to a small corridor. On the right hand side of the landing were four doors, and opposite them was a wall covered in flock wall-paper and embellished with a series of sporting lithographs. Jackson noticed that three of the doors, those furthest from him, sported brass nameplate escutcheons. He strode swiftly across and studied them. He then glanced at the lithographs. They were racing scenes and the first in the series was entitled *Vale of Aylesbury Steeple Chase.*

As he turned to retrace his steps to the staircase a maid appeared from the corridor that ran parallel to the landing. She stopped in surprise on seeing him.

'Just admiring these dashed fine prints, my dear,' he said lightly. 'Tell me, what is your name,' he went on, and made to catch hold of her arm. 'It's Ellen, isn't it,' he went on. 'Yes, Ellen. A very pretty name, if I may say so.'

The maid backed away from him in alarm, then dropped a quick curtsey before scuttling back into the corridor. Jackson glanced once again in the direction of the staircase then followed her into the corridor. About twenty minutes elapsed before he emerged again with an expression of annoyance on his face. He stared once more at the doors and their nameplates before moving briskly down the staircase to the hall.

'Rutherford,' he called out to a figure that was just emerging from the ante-room opposite the main entrance. 'Rutherford, care to join me for a ride in the park?'

And oblivious of the baleful stare of Anderson the butler, who was standing in the shadows by the door leading to the kitchen wing, he strode down the hall humming contentedly as he did so.

4.

Thursday 17th September 1964

Autumn term that year started on the 17th September. Nicholas returned from a summer holiday in Florence to find, amongst a whole pile of letters awaiting his attention, a note from Jane Emburey.

Dear Nick, it started. *You will be interested to hear, I hope, that my great work continues apace – and will be delighted to learn that you merit a credit for your heraldic efforts. I have found a man who will do me a map of the estate and a plan of the house itself. My tutor thinks it is going well too, so that must be a bonus. The other day my outsider came in - a letter from the Earl of St Boswells' secretary. Apparently they have four letters in their archives written by Lady Violet Sedgley to her sister, the Countess of St Boswells, including the one from 1897. The others are all earlier. She is going to send me a photocopy of the 1897* one. Apparently it is largely concerned with Elizabeth Howard, but it also has details about the horses the various members of the party backed as well as a bit of information about Charles S., and George J., who seems to have seduced one of the housemaids. What fun !!!

Now for some news that is rather more up your street. The Rector of Barcombe told me that his predecessor, who retired just after the war, attended the Drayfield Sale in 1939 and bought a rather magnificent heraldic tray there. Apparently it was solid silver and in the centre were the Sedgley arms. According to the rector it was 'an impaled coat with twelve quarterings on the sinister side'. Presumably this means something to you. I am sure that it must do. He says that anyone interested in Drayfield history ought to have a look at it. To cut a long story short, he gave me his predecessor's last known address, and although the old man has long since moved on to a happier heraldic hunting ground in the sky - I hope you appreciate the alliteration !!! – the tray is still in existence. It is now owned by the old man's daughter, who is married and who lives in Scotland, near Jedburgh, to be precise, and Jedburgh, in case you didn't know, is just over the border. I have to see my tutor before Christmas and so will arrange to spend an extra couple of nights up there and to visit Mrs Hick - the daughter – and see the tray. I have already phoned and she is agreeable. I will take a camera with me and show you the results of all this on my return.

And another piece of news,' the letter continued. 'I have met a Mrs Bridgewater who is the daughter of Anderson, butler at Drayfield until 1910 or thereabouts. She showed me a photograph of her father together with the rest of the staff. Thirteen altogether. A butler, a housekeeper, two footmen (in livery), a lady's maid, a cook and seven other maids. She wasn't sure, but she thought there were two parlour maids, a housemaid, three up-stairs maids and a still-room maid. What on earth is a still-room maid? Luv, J.

PS. By the way, I have found the rest of the doll.. Seven pieces altogether and no clothes to speak of. Much restoration required.

Nicholas thought long and hard and then responded.

Dear Jane - A tray with twelve quartering plus the Countess of St B, plus Mrs Bridgewater; your cup is positively cascading over. I should love to read the 1897 letter. Please keep it safe and sound until we next meet. Will you drive up to Newcastle, then Jedburgh? If so, and if you arrange your trip for early November – to be exact, my half-term, would you like company and shared driving? I have an aunt in Jesmond, a Newcastle suburb, who would love to see me, and then we could inspect your tray together.

He sat back and considered for a moment before signing off.

All the best, love Nick. PS, Delighted to hear about the doll but clothes absolutely essential.

CHAPTER FOUR

1.

Wednesday 2nd June 1897

A feature of the Derby House Parties at Drayfield Hall was the sweepstake, or Drayfield Sweep, as it had become known over the years. Derby Day itself saw the members of the house party assemble in the saloon after breakfast. Guests were greeted with the sight of a large punchbowl placed meticulously on the imposing oak table that graced the centre of the room. Beside it stood an upturned shako, once worn by Frederick Sedgley's father in the late 1850s, when he raised a troop of volunteer riflemen at a time of perceived national emergence. Within the punch bowl were placed slips of paper bearing the names of the runners in the day's big race. Lady Violet, who together with her husband stood on one side of the table, read out a list of the horses, and then invited her guests to step forward, one by one, and pick a slip of paper from the bowl. Guests then dropped a sovereign in the shako and returned to their places to discuss the likely fate of the horse that they had selected. The sovereigns remained in the shako until the end of Derby Day when, tradition had it, the winner handed the shako to Anderson and asked him to distribute the sovereigns amongst the staff.

Derby Day in 1897 was no exception to the general rule. After the usual excellent breakfast of porridge, eggs, kedgeree and fish, then cold pheasant and tongue, together with a choice of tea or coffee, the party assembled to hear 'Aunt Violet's reading', as Charles Sedgley described it. The three young officers chatted together by the window, the Rossdales, father, mother and daughter, seated themselves on chairs conveniently placed to the right of the door that led into the little drawing room. There they were joined by Elizabeth Howard and her daughter, Millicent. Sir Robert Carey strolled around the room admiring the heraldic frieze, while his wife, a trifle uneasily, hovered between the Rossdales and the Howards. She was well aware that her husband disapproved of gambling, and was still uncertain what his reaction would be to Lady Violet's 'harmless flutter', as Sybil Rossdale had put it the previous evening.

'Ladies and Gentlemen,' said Lady Violet, firmly, 'your attention please.' Sir Robert hastily seized a chair, sat down and motioned to his wife to occupy an adjoining one. The three young men stopped talking and turned attentively towards their hostess, and Frederick Sedgley gave the paper slips a quick stir. Victoria Sedgely tapped the shako suggestively and smiled at her friends by the window. 'Ladies and gentlemen,' repeated Lady Violet. 'The runners in today's race are as follows.' She picked up a sheet of paper from the table in front of her and read out a list of eleven names. Then:

'We have our usual problem this year, I am afraid. Our gathering outnumbers the horses by two. Fortunately, Sir Robert has offered to withdraw from the contest and so if Victoria and I share the last horse to be drawn all should be well.' She replaced the sheet of paper on the table and surveyed her audience. 'Good luck to you all. Lady Carey, would you be good enough to pick your horse?'

Lady Carey stepped forward, closed her eyes, and hastily drew a slip of paper from the bowl. She handed it to Lady Violet who announced, '*Prime Minister*, owned by Mr T. Wadlow'. There was a polite round of applause. 'Mrs Howard,' she went on. 'Your horse, if you please.'

2.

Tuesday 10th August 1999

'Mark Paddon-Browne will attend our next meeting,' said Councillor Barnes, 'and has asked for two further items to be added to the agenda, the picture hang and the question of catalogues.' I nodded and made an appropriate note. He continued, 'Have you made much progress with the Emburey woman and the question of a catalogue or something similar for the Sedgley Room?'

I rummaged in my case for my file. 'Not much, I am afraid,' I admitted. 'Newcastle University has no address other than the Barcombe one. I have drawn a blank on most of the names in the acknowledgements. Most were University lecturers of one sort or another, and her own tutor, who got most of the thanks, is now dead. There was a Nicholas Markham, who helped her with the heraldic decorations, and a J.A.Hignett, who provided a map of the estate and plans of the rooms. Markham is as elusive as Mrs Emburey and Hignett . . . well, he still lives locally. I have a Southwater address. At the moment he is visiting a sister in Canada, but I have arranged to meet him when he returns, which is shortly before our next meeting. Another sister, who lives in Barcombe, was happy to fix things up.'

Councillor Barnes nodded. 'Good, good,' he said. 'Keep me posted as and when things happen. I want to open next spring as part of the Millennium celebrations. I will be spelling this out to everyone at the meeting and if we can't find our missing author we will have to do something ourselves.' He stared at me thoughtfully. Perhaps a leaflet and a family tree. That sort of thing,' he said.

'May I ask how the things are progressing with the Carpenter portrait?' I asked.

'I will have news at the next meeting,' Councillor Barnes replied mysteriously.

As it turned out I met Mr Hignett three days before our next Fine Arts and Library Committee meeting. He lived in a modern bungalow on the outskirts of Barcombe and was a man of about 65 to 70, who wore a large hearing aid in his left ear. 'Can I tempt you to a sherry?' he asked as he ushered me into a sitting room decorated with model trains, pictures of assorted railway scenes and what I guessed were maps and plans of various railway lines. Above the mock fireplace was a huge sign, obviously from a station, bearing the legend *Eilden Halt.* 'My hobby,' announced Mr Hignett proudly. 'I do the maps myself and at the moment I am building this.' He pointed at a large model of a green locomotive that was taking shape on a table by the window.

'Yes,' he said. 'I remember Jane quite well. It must have been oh, nearly forty years ago. She wanted me to do a map of the Drayfield Hall estate. You know, farms, lodges, cottages, that sort of thing. She was particularly interested in who lived where and what they did. I wasn't much help with that side of things, but I did produce quite a competent map for her. Then she asked me to do a plan of the house, upstairs and downstairs. She wanted to show how it worked.' He paused for a moment. 'How it worked, yes those were her exact words. You know, she wanted to map out how servants moved around the place without colliding with their betters.'

I nodded and sipped my sherry.

'I was working on a project myself at the time, to do with the Sedgley family and the arrival of the railway.' He stared at me with the light of enthusiasm in his eyes. 'They made quite a killing, you know, when the London & South Coast arrived on the scene in the 1860s. The company had to buy several fields and Charles Sedgley – he was the owner at the time – cashed in. At first the Sedgleys were against the whole thing, but they changed their tune fast enough when they realised how much money was at stake. Then there was also the question of compensation.'

'Compensation,' I queried. 'For what?'

'The water table,' he answered. 'When they created the embankment they messed things up and the Sedgleys lost a couple of wells that totally dried up. Of course it didn't really matter as the Barcombe Water Company began to supply water at about the same time, or within a few years at any rate. Jane dealt with it in her thesis, and if you read it you will see that I get a credit in a footnote for pointing her in the direction of the Water Company Records.'

'Have you any idea what became of Mrs Emburey?' I asked, as he topped up my glass.

'I am afraid not,' he replied. 'She lived quite close to my old home in Hedge Lane, and her husband played for Barcombe 2nd XI cricket team. I do remember that as there was a bit of a problem because he missed the end of one particular season and they were short of whatever it was he did. Spin bowling, I believe, but I can't be certain. It was a very long time ago. But it must have been very shortly after she finished her thesis.' He thought for a moment. 'There was some talk of a love affair but whether it involved Jane or her husband – Victor, that was his name – I really couldn't be sure. Victor Emburey, yes that was it, and he was a leg-break bowler. Barcombe's answer to Johnny Wardle, they used to say. But that was before he was married. Wardle played for Yorkshire,' he explained, 'but was sacked after a row with the committee.'

'And Jane?' I prompted gently.

'Oh yes,' he went on. 'I think she moved away shortly after the love affair, whatever it was. I am sure Victor never reappeared, so perhaps he went off with a girlfriend and she decided to move out and start afresh elsewhere. Of course she probably married again and goodness knows what her name would be now. I suppose you could try and find

Victor. He might know what happened to her.' He shrugged his shoulders apologetically. 'I am sure she would have no objection to your using her work for your gallery, she wasn't that sort of girl at all. No, if I were you I would go ahead and use it.'

I passed on Mr Hignett's comments to the committee three days later. Mark Paddon-Browne had been giving everyone a lot of detail about his proposed catalogue and the general feeling was that the Sedgley Room required something equally professional if not containing quite so much detail.

'Perhaps, Richard,' said Councillor Barnes, 'you could have a good look at the Emburey thesis and see if you could re-hash the relevant chapter in a form suitable for publication yourself? After all, we have made every effort to find her, and as long as we make all possible acknowledgements I am sure that there could be no adverse come-back.'

'The Visitors Book she used would be a major addition either for the Sedgley Room or for the local collection in the Smoking Room,' said Mrs Vanstone, 'and there is a rather fine silver salver bearing the Sedgley arms that she certainly had sight of when she did her researches, which would be an added attraction for the Sedgley Room.' She paused for a moment then continued. 'I feel that it would be worth persevering in our search for her for that reason alone.' The committee members nodded and grunted their agreement. Mrs Vanstone's eyes lit up at this stage in a manner reminiscent of Mr Hignett when discussing his railways.

'Mrs Emburey used letters from the St Boswells archive that is now housed at Shropshire County Record Office. I have been in touch with them and the present Earl of St Boswells and it seems likely,' she went on with a note of triumph in her voice, 'that four letters written by Lady Violet Sedgley to her sister, the Countess of St Boswells, will be deposited here at Drayfield once the gallery is open. At first this will be a temporary loan, but I have been led to believe that it could well become permanent.'

A buzz of approval arose from around the table. Councillor Barnes looked around with a smile on his face. 'Given the good news we heard earlier regarding the Carpenter portrait and now this,' he said, 'I think we can congratulate ourselves on the highly satisfactory way in which matters are progressing. Now,' he shuffled his papers, 'item seven on the agenda – security. As you know the Council has appointed Mr Sam Kendle to be our security officer, and his flat, number 3, is now ready for occupation. Mr Kendle will take up his duties at approximately the same time that Mr Paddon-Browne moves into his apartment, that is to say the first week in September. In fact the only thing that is holding up further progress, and by that I mean the transfer of the Beckingsale Collection from Barcombe Lodge to Drayfield Hall, is the technical installations.'

Technical installations or rather the lack of them occupied the bulk of the rest of the meeting, and it was with a noticeable sigh of relief that the committee greeted the arrival of 'any other business'. Mrs McGinty's request that the question of the Gallery Shop be dealt with at the next meeting was granted and the time and date of that next meeting was fixed for the first week in October. Formalities having been dealt with, Mark leant across the table to me.

'Drop in and see how my office is progressing,' he said.

3.

Wednesday 2nd June 1897

The Countess of St Boswells,
Ashurst Lodge,
Bridgenorth,
Shropshire.
Derby Day June 1897

My dearest Kitty,

    Frederick, Vicky and I send you our warmest love and greetings in this my twelfth Derby letter to you. We trust that you and James have celebrated in suitable style and that this glorious weather has permitted the males in your family to have put in several hours on the river.

    Our Derby party this year has not been the great success for which I had hoped although on the surface all have enjoyed a tolerable time. The best news is that we had the good fortune, thanks to Mrs Howard, to meet the P of W. His horse, Oakdene, came fourth, and as Vicky and I had drawn him in the sweep HRH was vastly amused. He remembered the party at Dalkeith when you and I were presented by the Dss of Buccleuch, or at least he said he did. He remembered you in blue, which I knew to be quite wrong, but I thought it best not to correct him. Mrs H has promised to have a word with Lady Dudley and so I have high hopes that a visit to Drayfield might be arranged for next year. Just imagine if he could be persuaded to grace us at a Derby party! But I must not raise my hopes too high.

    Our stratagems for Vicky and Charles have I fear come to naught. Charles if anything shows an interest in Millicent Howard, Elizabeth Howard's girl, while Vicky seems to be besotted with a most unsuitable officer, formerly of the

Royal Welch Regiment, who was invited here at the behest of Edward Rossdale, who gets more obtuse by the minute and who has gone down in my estimation as a result.

My greatest faux pas, dear Kitty, has been to invite Robert Carey and his wife to a party including young officers. All was done for the best of motives and for the sake of Frederick, and at first all seemed to go well. Yesterday Sir Robert told us all about a piece he is writing for some magazine that was really quite amusing and even Edward R. joined in, but dinner was quite spoiled for me at least by the gentlemen arguing non-stop about the rights and wrongs of the infamous Raid.

You will recall that Charles was very much the prot_g_ of Johnny Willoughby, Jameson's military commander, and to make matters worse Sir Robert was one of the prosecutors who 'sent Johnny down' at the trial. Charles, as I confess I did not know although Frederick I am sure did, was a witness for the defence. Need I say more?

There was one exciting episode to make up for a somewhat frosty atmosphere. In an attempt to drag the conversation away from the Transvaal I turned to Mrs Howard whether she had any experience of the real 'wild west'. She admitted that she had travelled through the prairies and had seen several Red Indians. Someone, it might have been Tilly, then asked her whether or not she had ever handled a gun. She replied very archly that she had been shooting with the Prince of Wales on more than one occasion, but then on being pressed to admit whether she had shot Red Indians, she admitted that although she had not actually shot at Red Indians she did possess a revolver and that she had it upstairs!

Imagine our amazement when she turned to me and said 'May I?' and then to Anderson, who was standing behind Frederick.

'Anderson,' she said, 'would you be so good as to ask Broomfield,' (her maid), 'to fetch me the cedar-wood box from my portmanteau.'

We all waited agog until Anderson reappeared with the required box. She opened it and produced a small imitation-pearl handled revolver.

'A Smith and Wesson,' she said, and she spun the chamber round, extracted six shells, and then handed the gun to Frederick.

'My father gave it to me on my eighteenth birthday,' she explained.

We all passed it around, and the men in particular were most impressed. Mr Rutherford asked her whether she had ever fired it in anger and, I could hardly believe my ears, she acknowledged that she had once fired it to frighten off an intruder and once to stop unwanted attentions. 'It certainly ended the attentions,' she said, 'and I only winged him.' She was laughing when she said all this and I really do not know whether she was speaking the truth or simply joking. I very much hope the latter, but really, what an appalling life she must have led. They say that the Prince is quite captivated by her stories and I have to admit that I can quite see why, but at that moment I understood why Frederick said to me while dressing,

'My dear, we are not Marlborough House and we never will be.'

At any rate, my ploy had the desired effect. The Transvaal was forgotten for the rest of the evening and the conversation revolved around the so-called opening up of the West. We heard a lot about Elizabeth Howard's father, Mr Andrew Tritton, who made a lot of money building 'rail roads', as they are called. Millicent Howard opened up quite considerably. She is a very striking young lady with golden blonde hair and the young men were suitably impressed, and I include Archie Rossdale, who arrived yesterday morning, a day after the rest of the party assembled.

Somewhat to my surprise Archie took Sir Robert's side in our African debate about the rights and wrongs of the Raid. Luckily political differences did not affect friendships and Archie and Charles remain the best of pals. Tilly Rossdale lined up with the military versus the politicians when battle resumed after dinner, so while I endeavoured to play a rubber of bridge with Lady Carey and the Rossdales, a battle royal was being waged beside us.

As far as the sweep was concerned, the winner was Edward Rossdale. I teamed up with Vicky and as I have already mentioned, we drew Oakdene. I was hoping for Silver Fox, but was foiled by Sybil Rossdale. Her husband as usual generously handed his guineas to Anderson for distribution among the staff. His stock backstairs, as is to be expected, remains as high as it has ever been. At least one member of our party has not been so fortunate. The young officer who has so smitten Vicky has 'stepped out of line' with one of our housemaids. I am not supposed to know anything of this matter but I am well aware that the youngsters held a drumhead court martial and I am half expecting the disgraced lieutenant to decamp without further ado. I wonder whether dear Mama was ever faced with such problems.

Enough of Drayfield. What of Ashurst Lodge? And what of the government in such a pickle? The South Africa Committee has not given the Secretary of State a happy time, but as you know he was never one of my favourites. I could accept the Duke but not the man from Brummagem, I am afraid. However, as Frederick said to Sir Robert last night, once Mr Rhodes is back in Africa, the whole sorry episode will probably die a death.

Tomorrow the Rossdales visit Gatton Park then on Friday some of our party ride back to Epsom for The Oaks.

Others have elected to spend the day in the garden although Frederick and Sir Robert plan to walk across the park to the church. On Saturday we look forward to Lady Clonkerry's Ball at Hensford House. The young men will ride, Frederick and I will accompany the Rossdales in the landau, the girls chaperoned by Mrs Howard will travel in the double-victoria, and Sir Robert and Lady Carey have decided that the brougham will do them nicely. I cannot remember when we last had all three vehicles on the road together. I am reliably informed that no less a personage than the Lord Lieutenant is a guest so we are all looking forward to our visit with eager anticipation.

All the talk now is of the Jubilee Procession and the Devonshire House Ball, but Anderson is lurking at the door, doubtless to tell me that the walkers have returned from their turn around the gardens. I will dispatch this without further ado and remain, dear Kitty,

Your affectionate sister,
Violet.

4.

Thursday 19th November 1964

'You haven't really got an aunt in Jesmond, have you?' asked Jane as they drove north that November.

'No,' admitted Nicholas, 'but don't worry. I shan't force my attentions upon you. It just seemed too good to be true. The chance to spend a couple of days with you, I mean.'

'Where will you stay?' asked Jane. 'I can't see myself smuggling you into the hall of residence.'

'Oh I'll find somewhere,' said Nicholas. 'And while you have your tutorial I will explore Newcastle. When do we go to Jedburgh?'

Jane consulted her diary. 'Tutorial tomorrow at eleven, dinner with tutor and wife in the evening. Jedburgh, Saturday afternoon, and return home Sunday. You can buy me dinner somewhere on Saturday. And seriously, Nick, I am very flattered by your machinations, even though conversation and a heraldic tray will have to serve as your reward. I am a married woman, just, and I have got a family, so please, please, don't push things.'

Nick stared out of the window. 'Actually,' he said, 'I did have an aunt, but she lived well to the north of Newcastle and she died several years ago. As a child I spent a lot of time with her and so I do know my way around the borders. I have even been to Jedburgh,' he added. 'You know, it really is a very small world, isn't it?' He paused for a moment then turned to his companion.

'Jane,' he said. 'I have a confession to make.'

Jane reached across and put her hand on his knee.

'No confessions, please,' she said. 'Just enjoy the drive, and I shall be very grateful if you show me something of the borders. As you are perfectly well aware I lead a pretty gloomy life with Victor and this weekend will be a fantastic break, but no confessions, please. Life is complicated enough as it is. Live for the day, as the prophet said. No questions, no soul searching and definitely no confessions.'

Nicholas stared ahead and thought for a while.

'Fair enough,' he said, 'you're the boss.'

Jane's tutorial that Friday was clearly a great success and the following day they drove north to Jedburgh to view the tray. On the way conversation covered the food and accommodation at the hall of residence – 'primitive' – and the standard of B&B's in Newcastle – 'antediluvian'.

Nicholas also learnt more of late nineteenth century life at Drayfield.

'I have had three meetings with Mrs Bridgewater,' said Jane, 'and each one has produced more than the one before. It is absolutely fascinating. Apparently at the end of the day her grandfather used to stand at the foot of the stairs handing out silver candlesticks for the family and guests to light their way to bed. She also said that the house had gas from the 1880s, so I must check whether the candle routine preceded the gas installation or continued as well as. There were two footmen and one of them left Drayfield and became the first chauffeur in Barcombe, working for a doctor.'

The tray from Drayfield more than lived up to expectations. As had been reported, it showed the Sedgley arms impaling twelve quarterings.

'It must have been a wedding present,' said Nicholas. 'On the right you have the arms of the Earl of Storeton, Lady Violet Sedgley's father. Look,' and he pointed at the shield in the centre of the tray, 'the Storeton arms are in the first and twelfth quarters and all the others are families into which the Storetons married over the years, well centuries. You see that fifth quarter?'

Jane nodded.

'Those are the arms of the Norton family. *Azure a maunche ermine overall a bend gules.* That means a blue shield with an ermine maunche on it and over the maunche there is a diagonal red lion.'

'What on earth is a maunche?' asked Jane.

'A lady's sleeve.'

'It doesn't look like a lady's sleeve,' she objected. 'May I?' she said to tray's owner and she unhitched her camera and took some photographs.

Mrs Hick, the owner of the tray, was a well preserved lady in her middle sixties. She studied the tray carefully.

'Oh yes, I see,' she said at last. The arm goes through that top bit and the rest hangs down.' She thought for a moment then asked, 'Do you think the family would like it back? It is of no use to me and it would be nice if it could be returned.'

Jane smiled sadly. Nicholas opened his mouth as if to say something then closed it again.

'I am afraid the line has died out,' Jane said. 'I will certainly ask around. Maybe the council would be interested; after all it is a piece of local history. Why don't you find out how much it is worth and then let me know?'

'My father bought it just before the war,' explained Mrs Hick. 'He used to serve sherry from it when we visited him, my late husband and I.' She turned the tray over and stared at it. 'I have no idea how much he paid for it, but it must be worth something now. Prices were very low, you know, just before the war. I suppose people had other things to think about.'

I'd be very tempted to buy it myself,' said Jane, 'if it wasn't too expensive. Perhaps I could give it to Victor as a birthday present then he could hardly argue about the cost. But whatever you do make sure you get a decent price for it. Ask two or three reputable antique dealers what they think, and then at least you will have an idea of its true value.'

The promised dinner took place at the Wolflee Hotel in Roxburghshire about two miles from Bonchester Bridge. It was set in classic border country surrounded by its own timbered grounds and was about half and hour's drive from Jedburgh.

'What about tonight?' asked Nicholas. 'It will be quite a drive back to Newcastle after dinner. Shall I book us a couple of rooms here?'

'For a potential seducer you are far too tentative,' replied Jane. 'Make it a double and have done with it.'

'I am afraid I am not very practised at this sort of thing,' said Nicholas in some confusion. 'And I wouldn't want you to think . . .'

'I've thought,' said Jane, and so they stayed.

The conversation over dinner was largely taken up with matters to do with Drayfield Hall and for Nicholas, whose mind was in a turmoil as to exactly what was going to happen after the meal had concluded, the information that Jane was supplying went largely over his head. He had the sense, however, to congratulate her on her obviously satisfactory session with her tutor, and her pleasure at the discoveries she had made.

'When I am next in Surrey,' he said boldly, 'you must take me on another visit. I am intrigued by your Bachelors' Corridor and the interconnecting family bedrooms. Yes, another visit is definitely called for.'

He stretched out his hand and was relieved when the pressure was returned.

They made love that night for the first time and for Nicholas, who was relatively inexperienced in such matters, the whole procedure was as unnerving as it was exhilarating.

'You poor darling,' said Jane. 'I had no idea. Don't they teach you anything at University these days?'

The following morning they set out for Newcastle via Carter Bar and Otterburn. Nicholas was in seventh heaven. The weather was crisp and sunny, the landscape was breathtaking, and beside him sat, he was certain, the love of his life. The fact that she was already married and had a life of her own several hundred miles away seemed at that moment to be of little importance.

'May I call in this Christmas to see you again,' he asked.

She looked at him quizzically. 'Last night was last night,' she said. 'It would be lovely if you could but in this life one must grab what moments of happiness that one can.

Yes, I am sure we can work something out, but please, please don't think that this can develop into something it can't. If you were older and we had met ten years ago then perhaps we could have loved one another properly, but as it is . . .'

Jane paused and stared out of her window. 'Do come,' she said quietly, 'we'll think of something.'

Very shortly after they had set out they reached Carter Bar. Nicholas stopped the car and they climbed out.

'The Cheviot Hills in all their glory. The summit here is over 1400 feet high,' said Nicholas, 'and you have fantastic views all over the Borders. Down there,' he pointed south, 'is Kielder Water and as far as we are concerned it is a straight road to Newcastle. I think it is all so spectacularly beautiful. It is when I come to spots like this that I really believe in the spirit of place. I get a sense of belonging and a feeling that wherever I go here is a place to which I will always return.'

Jane smiled and shook her head. 'Breathtaking scenery, yes,' she said, 'but I am a wanderer by nature. I don't feel tied to places. People, perhaps, but not places. Still, I do agree with you. This is a magical part of the world and you were very lucky to have lived here. Where exactly was it,' she asked.

'Otterburn,' replied Nicholas. 'There was a battle there in 1388. The Douglas's of Scotland versus the Percys of England. All very romantic and rather like a football match. The Scots won,' he added. 'My parents were in Malta for some years and I stayed with my aunt, who was my father's sister, while they were away.'

'This has been a lovely morning,' said Jane as they drove into the suburb of Gosforth to collect her belongings from the hall of residence there. 'In fact it has been a positively idyllic few days that I will never ever forget.'

'What about this Christmas?' asked Nicholas, as they drove south after lunch.

'I must submit my dissertation next May and I have arranged to have another session with my tutor in January or early February,' replied Jane. 'I will drop you a line in a few weeks time and we will fix up a meeting at Drayfield this Christmas and then, if we both still feel the same, we could organise another holiday when I come up north next year. Now, enough of that. Let's change the subject.'

'Mrs Bridgewater?' prompted Nicholas.

'Ah yes, an absolute gem,' replied Jane, gratefully. 'I will now bore you with more details until we reach the station. Let me see. The outside staff at Drayfield included a coachman and two grooms, a head gardener with a staff of eight, a head cowman, a poultry farmer and several labourers at work in the park itself.' She counted on her fingers. 'There was a private laundry that employed three maids. Her grandfather, as butler, valeted for the family and the footmen valeted for the guests, at least if they didn't bring their own servants. Apparently the footmen were paid half a sovereign a week and white gloves were always worn for the serving of food.'

'I am suitably impressed,' said Nicholas.

'Oh, there's much more,' said Jane with a smile. 'The second footman cleaned the silver and the ladies' shoes. The first footman did the gentlemen's shoes. And talking of the footmen, did I tell you that she showed me a photograph of the staff in about 1907? It would have been nice to include the picture and reproductions of the portraits in the library in my dissertation, but it would cost too much to do it properly and anyway, my tutor says that illustrations are not required for a thesis. But I think I will have pictures for my own copy, whatever the expense.'

'Are you still comparing Drayfield with that other house?' asked Nicholas.

'Bearwood?' said Jane. 'Yes. Of course Drayfield is much smaller, but there was still a fair amount of division. As far as the house party was concerned the family, or rather Frederick and Lady Violet, had their own rooms. Married guests occupied two double rooms on the Barcombe side of the house. The chief guest suite was in the Chapel Corridor that started at the top of the stairs and further along this corridor was accommodation for unmarried ladies. Bachelors had bedrooms on the lower corridor which started half way up the staircase. You know, through that door which led to the room where we found all those bits and pieces. Both corridors led to the servants' quarters that were behind the proverbial green baize door, or rather doors. And of course there was a servants' staircase as well. I am working on that part of the house at the moment, but it's very difficult as it has been mucked around with to such an extent that it is difficult to sort everything out.'

'Oh well,' said Nicholas, 'you can go through all the problems with me when I see you at Christmas.'

It was evening when they reached Surrey and Jane drove Nick to the car-park where he had left his own car, three days earlier.

'I hate goodbyes,' said Jane, 'but it has been a lovely weekend and come what may we can always hang on to that. I don't know about you, but it is not going to be easy for me. Still, what will be will be,' and she kissed him on the lips before staring out of the window.

Nicholas seized her hand and kissed it as he clambered out of the car. 'Until next month,' he whispered as Jane slipped the clutch and the car began to move away.

'Until next month,' responded Jane, and she blew him a kiss as he raised his arm in farewell.

Nicholas stared after her until the rear lights disappeared from view. Already the events of the last four days were turning themselves into a delightful yet totally unreal dream. With his mind in a whirl and an aching sensation in the pit of his stomach he returned to his car and drove slowly off in the opposite direction.

5.

Wednesday 2nd June 1897

'I am very worried about Tilly,' said Lady Rossdale to Lady Violet as they sipped their coffee in the small drawing room after Wednesday's dinner. Beside them their respective husbands were playing a rubber of bridge with Mrs Howard and Lady Carey. Sir Robert Carey was dozing peacefully by a crackling fire and through the open door to the large drawing room the three young ladies were engrossed in conversation with George Johnstone and Lance Rutherford.

'Worried about Tilly,' said Lady Violet, raising her voice slightly for her friend's benefit, 'Whatever for?'

'You know she is a great friend of the Marlborough's daughter, Sarah Wilson?' replied Lady Rossdale. 'Well, Lady Sarah was in South Africa last year with her husband. They were there at the time of the Raid, as a matter of fact. They sailed back on the *Roslin Castle* and Tilly met Lady Sarah again a few weeks ago. I believe that she introduced Tilly to Cecil Rhodes at Lady Baxendale's. Tilly was with her aunt, of course, but you can't have eyes everywhere.'

'Go on dear,' said Lady Violet.

'The point is that Lady Sarah has filled Tilly's head with ideas of South Africa and she is determined to go there. Of course, it is all quite ridiculous. What Lady Sarah does is one thing – after all she is five years older than Tilly and a married woman. Tilly is not and there is no question of anyone taking her. But she mopes and, I suspect, plots. Her father is quite unimpressed but he has no idea of what girls these days can get up to. He has ideas about Tilly and young Lord Brenton, but she does not seem in the least bit interested. As I say, it is all very worrying.'

'So that is why she was taking Charles's part in last night's discussion,' mused Lady Violet. 'I thought she seemed very well informed.'

'Oh yes,' agreed Lady Rossdale. 'Lady Sarah apparently saw Jameson out there and speaks very highly of him. She will. I am sure, have given a glowing account to Tilly. And to think, my dear, the man is now languishing in a prison somewhere. The whole episode just does not bear thinking of.'

'No, Sybil,' said Lady Violet. 'He was released after four months, I think it was. Ill health, I believe. Charles told me all about it. I gather he is quite an acceptable figure in Unionist circles, although of course the Liberals take a very different view.' She cast a wary eye in the direction of Sir Robert. 'But what can Tilly actually do, my dear?'

'They could ask her to accompany them next time they travel to the Cape, the Wilsons, I mean,' suggested Lady Rossdale.

'Out of the question,' said Lady Violet, firmly. They are not family, and anyway who would pay? I am sure Edward would not countenance anything of the kind. No, what Tilly needs and Vicky too for that matter is a husband and a family. Of course Lord Brenton will be at Hensford on Saturday and she is no chicken now, is she, my dear? And as for Vicky,'

'Who is now 22, is she not?' put in Lady Rossdale quickly.

'Well that's even worse,' continued Lady Violet. 'Why oh why cannot either Archie or Charles come up trumps. It is reasonable to suppose that one of them could come up to the scratch. Perhaps they have tried and have been rejected,' she concluded sadly but in the tone of voice that suggested that she knew perfectly well that this had not been the case.

In the smoking room the subjects of her conversation were enjoying their cigars and talking intently. Just before dinner Charles had been cross-questioned by his aunt about George Johnstone's credentials, about which he knew very little, but to make matters worse he had already been forced to undergo a painful interview with Anderson on the same subject.

'Caught snooping on the upper landing,' Charles had said tersely. 'To make matters worse he messed around with one of the maids who happens to be Anderson's niece and is walking out with William, the first footman. I mean, he could hardly have done worse if he had made an indecent suggestion to my aunt or your mother. Poor Anderson buttonholed me before we set off this morning and I had the devil of a job mollifying him. Most embarrassing it was, for both of us that is. I mean Anderson is a stickler for protocol and all that, and he hardly knew which way to look and I felt so bad about the whole business that anyone walking in would have thought that I was the guilty party. Anyway, I had a word with Rutherford, who knows the fellow slightly, and he said that he would speak to him.'

'His father has taken Nuttall Priory,' said Archie gloomily, 'but I have never set eyes on him before. The old man wanted to do Johnstone senior a favour and your aunt was desperate for another man after I came up with Lance Rutherford, so that's why he's here. But you know all that, don't you?'

Charles nodded and he sipped his brandy. 'He appears to have some sort of understanding with Mrs Howard and this afternoon he was positively oozing charm all over her daughter at the races. I wonder if he is trying to get at Miss Howard through her mother?'

'Much good that will do him,' retorted Archie, bitterly. 'She appears to be in Westerdale's pocket, or so everyone says. Tilly thinks that he is hoping to ingratiate himself with Victoria and that she is rather taken with him, but if that is so what was he playing at with Millicent Howard?'

'She was extremely cool with him over dinner,' said Charles. 'Millicent Howard, I mean. I don't think Westerdale has anything to fear from that quarter. But Vicky! Oh,' he said angrily. 'Why on earth did Aunt Violet invite him?'

Archie Rossdale nodded miserably. 'It's a rotten business to let the side down like that, and in someone else's house. And you never came across him in Africa? I am told that he had quite a reputation in his regiment. Dashed good swordsman,' he added as an afterthought.

'I met him once,' said Charles, tersely, 'and I didn't like him. There was talk of cheating at cards amongst other things. And I don't think for a moment that he had to resign over the raid. He wasn't there, either at Pitsani or Mafeking. There's a brother as well and he's an equally bad lot. Got chucked out of the Royal Fusiliers, so I'm told. Anyway, I followed up whatever Rutherford said to Johnstone with a few choice words before dinner. I told him to mend his manners,' he went on. 'I spoke to Tilly about it and we agreed that it would be too embarrassing to ask him to leave. I mean there's the question of the ball at Hensford House. And if you're right and Vicky has taken a fancy to the man, heaven only knows what the outcome will be. All in all it's a shoddy business. We must hope that he knows how to behave at Lady Clonkerry's.'

'Miss Howard,' said Archie, changing the subject hastily. 'Now there's a girl I would like to see more of. Has she decided to join the race party on Friday? I hope so. You know that tomorrow we, that is the family, are going en masse to the Deepdene. I would much rather that we were here. What about the rest of you?'

'A ride in the morning for those under the age of thirty, Aunt Violet, Mrs Howard and Lady Carey will doubtless jaw in one of the drawing rooms, and Uncle Frederick and Sir Robert are off to visit some church or other,' said Charles succinctly. 'As for your first question about the races on Friday, everyone is going except Sir Robert and Lady Carey, thank the lord. Every time that man looks at me it is as if I had just murdered his grandmother. When I closed my eyes at dinner this evening I was listening to his voice and imagining that I was back in the Law Courts last July. Poor Johnnie! Fooled by Chamberlain and Rhodes, and probably by Jameson was as well. My God, politics is a dirty business. Give me soldiering any day.'

Archie Rossdale listened sympathetically. 'Come on,' he said. 'Let's join the others.'

They walked along the hallway to the two drawing rooms. Lady Violet was writing a letter at a table by the window and Sir Robert Carey had now joined the bridge players. The two officers moved towards the group in the large drawing room, Archie Rossdale taking care to head in the direction of Millicent Howard.

CHAPTER FIVE

1.

Saturday 4th September 1999

Mark Paddon-Browne moved into his new apartment as arranged during the first week in September and on that Saturday he threw a housewarming party. The members of the committee were all invited and on my suggestion he also included Mr Hignett, who appeared delighted to accept. Various individuals from the town hall were also present together with a handful of arty types including the curators of at least three well known galleries. Another guest was Sam Kendle, our recently appointed security man who lived around the other side of the house in flat number 3.

I arrived rather later than I had hoped, parking my car in front of the house, and walked to the door at the end of the loggia as instructed on his invitation – although as we had discussed the party at great length before it all happened I was well aware of the procedure as regards entrance. I pressed the doorbell and announced myself to a small metal plate to the right of the door. There was a distinct buzz and I was able to push the door open. I walked in, followed a short corridor that wheeled around to the right, and found myself parallel to the main staircase and facing down the main hall. A large notice in front of me carried the message; *Party Upstairs*. I ascended the staircase, passing another notice on a small wooden stand that announced *Office Only*, and reached Mark's front door. I rang the bell and was admitted by Tim Lewis, one of the two Barcombe representatives on the committee.

'I was just standing here,' he said, 'so don't run away with the idea that I am an official welcoming party.'

I thanked him and looked around me. The hall in front of me had been very tastefully decorated, and a row of *Ert_* prints had been hung on the wall opposite the four doorways that I remembered from my last visit. A notice on another little easel said *Ladies Loo* and pointed to the little corridor on the left, and a second saying *Gents Loo* pointed down the main hall, where I noticed a third pointing to the right. The rooms on my right, which I remembered as being the kitchen and the dining room, seemed to be fairly well populated, and further down the hall other guests were moving in and out of the sitting room.

'It's absolutely palatial, this place,' said Tim Lewis. 'No wonder he took the job. And he has some rather nice bits and pieces. Oh, and by the way, there's a chap here from one of the London galleries. You can't miss him. Dressed up to the nines with a purple bow tie. Keep your back to the wall when he approaches. There's booze in the kitchen, some rather good nibbles in the dining room next door, and then we are supposed to drift down the hall to that room on the left. Rumour has it that Councillor Barnes is going to say a few words, heaven help us.'

'Who's that lady over there in the black outfit?' I asked, pointing to a rather statuesque blonde who was emerging from the dining room.

'That, believe it or not, arrived with our colleague Edwin Hooper. I think it is his sister,' he replied. 'It only goes to show you, doesn't it? So he is worth talking to after all.' He laughed uproariously and disappeared into the kitchen.

'Mark!' I called out, as I saw my host appearing from the sitting room at the end of the hall.

He saw me and replied: 'Get yourself a drink and join me in here. Grab a plate and some goodies while you are at it, and can you fix one for me?'

I wandered into the kitchen and helped myself to a glass of white wine. There was a barman on duty, but he seemed to be fully occupied with Mrs Vanstone and Mrs

McGinty. I then moved next door to the dining room. There was a rather impressive oak dining table in the centre of the room surrounded by eight what appeared to be Georgian chairs. The walls were hung with very good reproductions of eighteenth century old masters, at least half of which I recognised but could not name, and on the table was a wide array of savoury snacks. Officiating was Mrs Donaghue, whom I had last seen wheeling a tea trolley in the Town Hall a few hours earlier. She greeted me cheerily and I appropriated two plates that I loaded with an assortment of items from the table.

'Not all for me, Mrs Donaghue,' I announced hastily. 'I have instructions from our host.'

I then beat a hasty retreat as I noticed Desmond Davies approaching from the hall.

'Hullo Desmond,' I said. 'Speak to you later.' And I moved down the hall to the sitting room in search of Mark.

There must have been about twenty people scattered around the room. Councillors Barnes and Lathom were talking in an animated fashion to two ladies, neither of whom I recognised, and a youngish man wearing the infamous purple bow tie. Mrs Fitter and Roger Collet were surrounded by another group of worthies, some of whom I knew from the Town Hall. Edwin Hooper and his sister, the glamorous creature in black, were studying a map of the county that hung in the centre of the wall on the right of the doorway, and Mark himself was holding forth to three ladies by the window. I also noticed that both Ken Belton from *The Barcombe News* and Leslie Davies from *The County Times* had turned up. When he saw me Mark extricated himself from his female listeners and came across to join me.

'It's going very well,' he said as he helped himself to one of the plates, thus enabling me to put the other on a conveniently placed side table and to take a sip of wine from my glass. He looked up.

'Ah, he said. 'Let me introduce you to John Dickinson, an old friend from the Courtauld. He runs the Halesborough Art Gallery and is staying the night here. My first guest, so he's very honoured.'

The rather languid individual with the bow tie proffered a hand to me and laughed politely.

'Hullo,' I said. 'I am ashamed to say that I had no idea that Halesborough had an art gallery. I associate it with fish and chips, an Edwardian Spa and a rather avant garde theatre. Is Mark picking your brains for ideas about our extravaganza down here?'

'The fish and chips are excellent and they do some good work at the playhouse,' John Dickinson agreed, 'but our gallery is very different from yours. We are based in a late Victorian house in a crescent on the cliff, and the collection is mainly nineteenth century British. We do have a Van Dyck, though, and we thought we had a Reynolds until very recently. We have now been told that it is *workshop of.*'

'I had heard that the latest is that it is only *circle of,*' put in Mark, mischievously. 'The next thing you'll know that it has been demoted to *follower of.*' He looked at me. 'After that its *manner of,* then simply *after.*'

'What happens then?' I asked.

'The basement,' said John Dickinson, gloomily. 'We've already had that scenario with something purporting to by Alma-Tadema. It was pretty awful, whoever painted it, and so I was not too unhappy when it was carted down the stairs to the cellar. This one is rather different. To start with it's really quite good. Anyway, at the moment I am sticking to *workshop of* and to hell with Claud Horwitz at the Tate.'

'Their Reynolds man,' explained Mark. 'Oh, excuse me a moment, I have just spotted Leslie,' and thrusting his plate in my hand he strode off towards the doorway.

'Yes, you've got quite a collection here, haven't you?' said John Dickinson. Mark took me over to Barcombe Lodge this afternoon. There's an excellent Wouvermans there and of course the Terborch is a masterpiece. Did you know that there are three other versions? One in Edinburgh, one in the Rijksmuseum in Amsterdam, and one in Berlin. I have seen the ones in Edinburgh and Amsterdam but not the one in Germany.'

'I am ashamed to say that I haven't set eyes on the collection yet,' I admitted. 'I must get Mark to take me over. Tell me more about the Terborch. Is ours as good as the others?'

'Undoubtedly. They all date from 1654, 1655, and the interesting thing is that the Scottish one is entitled *The Singing Lesson*, the Dutch one *A Company in a Room* and the German one *Parental Admonition*. Actually the subject is neither parental advice nor a singing lesson. It is a brothel scene. Berlin's father and mother are in fact a client and a procuress, and the lady whom Scotland thinks is being taught singing is the object of the gentleman's desire.' He smiled. 'You've also got a Dou, a definite Metsu and a 'circle of' Metsu and various Van Mieris's, two by Franz and one by Willem, and two others. Mark is going to have a wonderful time with the catalogue, believe you me. Oh and your Terborch, by the way, calls itself *Lady and Cavalier*.'

'Have you met Councillor Lathom?' I asked, as I saw my colleague on the committee approaching, clutching a mushroom vol-u-vent in one hand and a half empty glass in the other. I rather warmed to Councillor Lathom, a tall, balding and rather shambling individual, whose protestations that he did not know anything about the matter in hand usually disguised the fact that he knew rather more than the person to whom he was speaking.

'Councillor Lathom, this is John Dickinson from Halesborough Art Gallery. John, Councillor Lathom was an old friend of Brigadier Beckingsale, the donor of our collection.'

'Dr Dickinson,' said Councillor Lathom. 'I have heard all about you from Mark Paddon-Browne. Now, tell me. What did you think of the paintings? Were they up to your northern standards?'

I left them discussing the relative merits of Dutch 17th century and English 19th century genre paintings while the councillor liberally scattered the floor with puff pastry. Mark was still deep in conversation with the reporter from *The County Times*, and so I strolled across the room to Edwin Hooper and his sister who were standing by the door by the window. I introduced myself.

'This is my sister, Judith, Mrs Judith Fredericks,' he said.

'Hullo Judith,' I said. 'I may call you Judith, I hope?'

'Judy,' she smiled. Now do tell us. 'What happens in there?' and she pointed at the carved oak door.

I opened it slightly to reveal a small space and then another identical door. 'I have no idea what goes on in there,' I said, 'but it's Mark's bedroom. There are three rooms like this, overlooking the gardens. This one was the lady of the house's room, the next her husband's and the third his dressing room. They all connect in this way.'

'So if he was in luck his wife could slip into his room without going out onto the landing,' said Judith.

'And if he was scared he could retreat into his dressing room,' put in Edwin Hooper. It was the first joke I had ever heard him make. Clearly the white wine he was consuming was lightening his approach to life.

'The dressing room is now Mark's bathroom,' I continued, 'although I gather that tonight it is the ladies' loo.'

'I must say that curators do themselves very well indeed,' said Judith. 'Was that table in the dining room here already or is it his?'

'That's his,' I replied, 'and so are all those chairs. I am afraid the council did not supply any of the furnishings, although they did contribute the carpets and curtains. He was allowed to make suggestions, so I'm told. Tim,' I called out to Tim Lewis, who was standing nearby with Mrs Vanstone, 'Mark did have some say when it came to curtains and carpets, didn't he?'

'Indeed he did,' said Mrs Vanstone, as the two of them approached us. 'I think he has chosen very well. I gather that his friend from up north has to make do with a poky little flat at the back of his gallery. Although it does have glorious sea views, so he told me,' she added.

'You know, I don't think I would like to live in an apartment even if it was as spectacular as this one if I had to walk along a rather gloomy corridor and then climb a staircase in order to get to my own front door,' said Judy Fredericks.

'I had something very similar when I lived in the Circus in Bath,' said Mrs Vanstone. 'I used to work in the library there, you know. You soon get used to it, although there one had several doors to other apartments as one went up the stairs. My flat was on the third floor, and so I had considerably more climbing to do than Mr Paddon-Browne will have to put up with. He will be all alone in a sense, although he has all those flats just the other side of the building.'

'Can you get to them from the gallery?' asked Judy.

'No,' said Tim, clearly anxious to become involved in the conversation. 'Well, one,' he corrected himself.

'There's a door on the left just after you leave Mark's front door, which now leads to number 3, the security officer's flat. You see that chap over there?' He pointed to a short ginger haired individual of vaguely military bearing. 'He's Sam Kendle, our security man. He's only just moved in.'

Tim thought for a moment and then turned to Judy Fredericks. 'Come and have a look,' he said. 'I'll give you a quick tour.'

He ushered her in the direction of the hallway and somewhat to his annoyance Edwin Hooper followed.

'Have you met Mr Kendle yet?' asked Mrs Vanstone, and on receiving a negative reply the two of us walked over to him. 'How are you settling in, Mr Kendle?' she asked.

The security man all but snapped to attention. 'Very comfortably, thank you,' he replied. I waited for the 'ma'am' but thankfully it did not come.

Mrs Vanstone introduced us. 'We have a meeting next week with Mark Paddon-Browne, I think,' I said. 'Councillor Barnes wants us to talk about security and duty rotas so that I can report back to the next committee meeting.'

Mr Kendle nodded. 'He feels that some of the other flats should be earmarked for council staff. He said that we might need added back-up for security reasons. He said that when I was away it would be a good thing to have someone else who had access to the gallery from the inside. From my flat, that's to say.'

The suggestion was news to me, although on the face of it seemed a very sensible thing to do, provided of course that Mr Kendle was prepared to fall in line with the idea. I wondered why it hadn't been thought of before. I turned back to Mrs Vanstone and Sam Kendle listened politely.

'How are things going with your rooms,' I asked.

'Very well indeed,' came the reply. 'The display cases will be delivered during the next fortnight and we have packed up the books that we need for the Smoking Room. One of my deputies will be on duty here and responsible for both the Sedgley Room and the Smoking Room. She will also sell the catalogues and the postcards when the shop isn't open. Now you come to mention it, she would be an ideal tenant for one of the other flats.' She thought for a moment and then changed the subject. 'We really do need that Visitors Book though,' she said, fixing me with her gimlet stare. 'How are you getting on with tracking it down?'

2.

Thursday 3rd June 1897

Lady Violet watched from the riding block as the five riders trotted down the drive at the start of their canter around the park. The day, she considered, had started well. The protagonists in last night's debate at dinner had gone their separate ways. The Rossdales, including Tilly, had set out for their day at Gatton Park, her husband had taken Sir Robert Carey off in the brougham to visit Dunkerley Church, and Charles was now safely in the saddle. All that remained was to settle Lady Carey and Mrs Howard in the small drawing room and then her duties as a hostess would be complete. Tomorrow, she suspected, would take rather more stage management.

It was with interest tinged with annoyance that Lady Violet had noticed that it had been George Johnstone who had handed Victoria into the saddle, and that Charles had performed a similar service for Millicent Howard. Mr Rutherford had shuffled in slight embarrassment in the background. There were four young men at Drayfield that summer and her daughter had managed to pick the most unsuitable. Lady Violet was now firmly convinced that

Johnstone was up to no good. He had spent most of the previous day attempting, unsuccessfully she was sure, to ingratiate himself with Millicent Howard, to the obvious displeasure of her mother. Clearly, however, the absent attractions of the young Duke of Westerdale were more than a match for the efforts of George Johnstone. Today it was obviously to be Vicky's turn. Certainly he was 'playing the field', as Sybil Rossdale had put it before her departure. That he had tried and failed with Tilly had been made perfectly clear over the breakfast table.

'What is it exactly that you do in London, Mr Johnstone, now that you have no commission?' she had enquired sweetly, after she had been the object of his unwanted attentions over the porridge. His discomfiture with the question coupled with his obvious inability to answer it satisfactorily had even been noted by Edward Rossdale.

'Smarmy blighter,' had been his lordship's verdict. 'I wouldn't trust him as far as I could throw him,' he had observed to his wife, as they climbed into their carriage.

Lady Violet smiled at the memory of George Johnstone's treatment, but her smile rapidly turned into a frown. It was apparent that something needed to be done to persuade Vicky to adopt the same policy towards Johnstone as had Millicent and Tilly. Perhaps a little competition would be in order? Given that Charles and Archie were non-starters in the admirer stakes, the obvious solution was that Mr Rutherford needed to be given every opportunity to shine, if only for the duration of the house party. With plots beginning to ferment in her mind, Lady Violet re-entered the house and made her way to the small drawing room.

'The riders are away ladies,' she said brightly. 'We have at least two hours to study the papers, do our embroidery, or catch up with the latest novels,' and she sank into a comfortable chair. She adjusted the cushions and smiled at her guests. 'We might even indulge in a little uninterrupted conversation.'

By the time the young people had returned for a cold luncheon the three ladies had indeed enjoyed their hours of conversation and gossip, and Lady Violet had learnt that as far as Elizabeth Howard was concerned the engagement of her daughter to the Duke of Westerdale was a foregone conclusion. She also realised to her satisfaction that, despite Mrs Howard's irritation with George Johnstone, her American guest was enjoying her visit. While the riders enjoyed their meal she took the opportunity to ask Charles whether the outing had been a success. He replied in the affirmative and went on to remark,

'Rutherford is a fine horseman, you know. He led us for most of the way once Vicky had pointed him in the right direction. And Miss Howard is no mean shakes either. All in all an excellent morning's ride, Aunt Violet.'

After luncheon the party dispersed and Johnstone, taking advantage of the fact that Elizabeth Howard was alone in the ante-room, decided to re-establish what he hoped would be friendly relations. It was not a successful move.

'This is neither the time nor the place, Mr Johnstone,' said Elizabeth Howard with some acerbity as she smoothed down the front of her dress. 'I am not one of your many housemaids, you understand?'

George Johnstone opened his mouth to reply but Mrs Howard continued.

'And while we are on the subject of your amorous intentions,' she went on, 'my daughter is not to be considered as possible prey for your advances. Your reputation goes before you, as I am sure you know, and you would not want angry mothers as well as angry footmen pursuing you with meat cleavers. I have been married and what I choose to do with my life is entirely my own affair.

That is not the case with Millicent. I will tolerate no interference in that direction. I trust you understand the situation?'

'Mrs Howard, Elizabeth, I must protest,' interjected George Johnstone. 'I have absolutely no intention of interfering, as you put it, with a girl I respect utterly; as your daughter, if for no other reason. It is quite . . .'

But he was interrupted once again.

'Then we will close the subject,' said Mrs Howard. 'Enough of this chastisement. Spirited hounds make the best running but have to be curbed on occasions. Now, you may fetch me my book which, I believe, I have left in the small drawing room. I will await you under the trees where, I notice, Anderson has arranged some basket chairs.'

And with that Elizabeth Howard swept out of the ante-room door and into the garden. George Johnstone watched her with a mixture of emotions flickering across his face.

'Curbed indeed, Mrs high and mighty Howard. We will see about that. You may well find that your control over your spirited hounds is not quite as good as you supposed,' he muttered under his breath, and he turned on his heel and walked through the door into the saloon and in the direction of the small drawing room.

Clearly the malevolent influence of the Duke of Westerdale had meant that neither mother nor daughter were likely to succumb to his approaches, but equally clearly it was obvious that Victoria Sedgley offered the best chances of his successful advancement. Johnstone was not, however, prepared to forget the slight he had just received. He was not used to being overlooked by ladies whom he had favoured with his attentions and Elizabeth Howard would pay the necessary penalty. As he walked over to collect her novel he patted the inside pocket of his jacket that contained his notecase. His plans for Victoria Sedgley would need funding and Mrs Howard was the obvious person to supply him with the necessary finance.

As he walked out of the small drawing room into the hall he noticed a pensive Victoria Sedgley standing by the centre table. She was idly fingering the red leather bound Visitors Book. Johnstone strode over to her and casually kissed her hand.

'Miss Sedgley,' he said briskly, 'a capital ride was it not?'

Victoria flushed and pulled her hand away. 'Indeed it was, Mr Johnstone, but I am afraid that Mr Rutherford put us all to shame.'

'There are times, Miss Sedgley,' responded Johstone, 'when leading the field is not the best place to be. Personally I preferred the company a little further back.'

Victoria turned away from him in some confusion and said nothing.

'I see you have the Visitors Book there,' said Johnstone smoothly. 'None of us has signed it yet, I believe. Shall I?'

'Oh no, Mr Johnstone, that would not do at all,' said Victoria hastily. 'In the old days my grandmother filled in all the names in her own hand, that's why the early pages are so neat and tidy. Now Anderson brings in the book on Sunday when we have finished dinner and everyone signs. It is quite a little ceremony.'

Johnstone reached over and gently removed Victoria's hand from the book. Still holding her left hand in his right he turned over some of the pages.

'Your grandmother had a fine hand, Miss Sedgley,' he remarked, 'and so if I may say does her granddaughter.'

'Mr Johnstone,' began Victoria, but Johnstone continued.

'And now let me escort you to the lawn. I have a mission to complete for one of our older companions, and then perhaps we could take a turn around the gardens?'

He released her hand, offered her his arm, and the two of them walked through the ante-room and out on to the terrace, oblivious of Lady Violet's disapproving glare.

3.

Friday 1st January 1965

Nicholas had no very clear idea in his mind when he drove to Barcombe after Christmas, apart from a desire to prolong his relationship with a woman whom he found utterly desirable. Jane too must have been equally happy to see things continue, or so it seemed from her invitation.

Victor and Jane Emburey at Home for Drinks on New Year's Day at Noon, it read, and on the back Jane had scribbled, almost certainly with her husband's knowledge and approval, 'we have no idea where you usually spend Christmas but if you happen to be at the school please do drop in.'

Realistically there seemed little chance of anything permanent being created with Jane. She was some years his senior, was married and had two children. The state of her relationship with Victor was probably not too good, but she was obviously prepared to stick it out. On the other hand Nicholas was not thinking in terms of permanence. He was besotted and simply wished to perpetuate his good fortune.

Jane greeted him with a hand-squeeze and a quick kiss.

'Lovely to see you, Nick, happy New Year,' she said. 'Victor,' she called out, 'Nick has arrived. Now come on in, have a drink and meet everybody.'

The gathering seemed to be made up for the most part of cricketers and their wives and girl-friends, of whom

Nicholas recognised David Walton. Jane avoided the cricketers and introduced him to a couple who were standing by themselves by the fireplace.

'Nick,' said Jane, 'Let me introduce you to James and Eileen Hignett. James is doing the maps and plans for my great work. Nick teaches in Sussex and is helping me out with the genealogical bits.'

'Hullo,' said Nicholas. 'So we have both been dragooned into service on that front. As Jane says, I am the heraldic adviser.'

'How do you do,' said James Hignett. 'Sussex you say. Whereabouts?'

'Near Steyning,' replied Nicholas. 'My mother lives in Arundel, so it was quite convenient.'

'I spent some time in Sussex two years ago,' said James Hignett. 'There's an interesting branch line that runs from . . . '

But here he was interrupted. 'James,' said his wife, 'you haven't even allowed Jane to introduce me and you are already talking about branch lines. I am Eileen,' she said, turning to Nicholas with an outstretched hand, 'a notorious railway widow, as Jane has probably already told you. She usually warns people well in advance about James and his railways.'

Nicholas smiled politely.

'I didn't know you had a mother in Arundel,' put in Jane. 'So that is why you teach in Steyning?'

'For the short term,' said Nicholas. 'Like you I aspire to greater things. I would like to write – or rather I would like to persuade someone to publish what I already write – but until I am able to do so I need to earn my daily bread and teaching seemed the only answer.'

'Like Evelyn Waugh,' said Eileen Hignett.

'Like Evelyn Waugh,' agreed Nicholas.

'And what of your father,' asked Jane curiously.

'My father died two years ago,' replied Nicholas. 'He was a foreign correspondent for *The Daily Mirror*. Interesting really because at home we always took *The Daily Telegraph*.' He laughed and turned to James Hignett.

'So what exactly are you doing for Jane?' he asked.

'Maps and plans,' replied James Hignett, 'maps and plans. I am currently doing the layout of the ground-floor at Drayfield with little green arrows denoting servants' routes and red arrows showing the movements of the gentry. I should have preferred blue for the gentry, much more appropriate, but the lines didn't show up well enough.'

'We are going to have two plans for the house, ground-floor and first-floor, and a map for the estate. Three appendices altogether,' said Jane, 'but I am slightly worried that my tutor will think Drayfield is upstaging Bearwood. We may have to compromise, James, and ditch the estate map.'

'Jane,' shouted Victor from across the room. 'Could you dispense with the lecture and produce some more sausage rolls. David here is absolutely famished.'

Nicholas turned to see a red-faced Victor brandishing a glass beer tankard in one hand and a small cigar in the other, which he was waving around in a frantic fashion. Beside him stood David Walton, looking suitably abashed, and two other men whom he had yet to meet.

'Take no notice, Jane,' called out David. 'I am doing fine.'

Jane excused herself and moved away to the kitchen. Minutes later Sam Emburey emerged carrying a plate of sausage rolls.

'Hullo, Sam,' said Nicholas, as he passed, 'how are things with you? Is it Arsenal, Spurs or Chelsea?'

'I support Everton,' came the reply. 'We watch them when we visit my grand-dad. He takes us there.'

'Sam,' called out his father, 'what's keeping you. Mr Walton is dying of hunger.'

'I follow Brighton myself,' said Nicholas.

Sam stared at him in amazement. 'Brighton!' he said in a tone of deep incredulity, before moving towards his father with the sausage rolls.

'Now if you were a football man,' Nicholas said to James Hignett, 'presumably it would be either Swindon Town or Crewe Alexanda?'

James Hignett laughed delightedly. 'Railway junctions, my dear,' he explained to his wife, 'railway junctions.'

Nicholas excused himself and moved in the direction of the kitchen. Jane was in the process of arranging some small sandwiches on three large plates. She paused briefly as he entered.

'Would you believe it?' she said. 'Do you remember Mrs Hick's tray?'

Nicholas nodded. 'Yes,' he said.

'Well, I wrote to her to tell her that I would be interested in buying it and asked whether she had got a valuation, and she wrote back and told me that she had already sold it. Apparently she did what I suggested and had gone to three antique shops in Edinburgh and had accepted the third one's offer. I ask you, what rotten luck.'

Nicholas stared at her in astonishment. 'She said all that?' he asked. 'I don't believe it. Well, you have got to hand it to her.'

'Hand what to her?' asked Jane, but just then David Walton entered the room.

'Hullo, Nick,' he said, 'good to see you again. You haven't come across those cigarette cards yet, have you? Well, do keep looking, won't you. Happy New Year. Jane,' he went on, 'I really wasn't chasing you for sausage rolls, you know. I wouldn't . . .'

'Dare?' interrupted Jane. 'Don't be silly, David, of course I know you wouldn't. I haven't been Victor's wife for ten years without knowing that he would do anything to keep up his supply of food at a drinks party. Now be a couple of angels and hand round these sandwiches.'

The two men dutifully took a plate each and followed Jane out into the sitting room.

4.

Saturday 4th September 1999

'Mark must be very pleased with his party,' said Mrs McGinty, as she helped herself to a cheese straw. 'Now tell me. Do you think that Desmond Davies is any relation to that newspaper man?'

'Leslie?' asked Tim Lewis. 'Could be, I suppose. Does he spell his name with an 'E' as well? They don't look very alike though.'

We all stared at Desmond Davies, who was chatting to John Dickinson, and then at Leslie Davies, who appeared to be arguing with Ken Belton of *The Barcombe News*. As Desmond was tall, angular and grey haired, and Leslie was bald and rotund, we had to admit that there were few obvious similarities.

'Does Leslie pong?' muttered Tim Lewis, and then tried desperately to stop choking with laughter.

'How are plans for the shop and restaurant going?' I asked, hastily changing the subject.

'Shop and restaurant?' queried Judy. 'Where are you going to have your shop and restaurant?'

'Oh it's hardly going to be a restaurant, at least not to begin with,' said Mrs McGinty. 'You know the door at the end of the loggia, the one you came in by?'

'Yes,' said Judy.

'When you turned right to walk round to the main staircase, you could have turned left and continued down to the servants' wing. There you have the kitchen and the servants' hall.'

'And one will be your shop and one your restaurant?' asked Judy.

'That's right,' said Mrs McGinty. 'To start with we will use the kitchen for both functions. It's a far more interesting room anyway and the old range is still there. We will be able to make quite a feature of that. Whether everything will be ready for the opening I rather doubt, but Councillor Barnes always manages to achieve great things. Anyway, it will certainly be in business by the autumn.'

'And when is the grand opening?' asked Judy. 'Edwin said something about the spring.'

'That's right,' I put in. 'Easter weekend. And you'll never guess who we have got lined up to do the ceremony. I can't tell you because it's a state secret, but I gather that Councillor Lathom pulled a few strings. Councillor Barnes will probably tell all at next week's meeting.'

'I'm still not absolutely sure exactly what we will be selling in this shop,' said Tim Lewis.

'Ten picture postcards, one guide to the pictures, one history of Drayfield and the Sedgley family and all the assorted bits and pieces that we already sell in the library,' I explained. 'And any moment now Mrs Vanstone will catch my eye and ask me for the umpteenth time how I am getting on with my history and my search for the elusive Jane Emburey.'

'Jane Emburey?' queried Judy.

'Yes,' I replied. 'She wrote the thesis from which I am going to lift the vital details for the history of the family. She also had access to a visitors' book that Mrs V would dearly like to have in her display in the Sedgley Room, not to mention a silver salver that appears to contain the Sedgley coat of arms.'

'Emburey,' said Judy. 'Now why does that name ring a bell? I am sure I know somebody called Emburey.'

At that point I saw Councillor Barnes beckon to me from the other side of the room where he was in deep discussion with Mrs Fitter and Roger Collet.

'Mrs Fitter says,' he announced as I approached, 'don't forget to mention the orchids.'

'Orchids?' I asked. 'What orchids?'

'Charles Sedgley was world famous for his collection of orchids,' said Mrs Fitter. 'And they were still being grown in Mrs Rutherford's day. There used to be a huge range of greenhouses at the end of the gardens where they were produced, and certainly her grandfather won many awards. I was even told that he won a prize at one of the Great Exhibitions,' she added vaguely. 'They would make an interesting section in your booklet.' She stared at me expectantly.

'Excellent idea,' I said quickly. 'Many thanks for mentioning it. Tell me, have you any idea where I can get hold of some details? The orchids don't feature in the Emburey thesis. And what about the greenhouses? I was unaware of their existence.'

'Oh the greenhouses went just after the last war,' put in Roger Collet. 'The foundations are still there as are some of the old walls. As to the orchids, I believe there is a society of sorts you could contact. They may well have some details. And I am sure that there is something in Patterson's *History of Barcombe and District* written in 1909 or thereabouts. You could get a copy from Mrs Vanstone.'

I cursed inwardly at the thought of yet more work heading in my direction and produced an envelope from my pocket. I made a few notes.

'And what about the ghost? Will you be saying anything about the ghost in your booklet,' said Ken Belton, who had attached himself to our little group. 'It would be bound to push up the sales and I could do you a nice piece in the paper as well.'

'Mark,' called out Councillor Barnes, as Mark Paddon-Browne passed us carrying two bottles of wine, 'Mark, have you seen the ghost yet?'

'Not as yet,' said Mark, as he topped up our glasses. 'I know it's supposed to be Anne Boleyn, but for the life of me I can't imagine why she should haunt an eighteenth century house. Emma Hamilton once visited Drayfield, so I'm told. Perhaps she will pay me a visit. I think I should rather enjoy that,' he added thoughtfully.

'A portrait of Lady Hamilton used to hang in the house, you know,' said Mrs Fitter. 'My father told me that he saw it when he visited as a young man. They used to call it "the naughty lady". I believe it was a Romney and I think it hangs in an American museum at the moment.'

'Ghosts sell well,' said Ken Belton firmly. 'A section in your booklet on possible hauntings would do wonders for you. Is there any record of anyone actually seeing a ghost?'

'Jane Emburey never mentioned ghosts,' I said defensively. 'Perhaps Councillor Lathom would have some ideas on the subject?'

While Councillor Barnes scanned the room for his colleague I took the opportunity of having a quick word with Mark Paddon-Browne.

'Would it be all right if I leave the car here overnight?' I asked. I am going to try and cadge a lift home. I have knocked back quite a lot of your vino and I would hate to be breathalysed. A fine for drunk driving would hardly enhance my chances of promotion at the Town Hall.'

'No problem,' Mark replied, 'but don't bother to cadge a lift, stay here. John has got the spare room but you are welcome to a mattress in here. I have got another duvet and I can even give you a toothbrush. I stocked up well when I moved in, thanks to Rebecca. My sister,' he added hastily.

I thanked him and as I did so Councillor Barnes tapped on his glass for silence.

'Ladies and Gentlemen,' he began, and the hum of conversation died away. 'On behalf of everyone present I should like to thank Mark for inviting us to such a magnificent party.' There was a smattering of 'here here's and a few handclaps. 'I should also like to welcome both Mark and Sam Kendle to our team here at Drayfield.' More handclaps. 'As far as the Drayfield plans are concerned, perhaps I could anticipate one or two points I will be making at the meeting of the Fine Arts Committee next week. Firstly we are on course to open as an art gallery next Easter although our shop and tea room will probably not be fully functional until the late summer or early autumn. The pictures will be moved from Barcombe Lodge shortly after Christmas. I have a couple of surprises for our committee that I am unable to share with you all tonight, particularly as we have two bloodhounds or should I say truffle hounds of the local press in our midst – welcome Ken Belton and Leslie Davies.'

Councillor Barnes paused and acknowledged the perfunctory applause.

'But rest assured that once my committee has given me the all-clear then everyone, press included, will be fully briefed. Could I while on the subject of the press, through Ken and Leslie, thank the editors of both *The Barcombe News* and *The County Times* for running our story of the refurbishment of the Sedgley Room. The results have been highly satisfactory and we have acquired several artefacts for Mrs Vanstone's display. Almost all, I would add, have been in the nature of outright gifts or semi-permanent loans. Indeed, the only item for which the Borough Treasurer might be asked to make a financial outlay is a chair, and I remain hopeful that I will be able to twist his arm.' He smiled contentedly. 'Now, thanks again to Mark and have a safe journey home all those of you who were foolish enough not to order taxis.'

A rather more pronounced rattle of handclaps greeted the end of the councillor's 'few words' – clearly many present were expecting far worse. I looked around the room. In the far corner by the door that led to Mark's bedroom Judy Fredericks was in earnest discussion with James Hignett. She caught my eye and motioned me over.

'At your service,' I said.

'We think we have a breakthrough for you,' said Judy. 'James tells me that your Jane Emburey had a son called Sam and my ex-husband used to play cricket against a club whose President was a Sam Emburey. What do you think? Worth a few phone-calls, surely?'

'Judy,' I said, 'you are a marvel. Now lead me to Mrs Vanstone. I have news for her.'

5.

Friday 1st January 1965

'I have no idea what possessed you to invite that crashing bore,' said Victor. 'All he could talk about was railways. Main lines, branch lines, side lines; the list was endless. Never let him into the house again.'

'Victor,' said Jane in protest, 'he has been very helpful to me with my work.'

'Work,' snorted Victor in derision. 'Nick here has been helpful to you in your so-called work, but he doesn't blather on all day about family crests and the like.'

'Coats of arms,' interjected Nick.

'What?' said Victor, caught in full flow.

'Coats of arms,' repeated Nick. 'The crest is just the bit on the top.'

'My God, don't you start,' spluttered Victor. 'I've had my fill of railways, for the love of Mike don't let's start on crests or coats of arms or whatever you want to call them.'

'To be fair,' said David Walton, 'I don't suppose Hignett was riveted by our conversation either.'

'And his wife' went on Victor, 'talk about dowdy . . .'

'No,' said Jane firmly, 'let's not talk about dowdy. What about the Greta situation? What do we think about that?'

And the conversation moved away from the potentially dangerous subject of the Hignetts to the controversial, as it turned out, subject of Greta; wife of one member of the cricketing fraternity but shortly, according to Victor, to transfer her allegiance to another.

'Could play havoc with the make-up of the team next season,' said Victor. 'Rumour has it Don might leave the district.'

'Don?' queried Nick who, like David Walton, had been asked to stay behind for a cup of coffee after the other guests, Hignetts included, had gone.

'Opening bowler' responded David, 'and reputed lover of the aforementioned Greta. She was the girl in the red top. Her husband is Len. He bats at number three.'

'Why on earth should Greta walk out on Len?' asked Victor. 'Sound chap, good job, nice house, and Don is no Rock Hudson.'

'Boredom, perhaps,' said Jane. 'She hasn't even got a family. What does she do all day when he goes up to London? You know she wanted to continue working at the estate agents but he didn't want her to.'

'Not good for the image,' said Victor as he crossed over to the mantelpiece and selected a pipe, 'wife going out to work. He earns a very good salary, you know.'

'But that's not the point,' said Jane in exasperation, 'the poor girl wants more in life than just accompanying Len to cricket matches.'

'And anyway, she'd get that with Don,' added David.

Nick began to feel that the Greta, Don, Len conversation was going to turn out to be as divisive as the Hignett discussion. Jane was looking distinctly irritable, Victor was busy engulfing himself in a cloud of tobacco smoke while he considered the unreasonable behaviour of wives in general and Greta in particular, and David gave the impression of someone anxious to pour oil on troubled waters but having some difficulty in locating the oil. The situation was saved by the reappearance of the children from the garden.

'Daddy,' said Sam, 'did you know that Mr Markham supports Brighton?'

'Brighton?' said Victor in disbelief. 'What on earth possesses you to support Brighton?'

'Nearest team to Steyning,' said Nick, conscious that his stock with Victor, having suffered a body blow with the coats of arms controversy was now taking a further tumble.

'But you have got Portsmouth just along the coast, then at a pinch Southampton, but Brighton,' said Victor, shaking his head.

'Don't take any notice of the males in this family, Nick,' said Jane. 'You support Brighton if you want to. Why David supports . . .'

'Charlton Athletic,' said David, 'and nobody say anything.'

No one did, and Nicholas rose to his feet.

'Jane,' he said, 'I must be on my way. Thank you both for a lovely start to 1965. Cheerio, David, I'll be seeing you, and Sam, every time I see Everton's results I'll be thinking of you. Goodbye Bobbie' and he turned towards the door.

'See you, Nick,' said David, 'and don't forget about the cards,'

'I promise,' replied Nick.

Victor waved a valedictory pipe. 'Keep up the good work,' he said vaguely.

'I'll see you out, Nick,' said Jane, and she escorted him to the front door.

'If you can put up with any more of my company,' she said, as she gave him a quick and surreptitious kiss, 'we could meet in the gardens at Drayfield. The children are visiting their cousins tomorrow so I could get there just after lunch – say about two o'clock. Victor is involved with a golf match.'

'Drayfield it is,' promised Nicholas, and he walked down the lane with a spring in his step to collect his car.

CHAPTER SIX

1.

Friday 4th June 1897

'There are six races this afternoon,' said Lady Violet in the dining room after breakfast. '*The Mickleham Plate, The Chipstead Plate, The Oaks Stakes, The Acorn Stakes, The Walker Plate* and *The Glasgow Plate. The Oaks* of course is the one that interests us all and for those of you who do not know it is for three year old fillies.' She paused and then went on. 'My father achieved his greatest success with a filly at *The Oaks* about thirty years ago. Like Sir Robert, he never put a penny on a horse in his life, but he was intensely interested in breeding. Everything was in the pedigree, he used to say. Now I am sure you would agree with that sentiment?' and she flashed a dazzling smile in the direction of Sir Robert Carey.

'Indeed I do, Lady Violet, indeed I do,' he responded.

Millicent Howard placed her kedgeree fork carefully on her plate and said,

'Lady Violet, do tell me. Why *The Oaks* and why *The Acorn* stakes? Something to do with trees, perhaps?'

The Drayfield house party of 1897 was undoubtedly graced by good-looking young ladies, but of the three, Victoria Sedgley, Matilda Rossdale and Millicent Howard, the last named was certainly the one most likely to be described as a stunner. Millicent was blessed with blue eyes and golden hair and possessed a figure that had been admiringly described by George Johnstone as 'capital, quite capital'. At any rate, her question caused all four young officers present to give her their undivided attention.

'If I may, Lady Violet,' said George Johnstone, smoothly. '*The Oaks* takes its name from the Earl of

Derby's place about five miles away from Epsom. It was the same earl after whom the Derby itself was named.'

Millicent smiled at him graciously, 'You don't say, Mr Johnstone. How absolutely intriguing!'

'And what is more, Miss Howard,' said Archie Rossdale, anxious to shine in front of a lady who clearly took his fancy, 'the then earl tossed a coin to decide whether the race should be named after himself or his chum Sir Charles Bunbury.'

'So,' put in Charles Sedgley, 'if the coin had fallen the other way, Wednesday's classic would have been *The Bunbury*.'

'Indeed,' said Lady Rossdale, 'I did not know that.'

'I think the whole thing is quite perfect,' cried Millicent. 'Absolutely everything that goes on in this country is steeped in history. You wouldn't have a horse race in Kentucky named after someone's house.'

'Certainly not that of an English aristocrat, my dear,' put in her mother.

'And *The Acorn Stakes*, gentlemen?' said Lady Violet.

But *The Acorn Stakes* clearly stumped the young men.

'Mr Rutherford?' prompted Lady Violet, kindly, clearly anxious to draw the young man into the conversation.

'I understand it's for two year olds; fillies that is,' Lancelot Rutherford answered in alarm, 'but as to the origins of the name, I really don't know for sure. Surely it must be a play on words. I mean little acorns to great oak trees, don't you know?'

'So much for *The Acorn Stakes*,' said George Johnstone.

'Anderson,' said Frederick Sedgley. 'What are the weather prospects?'

'Somewhat threatening after luncheon, Mr Sedgley, Sir,' replied the butler, who had been hovering discreetly in the background. 'North-easterly winds, rather cloudy and the possibility of showers.'

'And transport?'

'The carriages will be at the main entrance at eleven o'clock, Sir.'

With over an hour to spare before departure the party adjourned from the dining room. Lady Violet and Lady Rossdale left in one direction for the drawing room. Frederick Sedgley, Lord Rossdale and Sir Robert Carey moved away in the other, heading for the library and the morning papers. The young men excused themselves on the grounds that they needed to see to their horses.

'Millie!' said Mrs Howard. 'Would you join me in the small drawing room? There is the small matter of an overdue letter to your aunt that must be attended to. It would be convenient to have it written before we leave for the races.'

Millicent gave her mother a resigned look and followed in the footsteps of the other ladies. Victoria Sedgley and Matilda Rossdale walked as far as the lobby that separated dining room and library and then turned right into the garden and on to the terrace. Ahead of them was the Rose Walk, a pathway arched over by an iron frame bearing climbing roses, which stretched out towards first a large circular lily pond and then on towards the kitchen gardens and the ranges of glasshouses constructed by Frederick Sedgley's father half a century earlier to contain the world famous Drayfield orchids. To their right the lawn dipped into an immense hollow that was a famed feature of the pleasure grounds. Indeed, the most famous views of Drayfield were invariably those taken from a vantage point on the far side of the hollow and looking towards the garden front of the house. The girls stood looking at the view for a moment and then,

'We must have it out with Charles,' said Victoria. 'What exactly has he done to make Sir Robert so annoyed?' And they started walking towards the Rose Walk.

'But we know,' said Matilda. 'We were told at dinner on Wednesday. Charles is a friend of Sir John Willoughby and Sir Robert sent Willoughby to jail. It's as simple as that. Well, not quite as simple as that, of course,' she went on, as Victoria opened her mouth to reply. 'Sir Robert is a Liberal who can't stand what he thinks the government is doing in South Africa with Cecil Rhodes, and poor Charles is a soldier who is doing it.'

'I suppose it is all to do with that dreadful Raid,' said Victoria.

'Vicky dear, you just don't listen,' said Matilda in exasperation. 'Dr Jameson and Sir John Willoughby were technically breaking the law when they invaded the Transvaal to rescue the people in Johannesburg. If they had succeeded then everything would have been fine, but they failed and so it wasn't.'

'And Charles?' asked Victoria.

'He missed the Raid because he had tummy trouble,' said Tilly Rossdale, 'but he was all set to go, apparently. He said that they all thought that the Imperial authorities were in on the scheme. And I'll bet they were,' she added angrily. 'If Jameson had reached Johannesburg, Cecil Rhodes would have been the lion of the moment, as it is he is in London pretending that it was nothing to do with him at all. Oh it makes me so cross. And now Charles has lost his commission as a result.'

By now they had reached the lily pond. Vicky Sedgley gazed into the water and then turned to her companion.

'George Johnstone lost his commission as well,' she said.

Tilly Rossdale looked at her suspiciously. 'I am not altogether sure that it was for the same reason,' she started, but Victoria Sedgley was not listening.

'I understand that he is regarded as the best shot in his regiment,' she said archly. 'He wants me to show him the Drayfield orchids. Just me, you understand. Not as a member of one of Papa's guided tours of the glasshouses.'

'I think you should be careful, Vicky,' said Matilda. 'You would not want to ruin your reputation. You know what they say went on with Ellen?'

'Oh how ridiculous,' retorted Victoria. 'Those maids will say anything for effect. He's told me all about it. He was just admiring the pictures on the upper landing and she thought he was chasing her. You know she is walking out with William, the footman? Well, I think she just made up a lot of untruths to work William up a bit. George Johnstone is a gentleman and he certainly would not behave like that when he was a guest in someone else's house. Or anywhere else at all for that matter. Anyway, I have promised him the first dance at Lady Clonkerry's ball. Mama won't like it but she will have to lump it.'

'Charles told me that William was very upset about it all,' said Matilda, anxiously. 'I do think that there is more to it than you imagine. And what about Mrs Howard? I am sure there is something going on between them. Did you see the way he looked at her over dinner?'

'Tilly,' said Victoria, sharply. 'If you are going to say nasty things about George Johnstone, I am going to join the others indoors. We will change the subject. Now, tell me all about Lady Sarah Wilson and your trip on the *Roslin Castle*. Were you sea-sick? And what about Lady Sarah and Cecil Rhodes? I know you met him at Lady Baxendale's because Mama told me. And is it true that you have been invited to travel to South Africa with the Wilsons? I feel so envious, you do such exciting things.'

'Lady Sarah did suggest it,' admitted Tilly, 'but Mama and Papa would never allow it, I know. And as for Mr Rhodes, he is very interesting and he has a rather squeaky voice. But for a man who lives in South Africa I didn't think he looked very well. Still, I suppose he had a lot on his mind. Oh,' and she made a sudden convulsive movement.

'What's the matter?' asked Victoria.

'I don't know, I suddenly felt as if goose-pimples were breaking out all over my body and the hair on the back of my neck, well, sort of stood on end.'

'Ah,' said Victoria, knowingly. 'Someone was walking on your grave.'

'Walking on my grave,' repeated Tilly, 'whatever do you mean?'

'It's true,' said Victoria. 'When you have a sudden shudder that you can't control, people say that someone has walked on your grave. It's rather creepy when you come to think of it. What to you is a sort of involuntary movement is really caused by someone who is not alive at all at this moment. Rather like a ghost, I suppose. Except that a ghost is someone from the past and this would be someone from the future. Did you know that Drayfield is supposed to be haunted?' she asked suddenly.

'No,' said Tilly. 'By whom?'

'They say Anne Boleyn, but I think it is Emma Hamilton,' replied Victoria. 'When I was little I used to stare at her portrait in the drawing-room. I used to get quite scared as her eyes seemed to stare out at me. Though I have to say that I have never seen her walking the corridors,' she admitted.

'Stairs,' said Tilly. 'The stairs are thought to be the most haunted part of the house, I believe.'

'And at least Emma Hamilton visited Drayfield,' continued Victoria. 'That's how the lodges got their names.

The Nelson Lodge at the Southwater entrance and the Hamilton Lodge at what were originally the Barcombe Gates. They are now the Hamilton Gates. Apparently great-grandfather Sedgley was a friend of Lord Nelson and he and Lady Hamilton rode over one day when they were living at Merton. Before then they, the lodges that is, were simply known as the Barcombe and Southwater Lodges. It must have been very confusing for the postman because there is a large house close by that is also called Barcombe Lodge.'

'She's certainly seen the world, that Mrs Howard,' said Archie Rossdale, as the four young men strolled in the direction of the stables.

'What do you mean?' said George Johnstone, suspiciously.

'All that talk about Dodge City and Wyatt Earp,' answered Archie Rossdale.

'The Gomorrah of the Plains,' put in Charles Sedgley.

'Her father made his first million building the Kansas City to Denver railway, or "railroad" as Miss Howard put it,' said Lancelot Rutherford.

'Pounds or dollars?' asked Charles.

'Does it matter?' replied George Johnstone. 'By the time the Yankees completed the line to California he had so much in the bank it wouldn't matter if it was dollars, pounds, or German marks.'

'And her daughter,' said Archie Rossdale, 'no wonder she's the talk of the town.'

'You know,' said Lancelot Rutherford, 'she told me that General Miles, the man who defeated the Sioux and the Apaches, was her godfather, then she said she was only teasing. But apparently he was a friend of her father. That was true enough. And what about that revolver of her mother's? She, Miss Howard that is, seemed to know a lot about it as well. She told me that it was a Smith & Wesson Model 63 and that it fired six shots and had a two inch barrel. She also knew the calibre. I mean, it's not the sort of thing that you expect a girl to know, is it? And those ivory grip plates. Apparently they were made specially to order by her grandfather.'

'And what about Mrs Howard's husband? Does anyone know anything about him?' asked Charles Sedgley.

'Nothing whatsoever,' said Lancelot, 'although Miss Howard did tell me that he died out west. She told Miss Sedgley that he wasn't "a major player", as she put it, and that the money for her education all came from old man Tritton. She went to a school in New York and then went on to Paris before they came over here.'

'You seem to know an awful lot about her,' said Archie, suspiciously.

'It was after dinner on Wednesday,' said Lancelot, hastily. 'You were all arguing about South Africa and Cecil Rhodes and I got into conversation with Miss Sedgley and Miss Howard. That was when she told me all about her mother's gun and General Miles and so on.'

'She seems a damn fine woman wherever she was educated and whoever her father was,' put in Archie Rossdale.

'Well, don't raise your sights too high, Rossdale,' said George Johnstone, drily. 'The lovely Millicent has been set up for the Duke of Westerdale and the Tritton millions, whether pounds or dollars, have been set aside to re-roof Westerdale Castle – so I am reliably informed,' he added.

'And your source?' asked Charles Sedley.

'Probably her mother,' put in Archie Rossdale. 'Johnstone favours the older woman, at least when housemaids are not available.'

George Johnstone flushed angrily and was about to answer when Lancelot Rutherford hastily said,

'Relax Johnstone, Rossdale means no harm. And you did rather let yourself in for that. I mean . . .'

'Oh, the devil take you all,' said George Johnstone. 'Penniless officers with no prospects have to take what opportunities that come their way. Added to which,' and he stared at Charles Sedgley, 'thanks to the activities of your misguided and incompetent friend Willoughby, I have no commission either. Can I help it if Mrs Howard appreciates my company, as do other and younger ladies in our party, if it comes to that,' he added with a note of self-satisfaction in his voice.

Archie Rossdale stared at him angrily as the four men reached the stables and headed for the stalls.

Meanwhile in the small drawing room the ladies who had been the object of George Johnstone's thoughts were themselves having a heated exchange under the portrait of Emma Hamilton that had so intrigued Victoria Sedgley as a child.

'I could not help but notice,' said Elizabeth Howard, 'that the envelope you were handed by that delightful butler after breakfast contained a ducal coronet on the flap.'

'It did indeed, Mama,' admitted her daughter, with more than a hint of annoyance in her voice.

'If you take my advice,' continued Elizabeth, 'you will be very guarded with those young gentlemen. I should hate you to do anything that might jeopardise the future of a very promising connection. And to think,' she went on contentedly, 'before we arrived in London this spring the duke had been earmarked by absolutely everybody for Lord Seamer's daughter.'

'I am sure that the Duke of Westerdale and Alice Seamer are perfectly suited,' said Millicent sweetly. 'The fact that their combined intellects are probably inferior to that of General Custer after the Indians finished with him could make existence tricky, but on the other hand Giles Westerdale has servants enough to do the thinking for them.'

'Millie, dear,' said Elizabeth Howard in alarm. 'The Duke of Westerdale is the finest catch of the season.'

'Not for me he isn't,' replied her daughter with asperity. 'I would sooner catch a cold.' She paused for a moment and then went on maliciously, 'I wonder if George Johnstone will ask me to open the dancing with him at Lady Clonkerry's Ball?'

Elizabeth Howard flushed angrily. 'You are not to fool about with George Johnstone, I positively forbid it . . .'

'You mean someone else has the monopoly,' broke in her daughter, then,

'Oh forgive me, Mama, that was nasty. I am only joshing. I have no intention of straying in that particular direction. But please, don't mention me to George Johnstone or to anyone else for that matter. I am quite old enough to manage my own affairs. We are Americans after all and are not hidebound by these ridiculous European conventions. It was bad enough in Paris but London is infinitely worse. Chaperones here, worried glances there, gossip everywhere. And yes, I am well aware that New York society was pretty strait laced as well,' she added as her mother opened her mouth to speak.

Elizabeth paused for a moment. 'We are on the same side, you and I,' she said. 'I only want the best for you and I would not want you to ruin your chances of a good match by a silly flirtation. The English love their rules and regulations and woe betide anyone who breaks them.'

'Especially a future Duchess of Westerdale,' replied Millicent quizzically.

'Particularly a future Duchess of Westerdale,' replied her mother firmly. 'Now, as you are probably well aware, we are invited to shoot with the Westerdales this August. Do I accept or are we otherwise engaged? Although I have to say that to be otherwise engaged would be something akin to a social disaster.'

Millie thought for a moment. 'I'll let you know on Saturday,' she said, 'after the Countess of Clonkerry's Ball.'

It was still some time before the party was scheduled to set off for Epsom so Millicent returned to the large drawing room. Lady Violet was in deep conversation with Lady Rosslyn and Lady Carey, and through the window Millicent could make out Victoria and Tilly walking along the Rose Walk. There was no sign of the young officers, but Lord Rosslyn and Sir Robert had taken their newspapers out on to the terrace and were taking advantage of the morning sunshine in two basket chairs.

Millicent thought for a moment and then made her way to the library. She paused outside the door then knocked gently.

'Come in,' called out Frederick Sedgley.

'Forgive my intrusion, Mr Sedgley,' said Millicent politely, 'but I wonder if I might look at some of your books while we are waiting to go?'

'The library is at your disposal, my dear,' replied Frederick Sedgley in a slightly surprised tone of voice. 'I am just leaving.'

'Oh, I'm not driving you away from your peace and quiet, am I?' asked Millicent anxiously.

'By no means,' responded her host kindly. 'And I am delighted to be able to offer you its comforts. Victoria comes in here occasionally to read her three deckers from Mudies and pretends she is ploughing her way through Sir Walter Scott. Lady Violet prefers to read in one of the drawing rooms. I hope you do not object to the aroma of cigar smoke? I should indulge in the smoking room next door, but my favourite chair is here and the flesh is weak.'

Millicent smiled at him. She felt quite at ease in his company and wondered whether it would be completely out of order to ask him to stay and talk to her. She was about to suggest something along those lines when he continued,

'Tell me Miss Howard, are you enjoying your stay at Drayfield Hall?' He pulled himself up. 'But what a foolish thing to ask. You could hardly tell me if you were not. Let me re-phrase my question. Is there anything you would like to do while you are a guest here that is not part of our current agenda?'

'I am enjoying myself immensely,' said Millicent truthfully. 'The races have been fun, I am greatly looking forward to the ball tomorrow, and I understand that you are to show us your famous orchids as well. No, everything is delightful.' She laughed mischievously. 'And with four young officers in attendance, what more could a young American lady expect?'

As Millicent settled herself down in the library two of the officers in question, their horses saddled up and ready to go, retraced their footsteps to the house.

'I really cannot stand the fellow,' said Charles with feeling. 'There is something not straight about him. And what did he mean by "thanks to the activities" of Johnny Willoughby? Johnstone had nothing to do with the Raid. The man's a blackguard and the sooner we see the last of him the better.'

'Do you think he is right about Giles Westerdale and Miss Howard?' asked Archie.

'Probably,' replied Charles gloomily. 'Though it didn't stop him trying to ingratiate himself with her on Wednesday, did it? Her mother was not happy with his behaviour at all, but whether it was on her daughter's account or on her owns I really would not like to say. Right, I will go and inform the others that we at least are ready for the off and that Anderson had better get the carriages organised,' and so saying he left his companion and entered the house.

Archie Rossdale continued to walk along the gravel path that wended its way around the side of the building. He noticed through the windows of the large drawing room that the older ladies were in conversation and as he watched the door opened and Charles entered the room. Tilly and Victoria were talking over by the lily pond but there was no sign of Millicent Howard. Muttering disconsolately to himself he walked on past his father, who was reading his newspaper on the terrace, and opened the lobby door. He turned right into the library and stopped just inside the doorway.

'Miss Howard!' he said in some confusion.

'The very same, Mr Rossdale,' replied Millicent, 'and please do not be alarmed. I have permission from our host to lurk in what I am well aware is a male preserve. I should not dream of upsetting the social niceties, you understand?'

She paused and looked at him humorously. 'I'll bet you didn't know that when they brought Lord Byron's body home from Greece in the,' and she consulted the pamphlet she had been reading, 'brig *Florida*, it was in a cask containing 180 gallons of spirits.'

Archie recovered his composure. 'Social niceties be hanged,' he said warmly, 'and as for Lord Byron, you know you never cease to surprise me.'

'Excellent,' said Millicent, 'then we shall never tire of each other's company.' She glanced out of the window. 'Now, judging by the antics of Mr Charles Sedgley, who is rounding everybody up as if they were so many head of cattle, I must go and find my hat and coat.' She handed him her pamphlet. 'Page 421,' she said. 'That gives you all the gory details. Then on page 426 there is an interesting snippet concerning Lord Nelson's breeches, the ones he was wearing at Trafalgar.'

She smiled at him, dropped him a mock curtsey and disappeared into the hall.

2.

Saturday 2nd January 1965

It was a cold, crisp morning as Nick drove his car into the car park behind St Peter's Church, Barcombe, and walked towards the church itself. His meeting with Jane was for two o'clock. The time was now ten o'clock, and he reckoned that a couple of hours or so in the church followed by a pub lunch at *The King's Head* would mean that he would be in the gardens at Drayfield well before the appointed time The church itself had been described by Pevsner as 'large and dull' while *The Little Guide* was equally uncomplimentary with its 'somewhat vulgar'. Nick had always felt that neither description was justified and that the structure seemed rather splendid, at least from the outside. The church had replaced an earlier building that had been pulled down in 1867, again according to *The Little Guide*, and the chancel of the old church had been retained as a separate chapel as it contained some important medieval monuments. Nick tried the door of the chapel, but as usual it was locked.

The Sedgley Memorial itself was located just outside the south door of the church. It was a large structure on a plinth surrounded by iron railings and took the form of an obelisk placed on top of a cube. The cube itself contained four recessed panels, and each panel commemorated a member of the Sedgley family, his wife, and in three cases assorted children. A final touch, which pleased Nicholas greatly, was that at the top of each panel was a small enamelled shield containing the arms of the male Sedgley in question, impaling those of his wife. The arms he now knew were identical to the ones he had deciphered for Jane in the house; a fact he felt that he might be able to put to good use at an appropriate moment.

The fourth panel, that of Frederick and Violet Sedgley, contained no more than their own names. Nick had always assumed that the family vault was now full. The existence of a grave with an ornate headstone in between the monument and the chapel seemed to confirm this opinion. It contained the remains of *Colonel the Hon. Lancelot Rutherford* and *Victoria his wife, the only daughter of Frederick and Violet Sedgley of Drayfield Park.*

The church was open and here too the Sedgley family had left its mark. The pulpit had been presented in 1937 by Mrs Victoria Rutherford in memory of her husband and her parents and there was an ornate coloured marble tablet on the wall of the south aisle that commemorated two brothers killed in the Great War. Nick contemplated the tablet in silence for a while then sat down in an adjacent pew and made a few notes in the pad he always carried in his duffel coat pocket.

Shortly after twelve o'clock Nick left the church. As he went he dutifully dropped half a crown into the small wall-safe in exchange for a short history and guide. He walked back to the lych-gate, crossed the car-park and headed for *The King's Head*, a rather attractive looking pub about five minutes walk away. There he lunched off a pint of bitter and a ham sandwich before returning for his car and setting off for Drayfield Park. He left the car just inside the gates and outside an obviously derelict lodge. He then made his way towards an old garden wall before entering the gardens through a small doorway. Ahead of him was a gravelled terrace that separated the house itself from the pleasure-gardens.

The ground floor windows were all closed and shuttered and the two doors that opened onto the terrace from the house were firmly locked. Nick tried them in a desultory fashion. The terrace gave way to a small path that circled round the side of the house and emerged to the right of the front entrance, where he and Jane had met Mr Innes just over six months earlier. Nick tried the main door and then the door at the end of the loggia that ran along the front of the building, but, like their fellows on the garden front, these entrances too were rigidly secured. So Nick followed the main drive along past the one-time servants' wing, which ultimately turned itself into a stable block. The drive then swung round to the right and he found himself back at the door in the garden wall. There had been no sign of Jane but, as it was still only a quarter to two, this was perhaps not surprising.

Nick entered the gardens for a second time but on this occasion he did not follow the terrace to its end. Instead, he turned left halfway along its length and walked down a rather attractive path that ran at right angles to the house and took him to a large goldfish pond. There he found his quarry, wrapped up in a heavy green overcoat and staring into the waters.

'Hullo, Nick,' she said, as he kissed her. 'Aren't you cold?'

'Not particularly,' he replied, as he glanced down and realised for the first time that he had left his own coat in the car. 'I seem to have been walking around quite a lot. Are you OK? You seem a trifle distraught.'

'I am a bit,' she admitted. 'I had a row with the children, an annoying letter from my tutor and some even more aggravating news from Victor, so altogether it hasn't been one of the best days. But it is much better now,' she went on with a smile. 'Come on, let's go for a walk. And by the way, do you see that little old lady over there?' and she pointed at a figure in black who was walking with the aid of a stick along a parallel path just inside the garden wall.

'Yes,' said Nick. 'Who is she?'

'That's Mrs Bridgewater, the butler's daughter,' said Jane. 'The one who gave me all that information about the staff.' And she laughed. 'Sounds just like *Happy Families*, doesn't it? Mrs Bridgewater, the butler's daughter. Mr Bull, the butcher, Mrs Bunn, the baker's wife and so on.'

Nick nodded. 'Snap,' he said. 'No, that's something else, isn't it? Now, tell me. What about all these problems?'

'The children was normal,' said Jane. 'The usual family traumas. The letter from my tutor was a nuisance because he says that I am spending too much time on the family and that it is unbalancing the chapter. I was cross because I was enjoying it, but he's probably right. It'll mean a bit of re-writing and cutting, but it's not the end of the world. Victor is the big problem. He's going for promotion and if he gets it, I am afraid it will mean a move. And not just any old move. He would be going to Milan and it would be for at least five years.'

'Milan,' said Nick. 'Italy?'

'Exactly,' Jane replied with a grimace. 'I suppose I would get used to it, but I really don't want to go. Victor's bad enough here in England where we have friends and family and interests, but in Italy where we don't know a soul and we would inevitably be left to our own devices, he'd be murder. Oh, I'm probably just being stupid and he probably won't get the position anyway. And please don't mention this to anybody, if you happen to see anybody. It's all very hush, hush. He certainly doesn't want the cricketers to know that he's going for it, and of course you will probably be seeing David, won't you?'

'Not in the immediate future,' said Nick, 'I hardly know him. He happens to be interested in some cricketing cigarette cards that used to belong to my father, that's all. But don't worry,' he continued, 'I won't breathe a word to anyone. When would you be going?'

'Apparently we would be given money and time off in May to go house hunting,' said Jane. 'Then he would be back to work in July and August, and would take up his new post in September. We would have to sort out a school for Bobbie in Milan, but Sam would stay on at his prep school as a border. They are holding interviews at the start of February, but he thinks that it is all a formality and that he wouldn't have been asked to put himself forward if they didn't want him to go.'

'It's all a bit sudden, isn't it?'

'You bet it is,' said Jane. 'He only told me last night after the party. We had been arguing about Len's job, for goodness sake, and how unreasonable Greta was to be dissatisfied with her life, and then he suddenly came out with it. "I suppose I have to be very thankful that I have a wife who is not quite so stupid", he said. He really is a patronising twerp. Then I thought of you and felt very guilty.' She laughed. 'Oh come on,' and she slipped her arm underneath his, 'let's go for a walk around the gardens.'

'Why don't we go back to your house?' asked Nicholas. 'If the children are away and Victor is playing golf we could, well, we could have a couple of hours together at least.'

Jane looked at him quizzically. 'Are you crackers? If the neighbours saw me sneaking in with you what on earth would they think? No, this afternoon you will get my company and that is all. Assignations with married women are all very well, but you will have to learn to put up with the attendant problems.'

Nick nodded morosely. 'I suppose you are right. Now if it was spring, we could always slip away somewhere and make mad passionate love in the grass. I have always fancied that.'

'If you go on like this I shall think that you are only after one thing,' said Jane severely. 'And for future reference, I am not one for frolicking in the grass, even if it happened to be high summer and blazing sunshine. There is a time and a place for everything, and the gardens of Drayfield are not the place for your nefarious schemes.'

'May I give you a kiss then?' asked Nick.

'You may,' replied Jane, primly, 'and then we will go for our walk.'

Nick held her for a moment and they kissed. She then released herself, ran her hands through her hair, which had become somewhat dishevelled. She turned, glanced back down the Rose Walk, and then suddenly went rigid with horror.

'My God!' she said. 'It's Victor.'

Nick followed her gaze. Sure enough, Victor was walking along the terrace from the doorway in the Tudor garden wall and quite clearly looking for someone, presumably his wife.

'He must have seen the car in the car park,' said Jane. 'His match has been postponed or something. I said that I was going to be working on Drayfield this afternoon, but I never told him that I was actually coming here. Look, there is no way he must see us together. It would make life far too complicated. You have got to disappear before he finds me.'

'How, for goodness sake?' said Nick. 'If I walk down towards the drive he could easily see me. Where's he going now?'

They watched as Victor reached the end of the terrace. He looked around but quite clearly could not see as far as the goldfish pond. Even though there were no roses in flower there was enough foliage entwined around the pergola to mask anyone doing anything in that area of the garden. There was a path that ran around the far side of the sunken lawn that would have taken him to the end of the Rose Walk, but luckily for the two watchers Victor chose not to take it. Instead he turned right along the path that led around the side of the house.

'He's doing what I did,' said Nick. 'He will check to see whether you are in the front of the house and then will walk around the servants wing and stables until he gets back to the garden wall over there,' and he pointed to the doorway in the Tudor garden wall. As he did so Victor disappeared around the side of the house.

Jane thought for a moment. 'Quick,' she said. 'I will stay here and wait until he finds me. You go to the end of the walk and then turn left when you reach the wall. There's a doorway in the wall just down on the right hand side. It says *Staff Only* and it takes you into the old kitchen garden. There will be nobody around there now, so wait for about twenty minutes and then see if the coast is clear. I will ring you later. Go on, quickly, if you get a move on you will be safe behind the doorway before he comes back into the garden.'

Nick stood up, bent down and kissed her briefly. 'OK,' he said. 'Ring me later' and he walked purposefully up the Rose Walk in the direction of the kitchen garden wall.

3.

Saturday 4th September 1999

After the party was over and the last guests had gone I sat down with Mark Paddon-Browne and John Dickinson and drank some coffee. It had, I felt, been a great success and from my point of view there had been the immense bonus that I had at long last been supplied with what could be a crucial Emburey lead.

Mark too seemed extremely pleased with the way things had gone. 'Not a bad evening at all,' he said, as he staggered into the sitting room with a large duvet. 'This should do you. Here is a towel that you can wrap round a cushion for a pillow, and I suggest that you share the bathroom over the way with John. That will save you crashing through my room in the early hours.'

'You've certainly fallen on your feet here, haven't you?' said John, as he sipped his coffee. 'It knocks my place into a cocked hat.' He walked across to the door that led to Mark's bedroom and opened it. 'I adore these double doorways,' he said. He closed the door, drained his cup and then walked across to the door leading to the hall. 'Well, that's me for the night. See you both in the morning, and thanks for a lovely party, Mark.'

'Got everything you want?' Mark asked me. 'Toothbrush, toothpaste and towel are in the bathroom and you can use my electric razor in the morning.'

I thanked him as he disappeared through the double set of doors into his bedroom. Then, in answer to John's shout of 'bathroom free', I made my way across the hall, first to the bathroom and then to the kitchen to collect a glass of water. Aware of the twin evils of too much alcohol and the effects of dehydration, I drained one glass and then poured myself a refill. Back in the sitting room I turned the light off and settled under my duvet. My final prayer was that that I should not wake up with a monumental hangover and that my stay at Drayfield Hall would result in a good night's sleep.

4.

Friday 4th June 1897

All in all Lady Violet felt that the second day's racing at Epsom had been an undoubted success. As her husband and Sir Robert Carey had elected to spend the day at St Martin's Church, studying the brasses, and Lady Carey had pleaded a headache, only eleven members of the party made their way to the racecourse. She herself travelled in the landau with the Rossdales and Elizabeth Howard; the three young ladies had the victoria to themselves; and the four officers provided a suitable escort. The journey from Drayfield to Epsom had been enlivened by the appearance of what Millicent Howard had excitedly described as a 'motor-carriage'. Their own vehicles had stopped by the side of the road to allow them to watch the progress of the locomotive, which made a lot of noise and caused a certain amount of alarm among the horses. Lancelot Rutherford's mount reversed into a hedge, much to the delight of the young ladies, and Charles exchanged words with the driver of the motor-carriage that seemed anything but friendly.

They arrived at the race-course in time to see *The Chipstead Plate* and to organise themselves for *The Oaks*, the chief race of the afternoon. No sweep had been organised, but Sir Robert's absence certainly lightened proceedings as far as the youngsters were concerned. They all placed bets on horses of their choice, the young men acting on the ladies behalf, and great was the delight when Tilly Rossdale was successful with her choice, *Limasol*, owned by Lord Hindlip. George Johnstone informed the group that the favourite, Lord Rosebery's horse *Chelandry*, was regarded as such a certainty that very few owners were prepared to start their fillies on what seemed to be a hopeless errand.

'More fools them,' said Archie Rossdale.

Lady Violet herself had been persuaded by her nephew to place a bet on *Flying Colours*, and he had been extremely apologetic when the horse had actually come in last. Millicent Howard then took control of affairs.

'I do think we should have another sweep,' she said. 'This time it must be *The Acorn Stakes*. I am quite determined. What do you think, Lady Violet?'

'We have never had two sweepstakes,' Lady Violet replied, doubtfully, 'but if everyone wants to join in I don't see why not. Has anyone got a list of the runners? And how long have we got before the race starts?'

A list of the runners was duly produced – by George Johnstone. 'He would have had one, wouldn't he?' said Lady Violet later to her husband. It was established that there was time to organise things, and Archie Rossdale volunteered to write out the names of the runners on slips of paper produced by Charles Sedgley with the help of his cousin's pocket nail scissors. Lancelot Rutherford offered the use of his top hat, and Lady Rossdale consented to take the first dip. She drew *Radical Party*, 'a most unsuitable selection', laughed her husband, who promptly picked Lord Cadogan's *Cranbourne Chase*. Rutherford next offered the hat to Mrs Howard whose horse turned out to be *Dainty*, and then to Lady Violet herself who drew *Lissa*.

'Luck is on my side on this occasion,' she said with a smile to Lancelot Rutherford. *Lissa* is Lord Ellesmere's horse and Lord Ellesmere is a great friend of my husband. In truth Lady Violet felt rather sorry for Rutherford. She could not help but notice that while he was busy handing round his hat the other officers were occupying the attentions of the young ladies, who were now making their selections.

'*Horatia*,' cried out Tilly Rossdale as Victoria showed her the slip she had just drawn. 'Now that is appropriate. We were talking about Emma Hamilton just before we left this morning, and Horatia was the name of her daughter.' She paused, 'by Lord Nelson that is.'

'Quite so, dear,' said Lady Rossdale, disapprovingly.

'Oh look,' called out Millicent. 'I have drawn *Cyanide*. How very macabre.'

'And do you know who owns her?' asked George Johnstone, leaving Victoria Sedgley's side and walking over to join Millicent and Archie, much to Lady Violet's relief and Elizabeth Howard's annoyance.

'No, who?' replied Millicent.

'Mr Jersey!' said Johnstone, knowingly.

'So who is Mr Jersey?' asked Tilly Rossdale. 'Not the Earl of Jersey, surely?'

'By no means,' said George Johnstone. 'Mr Jersey is the name used by one of the most popular performers on the English stage at this moment and, dare I say it, not so very long ago one of the leading lights of society.'

'Of course,' put in Charles Sedgley. 'Lily Langtry. Jersey Lily. One of the Prince of Wales's, well . . . set, shall we say.'

'I think we had better,' said Lady Rossdale, rather unhappily, clearly feeling that the conversation was drifting into highly unsuitable channels.

'And if I am not very much mistaken, the glamorous owner herself is taking a close interest in her filly's fortunes,' and George Johnstone motioned to a little group of figures on the edge of the Royal Enclosure.

Lady Violet followed his gesture and noticed the Prince of Wales in close conversation with Prince Charles of Denmark and two ladies, one of whom sure enough was the notorious Lily Langtry. It must have been twenty years since the Prince of Wales's liaison with Mrs Langtry had so scandalised society. Since then her fortunes had fluctuated. During the eighties and early nineties, when she was on stage, there were rumours of a highly unsuitable liaison with a Scottish millionaire, Mrs Langtry's name was not mentioned, certainly in the circles frequented by the Sedgleys. Now, however, things seemed rather different. She had amassed a fortune, had reinstated herself in society, and had become a leading patron of the turf.

The fortune and the horses had been acquired as a result of the convenient death of the Scottish millionaire, or so George Johnstone informed the party, but quite clearly the lady was back in favour with her former admirer. It was, as Johnstone pointed out to the annoyance of the older members of his audience, 'an open question' as to whether the prince was interested in the horses or their owner. 'Probably a bit of both,' he added with a smirk.

'Even so, despite his rather uncalled for comments, it was really very exciting,' said Lady Violet to Frederick Sedgley as they waited for their guests in the large drawing room before dinner. 'We all turned to look and at exactly the same moment the Prince turned to look at us. He smiled and sent over an equerry and we were invited to join him. He occupied most of his time talking to Elizabeth Howard, and then, when he was told about the sweep, he asked to speak to Millicent as well and he really spent quite a lot of time with her. He spoke to me, of course, and to the Rossdales, and then he had a chat with Charles. It was all highly satisfactory.'

'I am delighted to hear it,' said Frederick Sedgley.

'Then there was the race itself,' continued his wife. 'It was most embarrassing. When my horse won,' she paused and looked at her husband who was staring at her blankly. 'You know, *Lissa*; I told you, Lord Ellesmere's filly. Well, it was as if I had been riding her. Then Vicky's horse *Horatia* came third and everybody congratulated her. And do you know what? I had quite a long conversation with Mrs Langtry, who is not nearly as bad as one has been led to believe. Of course, she must be nearly as old as I am, but she has lovely blue eyes and is really very charming to talk to. Her horse wasn't placed, which was rather a pity.'

'And which horse came second?' asked Frederick Sedgley with an amused smile on his face as he made a slight adjustment to his tie.

'*Platonic*,' answered Lady Violet. 'And that was rather strange. George Johnstone had drawn her, and when he picked his piece of paper out of the hat and read the name he said "another very appropriate selection". Then he turned to Millicent Howard and said "surely this should be for you". He said it very quietly and I don't think anybody else heard, but you should have seen the look she gave him. Daggers that is the only way to describe it. It is a great pity that Vicky doesn't look at him in that way as well,' and she gave a brief sigh before turning with a smile to greet Lord and Lady Rossdale as they entered the room.

CHAPTER SEVEN

1.

Saturday 2nd January 1965

Nicholas glanced somewhat furtively around him but Jane was absolutely correct. The kitchen garden was deserted. It was a large area criss-crossed by small paths and a few low brick walls, which seemed to serve no apparent purpose. Most of the central area was covered with cold frames. A path ran alongside the wall separating the kitchen garden from the garden proper and Nicholas walked along it until he reached the corner. He calculated that he was probably roughly in line with the end of the Rose Walk so, taking advantage of a rusting iron tank, he clambered gingerly up until he was in a position to peer surreptitiously over the wall.

He was actually slightly to the right of the Rose Walk but he had an excellent view through gaps in the pergola and he could make Jane out quite clearly, still standing beside the goldfish pond. As he surveyed the scene Victor emerged from the direction of the terrace. Quite clearly he had done exactly what Nick himself had done rather earlier and re-entered the garden via the door in the Tudor garden wall. Nick shifted slightly to obtain a better view. Victor strode purposefully up the Rose Walk and as he reached the pond Jane turned to see him. They stood there talking for a while and then both turned and walked slowly back towards the terrace. Greatly daring, Nick climbed on to the wall itself and watched them until they disappeared through the garden door, clearly heading back to the car park. He waited for a further ten minutes, then left the kitchen garden.

This time Nicholas did not walk back along the Rose Walk but instead he ambled slowly along the path on the inside of the garden wall. Halfway down he came across the figure of Mrs Bridgewater, seated on a wooden garden seat. She was a small grey-haired lady and was well wrapped up in a dark coat and knitted muffler. She was obviously enjoying the strong January sunlight and was surrounded by four or five small birds, which she was feeding with seed that she was taking from a capacious handbag.

As Nicholas approached the birds, with one exception, flew away. Mrs Bridgewater looked at him.

'That's a robin,' she said. 'He's not frightened of you and he will get all the more now that his friends have gone. But they won't be long in returning. Just you wait and see.'

Nicholas approached her with his hand outstretched. 'Mrs Bridgewater,' he said. 'We haven't met before but I have heard all about you from Mrs Emburey, the lady who is writing about the Sedgley family. She told me that you had been a great help in giving her details about the staff here at the turn of the century.'

'A very nice young lady,' said Mrs Bridgewater, thoughtfully. 'She came round for tea one afternoon and we had a long chat.'

'May I join you?' asked Nicholas, and Mrs Bridgewater moved slightly to her right to make room for him. She paused to scatter some more seed in front of her, which the robin avidly devoured, and then she said,

'It's very peaceful here at this time of year. During the summer there are a lot of people that come into the gardens, but now there is just me and the birds. My father was butler at Drayfield you know, and I used to play in the park when I was a little girl.'

Nick nodded. 'Yes,' he said. 'Jane told me.'

'That was long before the war, the first war, that is,' said Mrs Bridgewater. Mr Sedgley owned the house then, Mr Frederick Sedgley. We used to go up there every Christmas for a party. I had thoughts of going into service there, to join my Dad as you might say, but then I met my Harold and then came the war. It was never the same after that. Those are chaffinches,' she whispered conspiratorially. 'They don't want the robin to have all the breakfast, cunning little birds.' And she scattered another handful of seed on the path in front of them.

'We had three members of the family working at Drayfield Hall.' Mrs Bridgewater thought for a moment. 'There was my father, and there was my cousin Ellen and my brother-in-law William, only he wasn't my brother-in-law then, you understand. He was Harold's elder brother, and by the time I married Harold, William and Ellen had moved on. He became butler in a big house in Norfolk. It was a good promotion, but my Dad said that he was worth it. He was very fond of Will, was Dad. He was killed on the Somme fighting the Germans, and then twenty years later we were all at it again.'

'What happened to Ellen?' prompted Nicholas.

'She married again,' said Mrs Bridgewater. They lived in Norwich but she came down to see us often enough. She died after the second war, but her lads still keep in touch.'

'And your father?'

'He retired before the first war and died before the second.' Mrs Bridgewater sighed. 'They didn't have a butler after he left. I suppose it was the money. But then everything changed after the war, didn't it? No more Derby parties, as I said to Mrs Emburey, we all had to pull our horns in and no mistake.'

'Mrs Emburey was telling me about the Derby Party of 1897, I think it was. She is using it as an example in what she is writing for her degree,' said Nicholas.

Mrs Bridgewater shot him a suspicious glance. 'That was a nasty one,' she said. 'Our William nearly lost his job over that, but it was all sorted out by Mr Charles. Now things might have been different if he had lived here. You need a man to run a place like this, and Mrs Rutherford meant well but it's not the same, is it?'

'Why did William almost lose his job?' asked Nicholas with interest.

'He got in a fight with one of the houseguests. A nasty piece of work he was by all accounts. Will gave him a good thrashing, but he was gentry, after all and Will thought he would be dismissed without a reference. Mr Charles fixed things up though, and Mr whatever his name was went to Africa. Yes, it was a great pity that Miss Victoria didn't marry Mr Charles and not that Colonel Rutherford. Things might have been very different then.'

'What did they have the fight about,' asked Nicholas.

'Ellen,' said Mrs Bridgewater, simply. 'He had been interfering with Ellen. He asked her to do some quite dreadful things as well, which I certainly will not mention now.'

'Quite,' said Nicholas, hastily.

'William came back that night with a cut lip and a black eye,' my father told me, 'and there was quite a to-do in the house next morning, but Mr Charles said that he got what he deserved and nothing more was done about it.'

'And the man who was responsible for all this went off to Africa?' asked Nicholas.

'Yes,' said Mrs Bridgewater, 'and good riddance to him, that's what we all felt. All that is except Miss Victoria, who was sweet on him, so they all thought. But that didn't last too long either for she went and married Colonel Rutherford, only he wasn't a colonel then, just a lieutenant. You see that chaffinch,' she went on, 'he's going to steal that bit of seed from under the nose of the robin. They're not stupid, those little birds, they've got more in their little heads than you'd think.'

'Indeed they have,' said Nicholas, mechanically.

2.

Saturday 5th June 1897

'It was the philosopher Theophrastus who first used the Greek word orchis to indicate a particular group of plants whose root, when dried and chopped were used in Greece and Asia Minor as anti-depressants and stimulants,' said Frederick Sedgley, as he led the party down the Rose Walk in the direction of the walled garden and the glasshouses. 'And as a result it is Theophrastus who is generally seen as the father of orchidology.'

'Orchidology,' repeated Lady Carey admiringly, 'what a splendid name.'

'Theophrastus,' said her husband, 'now let me see . . .'

'Circa 372 to 287BC,' went on Frederick Sedgley, warming to his theme. 'But no less than a person as Confucius commended orchids for their beauty and their scent. This was in China over two thousand years ago. Indeed, the first book on orchids that gives details about cultivation, species and varieties, was probably written in Chinese about fifty years before the battle of Hastings.'

'Which was fought in 1066,' whispered Archie Rossdale to Millicent Howard, who had dropped back from her mother to walk beside him.

'One in the eye for King Harold,' murmured Millicent. 'I did benefit from an excellent New York education, Mr Rossdale,' she said. 'I am particularly strong on the eighteenth century, you know. King George III and the American colonies and all that, but we ranged far and wide.'

'With special reference to the early nineteenth century,' put in Archie.

'The early nineteenth century?' queried Millicent.

'Lord Byron and his spirits, Lord Nelson and his breeches,' responded Archie.

Millicent laughed delightedly. The sunlight glinted in her hair as she threw back her head and Archie roundly although silently cursed the Duke of Westerdale, his castle and all his family. He searched rapidly for something else to say to captivate his companion.

'We have some interesting history in the library at Felton,' he volunteered at last. 'Gibbon's *Decline and Fall of the Roman Empire*, and there's the Hume and Smollett's *History of England to the reign of George III.* I used to like that as a child. It has some very good engravings.' He looked at her anxiously. 'There's one that shows the death of the Princes in the Tower. I used to be intrigued by that. In fact I have been told that I cried myself to sleep when I was first shown the picture. There's a figure in a helmet who's about to smother the boys and another holding a lamp who illuminates the scene. It's very theatrical,' he added.

Millicent looked at him mischievously. 'And what else is there in the library?' she asked.

'Armstrong's *History of Norfolk*,' answered Archie in all seriousness. 'It came out at the end of the last century. At least ten volumes and we get a mention. Well, two pages to be exact.'

'I shall look forward to reading it,' said Millicent.

Archie stared at her uncertainly. He could not make up his mind whether she was being serious or just joking. Millicent noticed the perplexity in his eyes and took pity on him. She touched him gently on his right arm.

'No, I mean it,' she said. 'I should be most interested to learn about your home. Now hush, we must catch up with the others and give our wholehearted attention to Mr Sedgley and his orchids.'

'Linnaeus, the Swedish botanist, is another giant in the field,' Frederick Sedgley was saying to his immediate audience. 'He, of course, is generally regarded as being the founder of modern plant taxonomy.'

'Taxonomy,' my dear?' queried Lady Violet.

Her husband looked surprised. 'The science of classification,' he answered. 'He wrote his *Species Plantarum* in the mid-eighteenth century, about fifty years before my father started his collection.'

By now the senior members of the party, who made up the advance guard, had reached the arched door that separated the flower garden from the walled gardens that contained the famous Drayfield glasshouses and their contents. Frederick Sedgley waited politely until the rest of the group had caught up with him before proceeding.

'My father always maintained that success in growing orchids depended upon six crucial factors; temperature, light, humidity, ventilation, watering and feeding. With this in mind he designed the range of glasshouses that you are about to see.'

Frederick Segley paused on this almost triumphant note and ushered his guests through the arched doorway that led into the walled garden.

'To our left,' he said, 'was once an old forty foot vinery that my father converted into two glasshouses. Beyond them is the cold orchid house and beyond that is the boiler and potting-shed. To our right is the intermediate house that fronts the warm orchid house and the cool orchid house. Beyond them is the peach house and then we have the fig and tomato house.'

'Tell me, Mr Sedgley,' put in George Johnstone in a slightly supercilious tone. 'Exactly what happens in the intermediate house?'

Frederick Sedgley seemed delighted with the question. 'The house was built to my father's own design for the purpose of growing *Cattleyas, Laelias* and other orchids that require an intermediate temperature. It has a very large tank in the middle, with small hot pipes running through it to supply water and keep a nice moisture in the air. This tank, when the rain collected from the roof gives out, can be replenished by water from a stand-pipe that has replaced the well that was in use during my father's time. My *Vandas* and other tall orchids live in the central bed directly above the tank. It is supported by oak props and formed of sheets of galvanized iron covered with broken coke.'

'Indeed,' said George Johnstone.

'The *Vandas* are my favourites,' cried Victoria. 'We have four varieties and the best are pinky-mauve in colour. I absolutely adore them.'

'Then we must see them, Miss Sedgley,' said Lancelot Rutherford firmly, before blushing at his own temerity. 'That is if your father is agreeable,' he added hastily.

'By all means,' said Frederick Sedgley, affably. 'Wander around for as long as you like. And keep your eyes open for Leicester.'

'Leicester?' queried Lady Carey.

'Our peacock,' said Victoria. 'He's rather old now but he loves the kitchen garden. He has three mates, although they are very dowdy by comparison. He used to have a brother until a fox got him. His name was Dudley,' she added inconsequentially.

There was a moment's silence, which was broken by Millicent, who said thoughtfully,

'And I'll bet there was once a third, whose name was Robert.'

'There was indeed, my dear,' said Lady Violet admiringly. She looked round her at a row of blank faces and at Sir Robert, who was smiling broadly. 'Well, really,' she said. 'Put to shame by our American guest. *Kenilworth* by Sir Walter Scott. Robert Dudley, Earl of Leicester, Queen Elizabeth's favourite. Surely some of you must have read it? We bought all three birds just after my parents gave us the collected works as a Christmas present.'

'Amazing,' said George Johnstone. 'Quite amazing. So, Miss Sedgley, lead us to the *Vandas*,' and at this point the party fragmented.

'My favourites are in the cold orchid house,' said Lady Violet decidedly. 'They are the *Masdevallias*. They have purple insides and they come from Peru.' And she led a group of four, comprising herself, Lord and Lady Rossdale and Lady Carey off in the direction of the cold orchid house. Frederick Sedgley, Mrs Howard, George Johnstone, Victoria Sedgley and Lance Rutherford dutifully trooped off in the direction of the intermediate house. Sir Robert Carey perched himself on an upturned wheelbarrow and consulted a small notebook that he produced from an inside pocket. Quite clearly he had had his fill of touring at least for the immediate future.

'Who's for the peaches and figs?' said Charles Sedgley. 'Raynsford,' he called out to an aged gardener, who had just appeared from the direction of the potting-shed. 'Raynsford, is the peach house open?'

'Come this way, Mr Charles,' came the answer.

Charles offered his arm to Tilly Rossdale while her brother provided the same service for Millicent Howard and the two couples followed the gardener along the path that ran along beside the wall. As they turned left towards the fig and peach houses he pointed towards a large tank on what appeared to be a wooden base.

'The old well,' he said. 'They covered it up when it fell into disuse. Grandmother was worried in case dogs or children might fall down it; probably in that order too' and he laughed.

'Took two of us to shift that tank, Mr Charles,' said the gardener. 'Six railway sleepers and then the tank. No dogs will ever fall down there, I'll be bound.'

'The tank's a relic from the intermediate house,' explained Charles. 'The first one that grandfather installed began leaking, so he replaced it with the existing one. I don't think that one's galvanized,' he added, pointing to the tank in the right angle of the wall. 'Whatever galvanized is.'

'Coated with zinc. It's a protection against rust,' said Millicent. 'And it is galvanized.' She tapped the tank with her knuckles.

Archie Rossdale stared at her in amazement. 'You are quite extraordinary,' he said. 'Why on earth should you know anything about zinc coated tanks?'

'Oh, my father was in that line of work,' replied Millicent vaguely, then changing the subject she asked, 'why isn't it used any more, the well, I mean?'

'The water table moved, so I'm told, and it dried up,' said Charles. 'Anyway, we are on mains water now so it doesn't really matter.'

'Miss Howard is bound to be an expert on water tables,' said Archie Rossdale, daringly.

Millicent smiled at him, then turned to Charles. 'Mr Sedgley,' she asked, Shall I be able to eat a peach?'

Raynsford, who had paused in front of the door that led to that particular glasshouse, chuckled.

'No. Ma'am, that you won't, begging your pardon, Mr Charles. Manure cart was here yesterday. Month's time will see some fine Alexander's, though.'

'Alexanders?' asked Tilly Rossdale.

'A species of peach,' said Charles. 'Raynsford's very proud of his Alexander's, aren't you, Arthur?'

'That I am, Mr Charles. Tree to be lifted and root pruned then the size and flavour will match anything John Gorman can produce for Lady Clonkerry, that's for sure.'

'Now there's a topic of conversation for this evening,' said Archie Rossdale, 'and talking of this evening, may I engage you for the first two dances, Miss Howard?'

Millicent glanced at him and smiled. 'I believe you can Mr Rossdale, yes I believe you can.'

3.

Saturday 4th September 1999

The events of that night are as clear to me now as they were when it all happened. Perhaps I should have talked about it, but I thought at the time that it was probably not the best of ideas. To start with people would think that I had imagined the whole thing. After all, I had consumed a fair amount of alcohol over the course of the evening, and if I had confessed to seeing pink elephants or green giraffes no one would have been in the least surprised. Then again, was it all just a bad dream? We had all been discussing ghosts at one stage and what would have been more natural than to have had a nightmare on the subject?

I was also well aware that my period of probation at the town hall was coming to an end and that there was every chance of promotion around the corner, what with the amount of work being generated by the art gallery project and all its ramifications. The last thing I wanted was for Councillor Barnes to run away with the idea that I had a screw loose or was someone liable to hallucinations. I did think of mentioning it to Mark the next morning and swearing him to secrecy, but pretty quickly decided against it. With the best will in the world it could slip out in conversation, or even worse when we discussed Sedgley family history or the proposed guide book in committee. No, in the end I took my own advice and kept silent. Anyway, I certainly hadn't seen either Anne Boleyn or Emma Hamilton, so from the local paper's point of view they weren't going to miss much.

I had awoken at four o'clock or just after. I remember glancing at my watch as I reached for my glass of water. I had, as I knew I would have, a raging thirst, and I polished off the half glass I had left and still felt I could do with more. A trip to the bathroom was also in order, and so I gingerly rolled off the couch and carefully made my way to the door. I turned the light on and left the door very slightly ajar so that a shaft of light illuminated the hallway and enabled me to get to the bathroom without turning on the main light in the hall and possibly disturbing the others.

The bathroom was at one end of the hall next to the spare bedroom that was currently occupied by John Dickinson. As I tip-toed passed his room en route to the kitchen, which was at the other end of the hall next to the front door, I heard him snoring. I remember making a mental note to let him know that he had been disturbing the peace then I entered the kitchen and replenished my glass. It was quite chilly, but I put it down to the fact that I was dressed only in my underpants.

As I left the kitchen clutching my water I distinctly felt a draught around my shins and ankles. I put my glass of water on the work surface and turned to my left, supposing that the front door must have been ajar. I recall quite clearly thinking that Mark's sense of security was not up to much, and I moved over to close it. It was then that I became aware of a shadowy figure dressed in what appeared to be evening clothes beside the door, which was in fact firmly closed. My first reaction was that it was either Mark or John and I was on the point of apologising if I had been the cause of them getting out of bed.

'Hullo,' I said. 'Is everything OK?'

Everything obviously wasn't for the man, and it was a man, of that I am quite certain, shook his head and stared behind me. It was then that I realised that it was neither Mark nor John who was standing there. I turned to look at whatever it was my mysterious companion was watching then turned to remonstrate. I remember thinking that it must have been an interloper and that I ought to shout for assistance, but as I turned I lost sight of him. It was as simple as that. One moment he was there and the next he had disappeared. He had not walked past me and the door behind him was still firmly closed.

Somewhat shaken I collected my glass, walked back along the hall, and returned to the sitting room. I sat on one of the easy chairs and tried to sort things out in my mind. I wasn't dreaming because I was quite clearly sitting there drinking my water. But had I been dreaming a few moments earlier, and if so when did that dream start and when did it finish? And surely the process of getting the water was intertwined with my seeing the interloper. If one was reality then so too must be the other.

I was well aware that many people would put my experience down to the amount of drink – both alcoholic and non-alcoholic - that I had put away over the past few hours. With my mind in turmoil I got up, walked over to the window and stared out. There in front of me I could make out quite clearly the Rose Walk and in the distance the wall marking the boundary of the kitchen garden. Half way down the Rose Walk was the goldfish pond, glinting in the early morning light; and standing there by the pond were two very shapely ladies in long white dresses. I moved rapidly across to the door and switched off the light to get a better view and then returned to the window. They appeared to be standing beside the pond staring into the water and obviously in deep conversation. I watched them for at least a minute before walking away from the window. I was in half a mind to go and wake up Mark, but decided against it and returned to my vantage point. It was as well that I had not disturbed Mark for, like the mysterious figure on the landing, my ladies had disappeared.

For the second time that night I sat in my easy chair and tried to work things out. I thought back to the conversation I had just before the party ended. I had been speaking with Mrs Vanstone about the Jane Emburey situation and then we both joined Mrs Fitter, who was still discussing ghosts with Roger Collet and Ken Belton. We listened for a while as Ken banged his former drum about the need for 'peppy', as he put it, coverage for Drayfield Hall in his paper, then Mrs Vanstone joined in.

'The librarian at Potters Bar was heavily involved with psychic research,' she said. 'I met him at a conference in York some years ago and he gave us a most instructive talk on the subject. I say "talk" but it was more of an informed chat one evening in the bar after a particularly tedious session on the weaknesses of the Dewey system of classification.'

'Yes, yes,' said Ken Belton, irritably, annoyed that the spotlight had at least temporarily moved away from him.

'He maintained,' went on Mrs Vanstone, 'that when people talk about ghosts they should realise that there are two quite distinct types of manifestation. He described them as "active" and "passive", and of the two the "passive" was the easiest to understand.'

'Go on,' said Roger Collet.

'The "passive" is rather like a film show,' said Mrs Vanstone. 'Something has happened and has imprinted itself on a background, and if you are able to tune in, so to speak, you will see it. Nothing can happen to you, the viewer, because that is all you are; simply a spectator watching something that was actually played in reality perhaps centuries earlier. He claimed that some locations provided suitable backgrounds and that certain people had the ability to tune in. It was as simple as that.'

'And the "active"?' asked Roger Collet.

'Ah, that's much more difficult to explain,' said Mrs Vanstone. "That is when things get thrown around and broken. That is actually happening, but I don't think that he came up with any examples of people getting hurt as a result of such activities, though he did give us several examples.'

'Poltergeists,' put in Mrs Fitter.

'Exactly,' said Mrs Vanstone. 'He did say that one was usually faced with either one sort of manifestation or the other but seldom both, though there were some examples of both happening at the same time and in the same place. Borley Rectory was a case in point.'

'Borley Rectory?' said Ken Belton, who had forgotten his initial annoyance and had been listening to Mrs Vanstone with obvious and increasing fascination.

'A haunted house on the Essex-Suffolk border,' explained Mrs Vanstone. 'It was built in 1863 on the site of a Benedictine monastery, and was supposed to be haunted by a nun. She had run off with a monk but they had been caught. Her lover was hanged and she was walled up in the monastery. There were several sightings of the nun from about 1885 until the 1930s, but there was also a lot of poltergeist activity, smashed glasses and stone throwing, that sort of thing. The rectory was badly damaged by fire in 1939 and finally demolished in 1944. I read an article about Borley in the paper, *The Times*, I think it was, some time ago. Apparently there is still trouble there to this day, but it seems to be centred round the parish church.'

After that the conversation reverted to the theme of whether or not something ghostly could be linked to Drayfield and used by Ken Belton in the paper.

Mrs Vanstone's remarks that evening remained in my mind and in the early hours of the following morning I sat in that easy chair for a good half an hour mulling over their significance. Had I seen in the hall and in the garden what Mrs Vanstone had described as a "passive manifestation" or had I just imagined it? I clearly hadn't dreamed it because I was wide awake. Or was it an "active manifestation" and had the figure been trying to communicate with me? One thing I did appreciate. Whereas in the hall the atmosphere was damp and creepy and I was clearly frightened, here in the sitting room the atmosphere was normal and there was no question of panic. Even when I was actually looking out of the window my feelings were more of curiosity than of fear. I could not understand it at all and finally, having established that it was now after five o'clock, I returned to my couch and my duvet, and this time slept through until breakfast time.

'How did you sleep?' asked Mark, as he fried some bacon and eggs in the kitchen.

'I have had better nights,' I answered truthfully. 'I had to get up once or twice, and I drank several glasses of water, which I suppose accounts for the getting up.'

Mark nodded. 'Yes, I thought I heard someone in the little corridor outside my bedroom. I suppose that must have been you.'

I shook my head. 'No,' I answered. 'My prowling took in the hall, the kitchen and the bathroom, but not your corridor,' but at that moment John Dickinson joined us, and we dropped the subject of nocturnal ramblings and reverted to the art gallery.

4.

Saturday 5th June 1897

'Archie,' said Tilly Rossdale. 'Come over here. I want you to do something for me. No,' she went one as both men moved in her direction. 'Not you Charlie,' you will only get all proprietorial and tell me I am not allowed to.'

Brother and sister disappeared around the side of the peach house and Charles Sedgley and Millicent Howard stared after them.

'He's a good chum of yours, Archie Rossdale, isn't he?' said Millicent.

'Very much so,' answered Charles. 'More like a brother, I suppose. We were at school together and when my father died I spent a lot of time with the Rossdales. They were very good to me. I used to spend the school holidays at their place in Norfolk, that is when I wasn't staying here or with one of my other uncles.'

'What happened to your father?' asked Millicent, curiously.

'Killed in Africa.' Charles thought for a moment. 'He was a soldier, like me. Well, not like me in truth. He was a good soldier whereas I suspect that I am a bad one, as you will have gathered from snippets of conversation over the last few days. No, my old man died leading his men at Majuba Hill when I was only five years old.'

'Poor you,' said Millicent. 'We have something in common, you and me. My father died a violent death, but not I am afraid a glorious one. What about your mother? No, I am very sorry. I should not be prying. Please forgive me.'

'It's quite alright,' said Charles. 'She married again. She has another family now. We don't see much of each other, but there's no estrangement or anything like that. It's just that our lives seemed to have diverged.'

'Nevertheless,' repeated Millicent, 'I should not have asked you.'

'I don't have to ask you about your mother.' Charles smiled. 'She is very much, how shall I say …'

'You don't have to,' replied Millicent. 'She is all of that and more. But I am very grateful. She brought me up alone and unaided, and here I am. But it's strange.' She paused and stared out of the side of the glasshouse. 'Well, not so strange really. When I think of my past and its upsets, and I see the stability of everything that is around me now, then I say to myself – that is what I want. I want to belong and to be part of something that goes on and on. Do you feel like that, having lost your father and drifted away from your mother? But I suppose that this place gives you the security that I would give my eye teeth for.'

Charles stared at her. 'Oh, Drayfield will never be mine. The entail ends with my uncle Frederick. Vicky will inherit. I have umpteen cousins anyway, and even if the house were to go through the male line I should be very low down the list. My uncle Charles has two sons and my uncle Reggie has one. No, unless I married Vicky, as the years go by Drayfield will go one way and I will go another. My uncle and aunt always hoped that Vicky would marry a cousin. Their wish was and I am sure still is to see Drayfield remain with the Sedgleys. But you can't choose who you fall in love with, can you?' He stopped for a moment.

'No, you can't,' said Millicent, quietly.

'Still, if you become the Duchess of Westerdale, you will get all the security you could possibly ask for.' Charles stopped when he saw the expression on her face. 'Now it is my turn to apologise,' he said. 'It is just that I thought ... well, your mother led my aunt to believe that you and the duke ...'

'My mother says some very silly things,' said Millicent. 'She also does some very silly things that I hope neither of us comes to regret. I accept your apology as I hope you have accepted mine. We have both delved too deeply into matters that perhaps do not concern us. Anyway, our friends are returning and,' she tapped him on his wrist with her fan, 'if you tell anyone that I am going to marry the Duke of Westerdale, I shall personally string you up on one of your uncle's peach trees.'

5.

Sunday 3rd January 1965

Next morning Nick was having a late breakfast when the phone rang.

'Hullo, Nick, darling,' said Jane. 'I thought that it would be as well to reassure you that all was OK yesterday. Victor said that he couldn't understand why I needed to see the crests on the down-pipes, which I explained was my reason for being there, but apart from that all seemed to be well.'

'Why did he turn up anyway,' asked Nick.

'The match was cancelled. Apparently three of their team had been taken ill after Christmas. Victor was livid that they hadn't been told about it. He was driving past Drayfield, and he knew I had said something about Drayfield research, so in he came. The rest you know. I am so sorry that your journey was wasted, but I have another idea that might appeal.'

'Go on,' said Nick.

'I have arranged to drive over to Bearwood next Thursday, that's the 7th. I was hoping that your term won't have started and that perhaps you could join me. I will have to be back by 6.00pm to collect the children, and anyway Victor gets home from work about then, but at least we could have a chat and a pub lunch. What do you think?'

'Yes, that should be fine.' Nick consulted his diary. 'Just! I am scheduled to be back on the 8th, that's when the borders turn up. What are you going to be doing at Bearwood?'

'They have found some household accounts that they thought I would be interested in looking at, and they said I could photocopy any I might need for the great work, which is very kind of them. It's going to be the last thing I do before I finish the whole thing and send it off to my tutor.

That is if you don't count cutting out a large chunk of Drayfield stuff.'

'Where shall we meet?'

'I have looked at the map,' said Jane, 'and it seems to me that the best thing would be for us to meet in Guildford and then take one car from then on. There's a car park by the new Civic Centre, or whatever it calls itself. Suppose we joined forces there at ten o'clock then we could be at Bearwood by 11.00am?'

'Sounds fine to me,' and Nick made a quick note. 'Guildford at ten, then.'

'Are you sure?' asked Jane. 'I realise that it's a long journey for just a pub lunch but you never know, we might be able to organise something else, who knows?'

'I am quite sure,' responded Nick with alacrity. 'I'll see you in the car-park at ten o'clock,' and feeling ridiculously pleased with himself he poured out another cup of coffee.

CHAPTER EIGHT

1.

Tuesday 5th October 1999

'Apologies for absence?' asked Councillor Barnes.

'Mr Collet and Mr Davies,' I replied.

The meeting of the Fine Arts Committee had been put back to the 5th of October at the request of the chairman. 'There have been one or two highly important developments that need to be resolved before we meet,' he had announced to me over the phone when I rang to arrange a time to work out the agenda. His decision proved to be a godsend as it turned out, for three significant things had occurred since the night of Mark's party and none of them would have been resolved if we had stuck to our original date of the 21st of September. The loss of Messrs Collet and Davies, owing to prior engagements, was as far as I was concerned more than compensated for by the amount of work I had been able to get through over the previous week.

In the first place I set to with a will and by the time of the meeting I was well underway with my Sedgley booklet. I sat down in my office on the Monday morning after the party with Jane Emburey's thesis, copies of Burke's *Peerage* and Burke's *Landed Gentry*, and Patterson's *History of Barcombe and District*, all courtesy of Mrs Vanstone, and by the end of the month I had written quite enough to earn plaudits when the committee met. I had even produced what I considered to be a more than workmanlike family tree, this time courtesy of the computer with which the council had provided me. I considered that the money spent on sending me on a beginner's computer course had been extremely well spent.

My second piece of good fortune was that I had been summoned to meet the powers that be at the Town Hall and had been informed that my period of probation had been satisfactorily concluded and that I was to be offered the post of Gallery Administrator. To do, in fact, what I was already doing, but this time on an official and permanent basis. The gods must have been smiling on me that day because there was more to come.

'The council is able to offer you accommodation,' I was told, and I was informed that I had the choice of the Hamilton Lodge, by the main gates of the park, or a flat in the servants' wing of Drayfield Hall itself, where I would be a neighbour of Sam Kendle.

The lodge was to be renovated, I was informed, funds being made available from a source as yet confidential but which would be revealed to members of the FAC at their next meeting. Given my recent experiences at Drayfield Hall and the fact that I always fancied the idea of a small garden, I quickly opted for the lodge.

The final thing was the fact that about a week after the party I received a call from Judy Fredericks, who gave me the phone number of *Emburey & Martin*, a Birmingham firm of solicitors of which Mr S.V.Emburey was senior partner.

'Judy, very many thanks,' I said gratefully. 'I owe you a drink, no make that two.'

'I'll hold you to that,' she said with a laugh, as she put the phone down.

I rang Messrs *Emburey & Martin* that same morning and was put through to Samuel Emburey, who was pleased to confirm that he was indeed the son of Jane Emburey and that his mother was both alive and well.

'You will understand if I don't give you her address and phone number,' he said guardedly, 'but I will contact her and give her your details. She will, I am sure, be in touch with you very soon. Let me just note down the gist of what you are saying. Drayfield Hall is shortly to open as an Art Gallery and you are hoping to make use of sections of her thesis for your booklet on the family that owned the place?'

I confirmed that this was the case and that there were various other questions that I would dearly love to put to her regarding the history of the hall and the family. He said once again that he was certain that his mother would be delighted to help in any way she could.

'Minutes of the last meeting,' said Councillor Barnes. 'You have all had copies so can I take it that these have met with your approval and that I can sign?' He waited for a brief moment, pen poised, then 'very well', he announced. He signed with a flourish, looked up and continued. 'Matters arising? I think that our agenda covers everything possible, but if there is anything else?' He paused again then shuffled his papers. Mark, who was sitting on my right, nudged me.

'If he goes on like this we'll have time for a swift one at *The Green Man*,' he muttered.

'Item four on the agenda. Staff changes,' said Councillor Barnes. 'I am happy to announce that our secretary Mr Tregaskes has been appointed Gallery Administrator as from this coming Monday. He will liaise closely with both Mr Paddon-Browne and Mr Kendle, and I am sure we all wish him well in his new post.'

There was a brief round of applause and Mark leant over and whispered 'well done, I hope you got a pay rise' while I distinctly heard Mrs McGinty whisper to Edwin Hooper, 'but I thought he was that already', but there was little time for preening as Councillor Barnes was moving the meeting along at his usual frenetic pace.

'Item five. Celebrity Opening,' said Councillor Barnes. 'As you all know, we have been giving much thought to the nature of our opening ceremony, which incidentally has now been confirmed as Saturday, 20th May 2000. We had very much hoped that we could persuade a member of the Royal Family to do us the honour, although I am aware that there was a body of opinion that favoured the idea of a film star who lives in the area.' He stared at Tim Lewis and cleared his throat in a theatrical manner.

'In the event,' he continued, 'we have been exceedingly fortunate in that we have been able to induce a member of the royal family to grace us with her presence. Please,' he said, as an excited murmur swept around the table. 'I am not supposed to say who it is until the Mayor has made a formal announcement to the council tomorrow, but the lady is a nearish neighbour, and I am reliably informed that her husband will be joining her as well.' He paused for a moment, clearly enjoying the build up of suspense. 'We made a great deal of the fact that Colonel Rutherford, the husband of the last owner, was a one-time aide to Princess Beatrice, Queen Victoria's youngest daughter, and that Drayfield used regularly to entertain royalty in the Edwardian period. Now, before you attempt to cross-question me and I give away information that I should not, we will move on to Item six on the agenda, Colleymore's Garden Centre.

'Colleymore's,' he explained, 'have taken a ten year lease on the old kitchen garden to the south of the house. At present, as you all know, access to the kitchen garden is through a door in the garden wall at the end of the Rose Walk. This entrance will still be used for pedestrian access to the garden centre but Colleymore's have received planning permission to make another access point to the south from the Barcombe Road and to provide parking facilities for fifty cars. The money the council has received from Colleymore's is being used to enhance the amenities of Drayfield Park as well as to enable our committee to spend a little more on our own refurbishment programme. In the short term, the first and very obvious thing to happen will be the renovation of the Nelson and Hamilton lodges.'

There followed an animated discussion on the financial implications of the Colleymore deal on our own activities, although during its course the committee was made aware of the fact that although it was intended to make some money by letting the Nelson Lodge, the Hamilton Lodge was being made available for use by a council employee, namely myself.

'You jammy so and so,' whispered Tim Lewis.

Mrs McGinty's rather long-winded account of progress with the shop followed next but had clearly been upstaged by Councillor Barnes's news. Then we briefly considered Desmond Davies's written report on the renovation of the restaurant before moving on to Mark Paddon-Browne's update on the pictures and the catalogue. The latter, he told us, would be ready for proof reading well before Christmas. The date for the removal of the collection from Barcombe Lodge to the new gallery had been confirmed as the Monday, 14th February and he had, he informed the committee, one rather exciting piece of information to impart.

'There is a Wouvermans in the collection that formerly hung here at Drayfield in the days of the Sedgleys,' he said, 'and so we are in the position of welcoming an old friend home. I am sure that Ken Belton will be able to make excellent use of that in his paper.'

His audience stared at him in stunned silence.

'Perhaps, Mark,' said Councillor Barnes gently, 'you had better explain to us exactly what a Wouvermans is.'

Mark cleared his throat. 'I do apologise, Mr Chairman,' he said. 'Philips Wouvermans was a Dutch seventeenth century painter who specialised in equestrian themes. He was much sought after in the eighteenth century by British collectors, and we think that this particular work was acquired by the first Charles Sedgley round about 1800. It is called *The halt of a hawking party outside an inn* and there is an almost identical version in the Royal Collection. According to Sir Denzil's records, he bought the painting at the time of the Drayfield sale on Mrs Rutherford's death, and he has noted inside his own copy of the sale catalogue that the picture hung in the Library, in this very room, in point of fact. Now I have discussed the matter with Mrs Vanstone and with our Gallery Administrator, and we all agree that it would be entirely appropriate if the Wouvermans were to hang here, exactly where it used to hang in the days of the Sedgleys.'

There were general grunts of approval and an 'excellent idea' from Edwin Hooper.

'I will of course be circulating a plan of the proposed picture hang in all three rooms, four if we count the Sedgley Room, in due course,' went on Mark, 'but this did seem like an particularly good idea, and there is just the one Wouvermans in the collection.'

I had paid my long awaited visit to Barcombe Lodge the day before the meeting and had familiarised myself with the paintings and so was in a position to nod wisely. Mark went on for a few more minutes outlining his ideas for the three main rooms of the gallery, and then came my turn. Councillor Barnes announced item ten, and asked for my update on the Emburey situation and the Sedgley Booklet. I was able to deal with both in a satisfactory fashion, and my observation that I was expecting to hear from Jane Emburey, possibly before the end of the week, met with universal approval. Mrs Vanstone positively beamed in my direction when she dealt with the Sedgley Room display, the next item on the agenda. Apparently the appeal for Sedgley mementoes publicised by Leslie Davies and Ken Belton in their respective papers had paid dividends. We had acquired on semi-permanent loan a pair of silver candlesticks, a long time Barcombe resident had presented us with a photograph album that contained several pictures of garden parties at Drayfield Hall, we had been given several turn of the century picture postcards that were in the process of being framed, and the Colleymore windfall had resulted in Councillor Barnes being able to purchase the chair he had mentioned at the party.

'I am told that it too used to live in this room,' he remarked. 'Apparently it was the desk chair and was originally purchased by Frederick Sedgley.'

'Could I ask a question?' put in Tim Lewis, as Mrs Vanstone replaced her notes in her folder.

'The floor is yours Tim,' responded Councillor Barnes in a genial fashion.

'Are there any clues in Sir Denzil's sale catalogue as to where other Sedgley items ended up?' asked Tim. 'I mean, if we felt that there were specific gaps in our display we could be proactive and see if we could persuade people to give, lend or if the worst happens, sell.'

Councillor Barnes tapped his pen on the table. 'That is certainly a thought,' he said. 'Mark, do you have any comments?'

'There are certainly plenty of notes in Sir Denzil's catalogue,' he admitted. 'Mainly next to the pictures but I will check when it comes to furnishings.'

Councillor Barnes chuckled. 'I should liaise with our Gallery Administrator,' he said. 'He's honing his powers of detection. If he can track down the author of a 1960s thesis he should have very little trouble with the occasional chair, or even occasional table.' He paused, clearly expecting laughter, and the meeting duly obliged. 'Now, any other business and time and date of our next meeting and then we are through,' he said. 'I am well aware that Messrs Lewis and Paddon-Browne are anxious to savour the delights of *The Green Man* and I should hate to disappoint them.'

2.

Saturday 5th June 1897

It was a tradition at Drayfield Hall that on Saturday mornings after breakfast the male members of the party adjourned to the library and the newspapers while the ladies retired to one of the two drawing rooms. The morning of the 5th of June 1897 was, however, an exception to this general rule. The tour of the glasshouses had thrown Lady Violet's schedule into temporary confusion and as a result it was only after luncheon that the gentlemen were able to subside into their comfortable library chairs and open the papers.

'I see the varsity has pulled itself together,' said Archie Rossdale, as he scanned the pages of *The Times*. 227 in the second innings. We only made 65 in the first though and Surrey made 192. If my maths are correct that means they only need 36 runs to win. Calamity, calamity, oh calamity!'

'Who made the runs?' asked Lance Rutherford.

'Fellow called F.H.Champain,' replied Archie. 'He scored 78 and Bromley-Martin made 35 before he was run out. I say, what rotten luck. The chap writing this talks about his "splendid batting".'

'That's rather peculiar,' said Charles Sedgley, interestedly. 'Champain was playing for Gloucestershire against Surrey earlier in the week. I remember noticing his name in Wednesday's paper, or was it Thursday. He made 3 and was bowled by Lees.'

'Well, this time he was bowled by Hayward in the first innings and he was lbw to Hayward in the second,' said Archie.

'You do realise, don't you that he has had six days on the trot against Surrey,' said Lance Rutherford. Monday,

Tuesday and Wednesday playing for Gloucester and Thursday, Friday and today playing for the varsity. Surely that must be some sort of record?'

Sir Robert Carey thought for a moment. 'I think that you are probably correct, Mr Rutherford,' he said.

'On a more serious note, gentlemen,' said Lord Rossdale, who was clearly no cricketer. 'I see that Cecil Rhodes has been giving more evidence to the Committee of Enquiry. He has admitted responsibility for placing troops on the Transvaal border but maintains that they were there to be used, and I quote, "in certain eventualities".'

'In my opinion the man's a charlatan, clever but a charlatan,' said Sir Robert with disapproval, 'but you all know my views on the subject.'

'Interesting what they say, though,' went on Lord Rossdale. 'Listen, "What would have been the condition of affairs if Dr Jameson had succeeded in getting into Johannesburg? Would the people have rallied to him? It did not necessarily condemn him to say that his action was rash and impetuous."'

'Rash and impetuous,' snorted George Johnstone, 'Well, he was that alright. What do you think, Sedgley, he was a friend of yours wasn't he?'

Frederick Sedgley, glanced anxiously at his nephew, who had flushed angrily, then turned back to Lord Rossdale. 'Go on,' he said.

'Where was I', said Lord Rossdale. 'Oh yes, "When Garibaldi landed on the coast of Sicily, he was as pure a filibuster as ever put on a red shirt; but his success caused his red shirt to be converted into a garb of honour, and laid the foundation of a new Monarchy in Europe". You have to admit, Sir Robert, that there is an element of truth in that?'

'An element,' responded Sir Robert, 'but there is a difference. Garibaldi was out to overthrow an iniquitous regime. Jameson and his men were out to further the interests of, in my opinion, corrupt racketeers.'

'Which is why he seems to have had the tacit backing of a good many members of the British government,' interrupted Charles Sedgley with exasperation. 'The men who followed Jameson did so because they were under the impression that they had Imperial approval, not to mention the fact that they were out to give some assistance to people who were being led a merry dance by Kruger and his Boers. That is something I do know about, Sir Robert. I have actually been there. I do not speak with the authority of men who simply read the morning papers in the Athenaeum Club. Excuse me uncle,' and he stalked angrily out of the room.

Frederick Sedgley stared unhappily after him. 'I do apologise . . .' he started, but Sir Robert Carey cut him short.

'No, No!' he said. 'The young man's heart is in the right place even if his head isn't, or wasn't. I should have kept my views to myself, but then I too have my ideas as to right and wrong, and if one feels as strongly about certain matters as I do, and indeed your nephew does, then it is difficult to remain silent.'

'Well, his head certainly wasn't in the right place,' said George Johnstone. 'From a purely military point of view the thing was a total fiasco. They just walked into a Boer ambush. Willoughby was totally incompetent. He wasn't fit to lead off in a polka let alone lead troopers into the Transvaal. I've no time for any of them.'

'What do you think, Sir Robert?' asked Archie Rossdale. 'Regardless of the rights and wrongs of it all, would Jameson have been a hero if he had reached Johannesburg?'

Sir Robert Carey permitted himself a wry smile. He stretched out a hand and picked up the paper from Lord Rossdale's lap.

'May I?' he said. 'I read this earlier,' he admitted, 'and was struck by the sad but alas true jingle that ends the piece:
>Treason doth never prosper, what's the reason?
>Why, if it prospers, none dare call it treason.

Now,' he went on, 'I think I must have a word with Mr Sedgley. I should not forgive myself if our gathering should end on a note of disharmony. Will you excuse me, Sedgley?' and with a nod to the others in the room he walked out into the corridor.

'F.H.Champain is clearly a man with a future, which is more I suspect than can be said for Charles Sedgley,' remarked George Johnstone.

Some minutes later Archie Rossdale came upon his sister and Millicent Howard on the terrace. They were standing still and staring at large and rather bored peacock that was pecking at the gravel in a desultory fashion.

'Look,' said Millicent, 'the elusive Leicester. And we have just seen one of his lady friends. She's skulking over there by the trees.'

'We are not sure which one,' said Tilly. 'Charity is very shy so it's probably either Faith or Hope, but they always stick together so if we are patient we will probably see all of them.'

Archie smiled for a moment then became more serious. 'Well,' he said as he approached them. 'It's all happening again inside.'

'What is?' asked Tilly Rossdale.

'The Jameson Raid,' replied her brother. 'Charles and Sir Robert have had the father and mother of a row in the library and Charles has stormed out in a fury. Lady Violet will not be pleased.'

'Oh that dreadful old man,' cried Tilly. 'Why can't he leave poor Charles alone. He goes on and on about that awful raid and all Charles was doing was following orders. I wish he would pack his bags and leave us all alone. He should go and live in the Transvaal if he thinks it is that wonderful.'

'Well, to be fair, I don't think he is a particular fan of Kruger,' said Archie, 'but he thinks that we are as bad as the Boers in our own way. The trouble is that he has strong opinions as well. Why father had to bring the whole thing up by quoting chunks from the paper is quite beyond my comprehension. He should have known what would happen. The trouble is he, Sir Robert that is, doesn't credit men like Charles with any other motives than either greed or sheer delight in fighting other people.'

'And where do you stand on all this, Mr Rossdale?' asked Millicent Howard curiously.

'Somewhere between the two of them,' replied Archie honestly. 'I think that there is more skulduggery there than Charles realises, but at the same time he acts for the finest motives. He wants to live up to his father, you see, and anything that smacks of Queen and Empire has his support. Particularly, I have to admit, if it involves the Boers. He has very little time for them, and I can't really blame him. If my old man had died fighting them I might see things his way as well.'

'I think he has behaved very honourably,' said Tilly fiercely. 'He stands by his friends as well. That's why he supported Dr Jameson and Sir John Willoughby at the trial.'

'Sir Robert said that he was all heart and no head,' said Archie, 'and to be fair to the old buffer, he did look as if he was going to try to sort things out with Charles after the row.'

'I think he is a dry old stick,' said Tilly angrily, 'and I hope that Charles throws him in the lily pond. He wouldn't though, because he doesn't like hurting his uncle and aunt. Oh, it really is too bad,' and she stormed off in the direction of the garden door. The peacock scuttled out of her way and then stalked imperiously off on to the lawn.

'She's just like a sister to him,' said Archie, as he watched her go. 'We were virtually brought up together, you know, and she has always had a soft spot for him.'

Millicent stared at him. 'A sister?' she said with interest. 'I rather doubt it. Oh look,' she went on, 'he's found two of his mates.'

Sure enough two peahens had emerged from behind the trees. Leicester approached them, and then circled them with interest.

'I wonder if he will display his feathers,' said Millicent.

'He might if we are lucky,' said Archie. 'That was very clever of you this morning,' he added, 'working out the Kenilworth reference. I should have spotted that myself. After all I have read the book.'

'And to be outdone by a woman, and an American as well,' said Millicent with a slight hint of exasperation in her voice. 'It doesn't bear thinking about, does it, Mr Rossdale?'

'Miss Howard,' said Archie suddenly, 'is it true that you are joining the Duke of Westerdale's shooting party in August?'

Millicent stared at him. 'Does Anderson steam open all the letters in this house before delivering them,' she asked coolly, 'and is it any business of yours Mr Rossdale?'

'No, it is not,' admitted Archie. 'I am sorry. I shouldn't have asked.'

'Heaven preserve us,' said Millicent with spirit, 'if there is one thing I have learnt about this household, it is that everyone is always apologising to everyone else. Sir Robert appears to be about to apologise to Charles Sedgley for annoying him. It is less than two hours since Charles Sedgley apologised to me for making assumptions which he had no right to do. Lancelot Rutherford has apologised for doubting my ability with a revolver. George Johnstone has apologised for doing something for which he had every reason to apologise, and now you are apologising for scrutinising my letters.'

'Please no,' said Archie miserably. 'I certainly have never scrutinised your letters. It was just that your mother gave mine the impression that, well that you had been asked and . . .'

'Oh, mother, mother, mother,' cried Millicent in a fury, then she controlled herself. 'Now it is my turn,' she said. 'I apologise for shouting at you. It was quite unnecessarily and very unladylike and I am trying very hard under immensely difficult circumstances to remain a lady. We will say no more about it.'

'Will you still dance with me this evening?' asked Archie hesitantly.

'I never go back on my word, Mr Rossdale, and so the answer is yes, however infuriating you have been.'

And Millicent turned on her heel and walked into the house. As she did so Leicester made up his mind and favoured Archie with a dazzling display of blue, green and golden feathers.

3.

Thursday 7th January 1965

'Do you remember that you said that Drayfield was haunted but not by Anne Boleyn?' said Nick, as they enjoyed glasses of house white wine in the bar at *The Rose Inn*, Wokingham, before lunch. 'It was when we first visited the house and you were giving me a conducted tour. Remember?'

'Yes,' replied Jane. 'We were in the smoking room. I just feel that the house has a rather eerie feeling about it. I don't know what it is. Perhaps it would be different if it was fully furnished and had pictures hanging on the walls and so on. As it is the whole place is rather bare and tomb-like. At that particular moment it seemed rather creepy, but somehow Anne Boleyn didn't seem to have anything to do with the general air of sadness that seemed to pervade the place.' She paused for a moment and thought. 'Yes, that must have been it. But it's true about the atmosphere. I just don't fancy wandering about the place by myself. Well, I won't have to any more. I'll incorporate these last few Bearwood bits into chapter seven, then off it can all go to Dr Waterman. Bob's your uncle,' she added, inconsequentially.

'Then what?' asked Nick.

'They'll appoint examiners who in the course of time will report back - I hope favourably - to the department, or faculty, and then I will be awarded an M.Litt., which will be given at a congregation in the winter, or *in absentia* if I can't make it. Of course, if I'm living in Italy it is almost bound to be *in absentia*. Pity! I rather fancy going up there. I should buy a new dress and have my hair done and look the most glamorous mature student on the campus,' said Jane.

As they enjoyed their scampi about half an hour later, Nick suddenly said,

'Look, you have got to pick up the children at six o'clock, which is approximately the time that Victor gets home. If we left here in about twenty minutes we could be back in Barcombe between three and four. If I arrived shortly after you did, everything quite open and above board in case anyone saw me, we would have a couple of hours together in comfort. What do you think?'

'I think you've got a one-track mind,' replied Jane. 'Why on earth should you have arrived at the house out of the blue?'

'I will have unearthed a snippet of information that I thought would be of use to you,' replied Nick, 'and as I was driving back from London I thought I would make the detour to tell you in person. And to make things even more transparent, when you leave to pick up the children I will wait in the house – at your suggestion. When Victor arrives I will tell him everything. He will think we are both crackers, but he does already. The important thing is there is no way he would think we are, well, lovers. I mean no one in their right minds would ask their lover to hang around for evening drinks with their husband, would they?'

'Quite ingenious,' said Jane with admiration. 'OK, you're on. But what will be your snippet of information?'

'We'll save it up for Victor,' replied Nick mysteriously. 'You know, I think I could give the sweet a miss, what about you?'

'I never touch the stuff,' said Jane. 'Catch the girl's eye and ask for the bill.'

Almost exactly two hours later Jane was drawing the curtains of her bedroom. Nick's car was parked in the road outside the house; the Emburey's Ford was in the drive in front of their garage. Given Nick's meticulous planning, he was rather disappointed that his arrival at the house, as far as he could make out, had not been noticed by anyone. No neighbour had been working in his or her garden, no one had been passing by, and a battalion of boyfriends could have turned up without causing a stir.

'I am afraid I am not exactly Sophia Loren,' said Jane as he unzipped her and her dress fell in a pool around her ankles.

'I have always been an Audrey Hepburn man myself,' replied Nick as he gazed at her admiringly, 'but I do go for black underwear, I really do.'

'Come on darling,' whispered Jane, 'let's race.'

Later, as they dressed, Jane remarked, 'You know, Victor does not enjoy life the way you do. Now, how about a cup of tea before we put plan B into operation?'

At just after ten past six Nick heard the sound of a key in the front door. 'Hullo Victor,' he shouted as the door opened. 'I am making free with your living room.'

Victor entered the room. He was wearing a dark suit and he carried a small brief-case. He looked around.

'Where's Jane?' he asked.

'She had to go to collect the children,' replied Nick. 'She asked me to wait. She told me that you would be home directly, and I promised not to steal the silver.'

'What brings you to this neck of the woods?' asked Victor.

'I was driving back from London,' replied Nick, 'and as I had some information that Jane might find useful, I thought that I would drop in and tell her. I was going to ring to see whether she was in, but your number is in my address book at home. Anyway, I took pot luck, and luckily I caught her as she was on the way out.'

'Well, have a drink while we wait,' said Victor. 'Beer OK?'

'That's very good of you,' answered Nick. 'I didn't come to cadge drinks off you, but if you are going to have one I should be delighted to join you.'

Twenty minutes and half a pint later the front door opened once again and this time Jane entered the room preceded by her two children. They rushed over to their father and kissed him, then turned politely to Nick.

'Good evening, Mr Markham,' said Sam. 'How are you?' Then without waiting for a reply he said 'who are Brighton playing on Saturday?'

Nick looked uneasy. 'I am afraid I have no idea,' he admitted. 'How are Everton doing?' he asked quickly.

'Excuse me, gentleman,' said Jane, 'could we leave Everton out of things for the moment. Victor, Nick has found something out for me and I am absolutely intrigued – although I have to warn you, Nick, I can't fit any more

Sedgley family details in – tutor's orders. I've even lost my family tree.'

Nick looked disappointed, so Jane quickly went on, 'but I am still very interested in Sedgley family details, so go on, surprise me.'

'Go on, surprise her,' said Victor in a resigned tone.

'Here goes then,' said Nick, with a look of self-satisfaction on his features. 'You know you said that no one knew what happened to Charles Sedgley, the nephew who took part in the Jameson Raid?'

'Yes,' said Jane.

'A friend of mine who is interested in the Boer War rang me up the other night. He's just got hold of a book called *Mafeking – A Diary of the Siege*, which was written by someone called Major F.D.Baillie in 1900. Apparently it contains a list of the officers who were present in Mafeking with Colonel Baden-Powell, and you'll never guess who was serving there,' and he pulled his note-book out of his breast pocket and consulted it, 'on the 1st November 1899 with the Protectorate Regiment and mounted Bechuanaland Rifles?'

'Not . . .' began Jane.

'The very same,' said Nick. 'Major Charles Sedgley, late of this parish and obviously very much alive and kicking.'

4.

Tuesday 5th October 1999

After the meeting Mark, Tim Lewis and I adjourned to *The Green Man* as Councillor Barnes had suspected. The pub was nearly opposite the Hamilton gates of the park, another good reason, I thought for opting for the Hamilton Lodge as my new home. It had a pleasant old world feel to it and from the outside it possessed the rather unusual feature of three doors. Originally these had led to the saloon bar on the left, the snug bar in the centre and the public bar on the right. In the enlightened year 1999, however, such divisions had long since been swept away, the centre and right hand doors and been permanently shut, and the left hand door led to one long bar. Having said that, the landlord had turned what had been the old public bar into a rather nice sitting area, and we made a bee-line for a table and three chairs alongside the fireplace.

'Three pints?' asked Tim.

'And some dry roasted,' called Mark, as our colleague made his way to the corner of the bar and we settled back in our seats.

'My money's on the Countess of Wessex and Prince Edward,' said Mark, 'and well done, once again, on the promotion, if it is promotion.'

I opened my briefcase and took out the notes I had made at the meeting and a blue folder containing a wad of A4 paper. 'Job description,' I announced, tapping the folder. 'Apart from anything else I have got to have regular meetings with your good self, Sam Kendle and the ladies – yet to be appointed - who will be running the shop and restaurant. Until they appear it will have to be Mrs McGinty and Desmond Davies. And,' I paused expectantly, and then waited while Tim brought over first two pints of beer, then the third pint plus three packets of peanuts. 'And,' I went on, 'I am to have an office on the ground-floor. It will be on the left hand side of the front entrance in what, according to the Emburey thesis, was the butler's pantry. How about that?'

'Tell me,' asked Tim, 'have you handed Councillor Barnes a hefty backhander, or is it just a sexual relationship?'

Just then my mobile phone rang. I picked it up. 'Hullo?' I said. There was a short silence and then a voice said,

'Hullo, this is Jane Ward speaking, Jane Emburey that was. Am I speaking to Mr Richard Tregaskes . . .'

'Mrs Emburey, I am sorry, Mrs Ward,' I said excitedly. 'I am delighted to hear from you. Yes, I took the liberty of approaching your son and asking him to get in touch with you. It is very good of you to contact me so soon.'

'It's no trouble at all,' said the voice. 'I am delighted to be linking up with Drayfield Hall again after so many years and yes, by all means make use of my thesis in any way you see fit. So you are turning the house into an art gallery. How very exciting.'

'Yes,' I said, 'and one of the rooms is going to be called *The Sedgley Room* and will contain an exhibition relating to the family. We already have a few pictures, you know the ones that you probably saw when you wrote your piece plus one or two others that we have since acquired. We are also on the look out for pieces of furniture and really any objects that were at one time in the house, and I have drawn the short straw and am supposed to be writing a booklet about the family.'

'I wish you well,' said Mrs Ward, 'but I am not sure how else I can be of assistance. I mean it is a very long time ago and I have forgotten an awful lot. Though I dare say,' she went on, 'bits will come back to me if I re-read the thesis. I have it stashed away somewhere upstairs. Oh I know what I have got, and you are very welcome to them. Five or six bound copies of Punch, all of which contain the Sedgley bookplate. My daughter lives in London but comes down to see me very regularly. I could give them to her and she could pass them on to you.'

'That would be marvellous,' I said. 'They would be a splendid addition. Now, there were two further items. My colleague who is responsible for the exhibition would dearly like to display the Visitors Book that you used for your work, and also the Drayfield Tray that you photographed. I don't know if you remember but you left a packet of photos with your thesis when you presented it to the library.'

'Oh yes,' said Mrs Ward. 'Yes, I do remember. I am very sorry but I have no idea what happened to them. The tray, it was really a silver salver and it had a coat of arms on it, I last saw in Scotland and the then owner, as far as I know, sold it to an Edinburgh antique dealer. The Visitors Book I passed on to a friend of mine, a Mr Nicholas Markham. I believe he was going to present it to the Record Office, but I couldn't swear to it. I am afraid that I don't know where he is now either. We haven't been in touch since I went to live in Italy shortly after writing the thesis.'

'Hang on a moment,' I interrupted. 'You gave the Visitors Book to Nicholas Markham? Wasn't he the man who helped you to identify the heraldry?'

'Yes,' she said, 'that's right. He was a teacher who lived and worked in Sussex. Steyning, I think. That was where he worked and he lived in Arundel.'

I wrote all this down. 'Got it,' I said. 'I will try to track him down.'

'Look,' Mrs Ward went on, 'let me give you my address and phone number. I will ring you if I have any bright ideas, and you can get in touch with me if you need to. Do please keep me informed as to your progress and I should very much like to visit the gallery when it opens.'

I thanked her profusely and wrote down her address and telephone number. She lived in a village just outside Ludlow in Shropshire. I thanked her again and said goodbye. Then I closed the mobile phone and turned to my companions.

'How on earth I am I going to locate this Nicholas Markham?' I asked my colleagues, who had been following my conversation with interest.

Mark stared at me. 'Have another beer,' he said. 'It will oil the wheels,' and he stood up and made his way to the bar.

CHAPTER NINE

1.

Saturday 5th June 1897

Hensford House, the seat of the Earls of Clonkerry, was situated in the little village of Hensford, about eleven miles from Barcombe. It had been built for the 4th earl to the designs of Bonomi in the 1790s, and was a handsome square mansion, built of white brick with stone dressings, and had a portico on the northern front. The latter proved most efficacious as far as the party from Drayfield Hall was concerned because, when their carriages swept up the imposing driveway at ten o'clock that evening, a light drizzle had set in.

The ball at Hensford House was a traditional feature of the Derby Party organised by the Sedgleys. Lady Clonkerry was an old friend as well as a close neighbour, and her late husband had been a keen rival of Frederick Sedgley's father when it came to horticultural matters. As far as orchids were concerned, Charles Sedgley was the clear winner, but he had no trees in his park to match either the Earl of Clonkerry's famous Spanish chestnut trees or the renowned Hensford elm, a tree of enormous size that was forty feet in circumference round its base.

The countess received her guests in the entrance hall at the door leading into the saloon where they were announced in stentorian tones by Archbold, the house steward, who was almost as old as his mistress.

'Why he can't be called a butler, goodness only knows,' whispered Lady Violet to Lady Rossdale, as they waited to be presented to their hostess. Lady Rossdale, who only caught the word 'butler', smiled knowingly.

Millicent, who was ready to admire anything old and English, was intrigued by the formality of the occasion and even more so by the splendour of the saloon, which was Roman in style and featured alternate niches and recessed pairs of Roman Doric columns. A small orchestra was tuning up at one end of the room, and it was here that the dancing was to take place. Lady Violet had explained to her that refreshments would be available at a later stage in the dining room, and that the drawing room was used as a sitting room for those chaperones who felt disinclined to spend the whole evening watching the dancing. Lady Clonkerry invariably arranged for bridge tables to be set out for those so inclined, and whisky and soda was always served in the library to gentlemen who favoured a little quiet conversation as the evening progressed.

On the right hand side of the door leading from the main hall to the saloon was a table bearing a pile of dance programmes contained within attractive blue covers; blue being the colour of the Clonkerry livery. On the front cover of each programme was an embossed representation of the Clonkerry coat of arms, and attached to each programme by a thin blue cord was a tiny golden pencil. Millicent had been thoroughly briefed, not just by Lady Violet but also by Victoria and Tilly Rossdale, and when she opened her programme saw, as she had expected, that there were twenty dances with an intermission after the first ten and that the first dance of the evening was to be a *Grand March – Quadrille.*

The *Grand March – Quadrille* was an opening spectacle in which the Countess of Clonkerry took the arm of the most important male guest present, almost invariably the Lord Lieutenant of the county. This was the only dance of the evening in which all guests were expected to take part, and as there were always over one hundred and fifty guests at Hensford House for a Derby Ball, the saloon was inevitably extremely crowded. Millicent studied her programme and then wrote the initials AR beside the opening dance and the waltz that succeeded it. She noted with interest that dance number thirteen was a *Rye Waltz – Ladies' Choice.*

Lady Clonkerry had distinct reservations about allowing such a dance to be included in her programme. The idea that a young lady should be so forward as to ask a gentleman to dance was one that was quite foreign to her, but she was determined to move with the times, especially as the Derby Ball was to be the occasion for the coming out of her great-niece. Lucy Fitzhenry was a house guest at Hensford and had pressed her aunt to allow the dance to be featured. As Lady Clonkerry was determined that her young relative should be given every opportunity to make her mark on the dance floor, she gave in to Lucy's request.

When it came to her guest list the Countess of Clonkerry had as always taken into consideration that her ball was regarded by county society as one of the major events of the year. Matches were to be made at Hensford House in exactly the same way as they were in any of the great town houses to which many of her guests were likely to be invited. She had made careful note of the various young ladies on her list, and she was determined that Lucy Fitzhenry would not be the only eligible female to be grateful that she had attended the Hensford Derby Ball.

The countess had been delighted to learn that as many as four young officers were part of the Drayfield contingent to be invited and that as far as Lady Violet had been aware all four were available when it came to working out possible matrimonial stakes. Archie Rossdale was the only one to be in line for a title, to be sure, but Lady Clonkerry had already welcomed Viscount Brenton and his brother, the honourable Lionel Vaughan, sons of the Earl of Eversleigh, and she understood that Lancelot Rutherford was a younger son of Lord Rutherford. Taking everything into consideration, she felt that the Sedgleys had as usual done her proud on the male front. When it came to the young ladies from Drayfield, the countess was even more content. Victoria Sedgley, though nice enough in her own way, was something of a bluestocking and would be no competition for Lucy, Matilda Rossdale was far too headstrong for most male tastes, and Millicent Howard, though undoubtedly a threat in terms of beauty, was, Lady Clonkerry had been confidently informed, on the point of being snapped up by the Duke of Westerdale.

The Countess of Clonkerry was not the only one to have planned the evening with military precision. George Johnstone had organised not just that evening but his whole week with great care and forethought. His casual relationship with Elizabeth Howard, the result of an assignation following a ball at a London town house, had given him the idea of using either mother or daughter or both to further his social and financial ambitions, both of which had been severely dented in South Africa. The knowledge that the Howards had been invited to Drayfield for Derby week led him to strive for his own invitation. This he successfully achieved as a result of his cultivation of Lancelot Rutherford, who in turn was able to introduce him to Archie Rossdale. Johnstone was also assisted in no small part by his own father's social ambitions.

George Johnstone senior was a self-made man who had leased his East Anglian estate and his town house in Wilton Crescent on the proceeds of a highly profitable trade in guano. He was anxious to establish his family in society and to that end had educated his two sons at a good albeit minor public school and financed their entry into the army; Clive into the Royal Fusiliers and George into the Royal Welch Regiment. Both men were seconded for duty with the British South Africa Company's police in the mid 1890s, a situation which greatly pleased their father as they had gained a reputation in London that was far from creditable;

Clive as a womaniser and George as a gambler. Indeed one of the reasons that Clive had applied for his secondment was that his involvement with the wife of a senior officer had proved highly embarrassing to his regiment.

Their sister Mabell was quite a different personality, and George Johnstone felt that it was money well spent when he arranged for a highly placed yet impoverished countess to take his daughter under her wing for the 1897 season. That spring Johnstone lived the life of a country squire in Norfolk while the news of his daughter's progress on the London social scene seemed eminently satisfactory. It made up to some extent for the depressing news from South Africa the previous autumn. Not only had he learnt to his annoyance that Clive had left the Company's police after a drunken brawl and was working for a newspaper in Cape Town but he also discovered that his younger son was returning home from South Africa without a commission and with what the father had hoped would be a worthwhile career in tatters. Clearly the young man had no intention of confronting his father with his news for that spring he appeared to be keeping as far away from Norfolk as possible and spending his time skulking in London. Had he not been regularly drawing his allowance from Coutts Bank, George Johnstone would not even have known that his son was in town.

The information, again obtained from an intermediary, that George junior was anxious to attend a house party at which their neighbours, Lord and Lady Rossdale, were also guests, was the first ray of sunshine to illuminate the scene as far as his sons were concerned, and when he subsequently learnt that Elizabeth Howard, a friend of the Prince of Wales, was also to be present, he was positively delighted. He revoked his decision to cancel his still existing and extremely generous allowance - Clive had lost his the previous year - and made it clear to Lord Rossdale, when they met at the Norwich Quarter Sessions, that he would be more than grateful if an appropriate word to the Sedgleys could be forthcoming.

'Let them know that he doesn't eat peas with a knife; that sort of thing,' he said with a laugh, as he offered Lord Rossdale a particularly fine cigar. 'And if you see him there, mention the fact that his father would appreciate a visit. I'm damned if I'm going to the trouble of tracking him down at his club,' he continued.

Once at Drayfield it did not take the young Johnstone long to realise that Victoria Sedgley was the young lady most likely to serve his purposes. An heiress to a substantial estate was easier game than a dollar princess with a wronged mother in her wake. Marriage of course was out of the question for in the end the Johnstone brothers' saga would come to light, but a substantial pay-off could be virtually guaranteed. That he had made his decision after an abortive attempt to seduce a housemaid resulted in the need to make up lost ground, but Victoria was gullible prey and was very ready to believe that the stories emanating from the servants' hall were no more than malicious gossip. The only drawback to his plan of campaign was that Millicent Howard was without a doubt the better looking of the two girls and Johnstone disliked the idea of seeing other men monopolising her attentions. It might appear to a casual onlooker that he was a loser, and that was one thing that he could not abide.

When he arrived at Drayfield, Johnstone's biggest worry revolved around the fact that Charles Sedgley was also a guest and that Sedgley had served in the British South African Company. In fact neither of the Johnstone brothers had knowingly come across him in Africa, but it was always possible that one or other of them might have been pointed out to him, either at Bulawayo or the Cape, where officers often mingled with others from different bases. The other difficulty could have been that Sedgley, or someone else for that matter, might have learnt of the circumstances of George Johnstone's resignation of his commission. It had come, annoyingly enough, after he had successfully fulfilled a couple of missions for the Cape Government that would probably have ensured his rapid promotion had he not been caught cheating at cards at a baccarat party in Cape Town.

In order to avoid unnecessary scandal it had been agreed by those present that the matter would go no further provided that Johnstone resigned his commission and gave his word never to play cards again. This he did with as much grace as he could muster, but rumours of his behaviour began to spread and there was no knowing how far they might have travelled. In the event Johnstone's worries appeared to have been groundless. Sedgley clearly did not recognise him. When he was reprimanded over the Ellen business there was no reference to previous misdemeanours of a similar nature, and like everybody else Charles Sedgley seemed to have accepted the fact that he had resigned his commission as a result of complicity with Dr Jameson, but exactly how and why was something of a mystery.

At half past ten precisely the orchestra struck up and the Countess of Clonkerry's *Grand March - Quadrille* opened proceedings at the Hensford House Ball. All members of the Drayfield houseparty took their allotted places, Lord and Lady Rossdale, Frederick and Lady Violet Sedgely, Sir Robert and Lady Carey, Elizabeth Howard partnered by the Earl of Eversleigh, Archie Rossdale and Millicent Howard, Charles Sedgley and Matilda Rossdale, George Johnstone and Victoria Sedgley and Lancelot Rutherford who, at Lady Clonkerry's suggestion, had asked Miss Clarissa King-Montagu to be his partner.

The waltz that followed saw the younger members of the party retain their respective partners, but the more senior members withdrew, either to the seats that surrounded the saloon or as in the case with many of the gentlemen to the safe haven of the library.

'Miss Howard will not want for partners,' observed Lady Clonkerry drily, as she took a seat beside Lady Violet and Lady Rossdale, and scanned the floor for Lucy Fitzhenry, whom she finally spotted dancing with the hon. Lionel Vaughan. Satisfied, she snapped her lorgnette closed and turned her attention to her companions.

'No,' agreed Lady Violet, 'and her mother appears to have found another admirer,' and she glanced across the floor to the other side of the room where Elizabeth Howard was in conversation with Lord Eversleigh.

'I understand that your daughter is a great favourite of Lady Sarah Wilson,' went on Lady Clonkerry to Lady Rossdale. 'I met the Wilsons at a function at her mother's house in Grosvenor Square quite recently. Of course he's in the Blues as well. Tell me,' and she turned back to Lady Violet, 'I am told that your nephew has resigned his commission as a result of being involved in Dr Jameson's stupidity. Is that so?'

Lady Violet nodded unhappily. 'I am afraid so,' she admitted.

'And that other young man, the one who is dancing with your daughter, was he involved as well?'

'I believe so,' replied Lady Violet.

'I am not so sure about him,' put in Lady Rossdale. 'I understand from Archie that there is more to it than that, but exactly what I do not know. The young people have not included me in their confidences.'

'It seems strange, does it not, that men who appear to have broken our laws have been positively lionised by society,' said Lady Clonkerry. 'There is a great deal about this South Africa business that we are not told. Now, you must excuse me. I must make sure that all is well in the library where, no doubt, your husbands are talking estate business or something equally mundane. I suggest that a little bridge after the refreshments might be in order?' and the countess rose to her feet and moved in the direction of the doorway.

The two ladies stared after her somewhat discomforted.

'How very embarrassing,' said Lady Violet at last. 'She would have heard about Charles and his problems, wouldn't she?'

'She can hardly ask him to leave, can she?' said Lady Rossdale. 'After all, she herself pointed out that Society has taken the Charles's of this world to its heart. Most of her guests would give him a round of applause if they knew. But I do hope that Tilly is not talking about South Africa to Charles. She has learnt quite enough about that continent from Lady Sarah.'

'I doubt whether they are exchanging sweet nothings,' said Lady Violet sadly. 'They have known each other far too long. Tell me, my dear,' she went on, 'who is that young man dancing with Lucy Fitzhenry? I must be very old fashioned, but the way he is holding her is positively, well the word that springs to mind is indecent.'

At approximately twenty to twelve George Johnstone glanced at his half-hunter and scanned the saloon for Elizabeth Howard. He had just completed the *Lancers – Saratoga* and had escorted his partner back to her party, and felt that the moment was ripe for the business he had planned. He had partnered Victoria Sedgley in the opening two dances, had engaged her for a *Schottische* in the second half of the evening and had accepted the invitation to partner her in the *Rye Waltz*, the ladies' choice, which was dance number thirteen. 'Unlucky for some,' he had muttered to himself as he wrote his name on her card. Johnstone felt that had more than done his duty by Miss Sedgley, and his failure to engage her for the *Waltz – Quadrille* that preceded the intermission would not be counted too heavily against him. As it was he had even prepared his defences in case of problems.

'Rutherford, old man,' he had said to his friend. 'Do me the very great favour of engaging Miss Sedgley for number ten and then take her in to supper. I have a little matter of business to attend to, and supper would provide me with the necessary opportunity.'

Lancelot Rutherford had looked slightly surprised but, as Johnstone had suspected, was more than happy to oblige. Rutherford had been on the floor for all eight dances, but with one exception, the *Double – Quadrille*, had been partnering young ladies at the behest of either his hostess or of Lady Violet. Added to which he was not a good dancer, having very little sense of rhythm, and more than one of his partners had made it perfectly obvious that she had not enjoyed the Rutherford experience in the slightest. The *Double – Quadrille* had given him the opportunity to partner Victoria Sedgley and, although she would clearly have preferred to be dancing with George Johnstone, Rutherford himself counted that dance as the best of the evening.

Elizabeth Howard was sitting with three other ladies on the far side of the room by the door to the main hall. Johnstone recognised one as Lady Carey but the other two were strangers to him. He strolled casually around the ring of dancers, currently engaged in the *Newport*, until he reached her. He waited patiently for his opportunity and then quietly said,

'Do excuse me, ladies. Mrs Howard, might I have a word with you if it is no trouble.'

Elizabeth Howard looked slightly surprised, and then rose to her feet.

'Certainly Mr Johnstone,' she replied, and she walked in front of him to the doorway. Once within the hall she looked around then moved decisively towards the drawing room. To her dismay it was already well populated. Several games of bridge were in progress and there was a general hum of conversation from several small groups of ladies who had escaped from the routine of the dances.

Elizabeth Howard paused for a moment then swept on through the drawing room to the conservatory, once the pride and joy of the late Earl of Clonkerry. It was a large and spacious room, constructed of iron and glass, and had been designed by no less a person than Joseph Paxton in 1837. There was a strong fragrance of flowers in the air, curved iron chairs and tables were dotted around amongst the rich green foliage, and flickering gas lamps added vital illumination to the moonlight that filtered through the barrel vaulted roof. Under any other circumstances Elizabeth Howard would have found it immensely romantic, as obviously did the various young couples, who had slipped away from the eagle eyes of chaperones in the saloon.

'If you were intending to ask me to dance,' said Elizabeth Howard, as they stood in front of a mass of exquisite hot-house ferns, 'I think that it would probably be inappropriate. Indeed, I have to say that our present conversation is not the wisest thing that we should be doing.'

George Johnstone smiled. 'Indeed,' he said. 'By Jove, they've even got a fountain in here,' and he pointed at a splendid structure in the centre of the room surmounted by a winged victory, which was disgorging water into an ornamental goldfish pond. 'No,' he went on smoothly. 'I felt that a short meeting at this stage would clarify one or two points and it has proved difficult to seize a convenient moment at Drayfield.'

'One or two points?' queried Elizabeth Howard.

'The card you left with me on Monday,' said Johnstone as they walked towards the fountain. 'Your name on the one side and that rather curt note "Not tonight" on the other. Am I to assume that your sentiments remain the same today?'

Elizabeth Howard stared at him icily. 'Indeed they are. We both are in the habit of seizing the moment, but as I have said before I feel that it would be best if we were to resume the roles of indifferent acquaintances.'

'Indifferent acquaintances,' repeated Johnstone. 'Oh come now Mrs Howard. Surely friends at the very least. From lover to acquaintance in one fell swoop. It would make a fellow dashed miserable, you know. And besides, it is as a friend that I am approaching you now, with what I hope will not be too onerous a request.'

'Which is?'

'A loan of five hundred guineas,' said George Johnstone. 'I am finding things rather tight at the present moment, and if friends such as you could rally round it would make life so much easier.' He picked a leaf from the ground beneath his feet and casually flicked it into the water.

'Out of the question,' Mr Johnstone, said Elizabeth Howard shortly. 'And now I think it would be best if we returned to the ballroom, and separately if you do not mind.'

George Johnstone stared at her sadly. 'Oh dear,' he said quietly. 'I do hate to discuss matters of business at an occasion such as this, but really you leave me no option. If you feel unable to oblige me with a loan perhaps you could be persuaded to make a small purchase?'

Elizabeth Howard turned to face him once again. A tremor of trepidation crossed her face. 'What purchase?' she asked angrily.

'The card I have just mentioned,' replied Johnstone, 'together with the letter you sent me shortly before our visit to Drayfield commenced. I am sure you remember the one I mean. You wrote it after we first met at that function in Carlton House Terrace. Shall we say eight hundred guineas for the two? Please feel under no obligation,' he continued with a smirk on his face. 'There are others who are avid collectors of such curiosities. The Dowager-duchess of Westerdale is one who I am sure would be more than interested to cast her eyes over both documents.'

'You are no gentleman,' responded Elizabeth Howard furiously. 'I demand the instant return of my letter and my card.'

George Johnstone paid no attention to the order. 'Neither an officer nor a gentleman,' he went on. 'Alas, a second son has so few prospects, and living like a gentleman is a very expensive occupation.' He paused and looked at her maliciously. 'Perhaps your daughter would have a view of the matter,' he said. 'I am told that her relationship with the duke is at an interesting stage and I feel certain that she would not wish family difficulties to jeopardise what could result in a most happy outcome.'

'Don't you dare speak to my daughter about this,' began Elizabeth Howard, but it was to no avail.

Johnstone glanced at her once again and twirled the end of his moustache with panache. 'Be so good enough to let me know whether or not you would be interested in the purchase. By tomorrow's luncheon if you would be so kind. I will then have time to consider other interested parties. And now, if you will excuse me, I think a trip to the supper room is in order,' and he turned on his heel and strode off in the direction of the dining room.

Elizabeth Howard stared after him in dismay. As she did so her daughter emerged from the shadows beside the fountain.

'Oh mother, what on earth have you done?' she said, and her eyes narrowed as she watched George Johnstone disappear into the drawing room.

'You know, I feel rather sorry for young Charles Sedgley,' said Lady Carey to Lady Rossdale, as they sipped their soup at a small table in the dining-room. 'Sir Robert showed him no mercy in the courtroom, but he admitted to me last night that the young man did have the courage of his convictions, however misguided. Apparently he never actually took part in the raid, but chose to defend his friends anyway. He could have kept quiet and not become involved.' She looked across the room to where Charles Sedgley was standing with a group of young people. She noticed that he was not paying much attention to his own party but had eyes only for Matilda Rossdale, who was talking to Viscount Brenton by the doorway into the hall.

'I believe he rather likes your daughter,' she observed to Lady Rossdale.

'They spent a lot of time together as children,' said Lady Rossdale, 'and I think Tilly envies him his South African experiences. I am told Lady Sarah Wilson would like her to accompany them when they next travel to Cape Town, but that would be quite out of the question. Gordon Wilson is in the Blues like Archie,' she went on. 'Charles of course follows the Sedgley family tradition and is in the Grenadiers.'

'Rutherford,' said Archie Rossdale, 'Rutherford, have you seen Miss Howard?' I engaged her for the *Waltz-Quadrille*, but have not set eyes on her for at least twenty minutes. You have no idea where she can be Vicky?' and he turned to Victoria Sedgley, who was munching a stuffed roll in a somewhat morose fashion beside her partner.

Vicky Sedgley muttered something indistinctly and then looked rather alarmed as Lance Rutherford went on,

'Perhaps she's with Johnstone. I haven't seen him since we were all dancing together in the *Lancers*.' Then, realising too late that he had committed something of a faux-pas, he hastily went on,

'No, she's probably with her mother. Why not try the drawing-room or the conservatory. There's quite a crowd there,' and solicitously turning his attentions to Vicky Sedgley he asked,

'Would you prefer an ice or a jelly, Miss Sedgley?'

Archie Rossdale glanced at them in annoyance, and then walked away in the direction of the hall. As he did so he passed George Johnstone strolling languidly in the opposite direction. Archie nodded curtly as they passed and Johnstone joined Lance Rutherford and Victoria Sedgley.

'I have been looking for you everywhere,' he said. 'Miss Sedgley. I see that the next dance will be a *Danish Polka*. If by any chance you are not already engaged, may I ask you to partner me?'

Victoria blushed. 'I should be delighted to, Mr Johnstone,' she replied.

Lance Rutherford opened his mouth then thought better of it. Well, if you will both excuse me,' he said sadly. But his misery was soon to be compounded.

'Mr Rutherford,' called Lady Clonkerry. 'Mr Rutherford, may I beg a moment of your time.' Lance Rutherford turned to see his hostess bearing down upon him and in her wake was a rather angular female of indeterminate age and earnest expression.

'I am afraid that when it comes to the polka,' he started, but it was to no avail, and he patiently wrote his name on the proffered programme.

2.

Wednesday 3rd November 1999

Hamilton Lodge was not going to be ready for occupation before the New Year, but I was able to move into my new office at Drayfield Hall – according to the plan in Jane Emburey's thesis, the former butler's pantry – early that November. It was there that I met Roberta Clarke. She had rung from her office in Bromley to say that she had a parcel of books from her mother, and we arranged that she should call in one Friday afternoon. I understood that she was leaving work early to drive down to Ludlow.

I was very pleased with my new accommodation, a long and rather narrow room that looked out onto the loggia that ran along the front of the house. From my window I could see down the drive quite clearly. This was an obvious asset for the butler in days gone by, for the entrance hall was just beside the door to my office, and had I been the butler I should have had all the time in the world to station myself by the front door in time to welcome any guest. I remembered reading in the thesis that the Sedgleys prided themselves upon the fact that their front door always opened as if by magic and guests never had to trouble themselves with using the grandiose bell-pull.

I was able to put all my thoughts into practice when a small blue Fiat drove up the drive shortly after three o'clock and a rather smart lady with wavy chestnut hair got out.

'That was very impressive,' she said, as I opened the door with a flourish. 'Hullo, I am Roberta Clarke, and here are the goodies,' and she shook hands and passed over two neatly wrapped packages.

'Do come in,' I said after I introduced myself. 'Welcome to Drayfield Hall, former semi-stately home, present or rather future art gallery.'

'My mother has told me all about this,' she said as I opened the door of my sanctum and ushered her in. 'She has even dug out her thesis for me to read, and I might do just that this weekend. I gather you are streamlining bits of it to use as a guide for your gallery?'

I admitted the truth of this as I made her a cup of tea and offered her a chocolate digestive biscuit. 'It's a bit primitive,' I said, 'but I have only just moved in.' I then unwrapped her first parcel. The books, bound volumes of

Punch, contained the Sedgley bookplate as her mother had explained, and would quite clearly be welcome additions to Mrs Vanstone's exhibition.

The second was a bulky object carefully protected by layers of bubble wrap. I undid it carefully and there inside was a beautifully costumed china doll.

'Her name's Jemima,' said Roberta Clarke. 'Mother found her in pieces in the old housekeeper's room and had her restored. She made the dress herself. She said that if you wanted to display her that would be fine but if not she would like her back. She's rather fond of her.'

'She is absolutely delightful,' I answered. 'We will take great care of her. Now, before I forget I must give you a receipt for all these.'

'Mother wondered whether you had managed to track down Nick Markham,' said Mrs Clarke, as I scribbled the details down on a sheet of headed notepaper.

'Not as yet,' I admitted, 'but I haven't given up. It's really a hunt on behalf of a colleague who wants to display the old Visitors Book in the Sedgley exhibition she is organising. I must show you before you go how we are going to lay out the whole experience and then you will be able to give your mother a progress report.' I handed her the receipt.

Roberta Clarke thanked me and carefully folded the paper, which she stowed away in her handbag. 'She would like that,' she said. 'My brother, who I believe you spoke to on the phone some time ago, told me to tell you that there are a couple of things that might be useful to you in your search. Nick Markham was a supporter of Brighton and Hove Albion football team, and he was also a follower of Worcestershire County Cricket Club. Sam seems to think that he might still be, and that he could be on somebody's membership list. Personally I have my doubts, but there it is for what it is worth.'

I thanked her and then took her on a short tour of the rooms that were all but ready for the reception of the pictures. They were now adorned with various pieces of furniture from Barcombe Lodge that Mrs Fitter had kindly loaned to the Council. Once the paintings were in place the Drayfield Gallery really would be something to shout about, I felt. We moved on to the Sedgley Room, with its empty display cabinets, and the Smoking Room, with its bookcases ready for Mrs Vanstone's local collection. 'Mother spoke to me about the old housekeeper's room,' said Roberta Clarke, so I took her upstairs and showed her Mark's office and the blank wall that sealed off the old servants' wing.

'Mother will be most impressed with all you have done,' said Mrs Clarke, as I escorted her to her car. 'Please keep us informed as to future progress, and I will make sure that she is able to attend your grand opening. She will be thrilled to come.'

I waved her goodbye and returned to my office. Over the next few days I contacted the Brighton and Hove Football Club to no avail and the Worcestershire County Cricket Club, who were also unable to help. Then, a week or so after my initial enquiry, I received a call from a lady from the Worcestershire Club.

'It's quite a coincidence,' she said, 'but shortly after I last spoke to you I was in the archives and I came across a magazine called *The Cartophilic News,* or something like that. It was a magazine for collectors of cigarette cards, and the reason why we have a copy in our collection is that this particular issue contains an article about members of the Foster family, who played for the county and who feature on a set of Wills cigarette cards that came out at the turn of the century. Anyway, to cut a long story short, this particular article was written by a Nicholas Markham. The date of the magazine was July 1986 and the blurb about the author says that he was a schoolmaster in Winchester.'

3.

Sunday 6th June 1897

'When Archie Rossdale rode back to Drayfield early the next morning his mind was in turmoil. Beside him rode a thoughtful Charles Sedgley, a rather morose Lancelot Rutherford and a surly George Johnstone. In front of him rattled the carriage containing the young lady of his dreams, but he was none the wiser as to how she felt about him. After failing to secure her for the *Waltz – Quadrille* before the intermission and thus the supper itself, he was faced with the further ignominy of seeing her dance the *Rye – Waltz* with no less a person than George Johnstone. Finally matters improved. She partnered him in dance number seventeen, the *Lancers* then, before she was whisked away to dance a waltz with Viscount Brenton she turned to him and said,

'Did you forget to engage me for the *Waltz – Home Sweet Home*, Mr Rossdale, or was it an intentional omission?'

Hardly believing his luck Archie instantly signed her dance card, and his evening ended as he could scarcely have hoped after the supper debacle with Millicent Howard in his arms. Yet as he rode he heard the rasping voice of Lady Clonkerry echoing in his ears,

'Of course, Miss Howard is all but engaged to the Duke of Westerdale and I am told that an announcement is expected after the shooting party in August.'

In the carriage just ahead of him conversation was of necessity restricted as a result of the presence of Elizabeth Howard, but in truth none of the ladies felt in the least like talking. Millicent had already attempted, with very little success, to restore her standing with Victoria Sedgley.

'I had engaged Mr Johnstone for the *Rye – Waltz*,' said Victoria furiously, when the two had exchanged words shortly before the final dance, 'and then he partnered you. I don't understand it.'

Millicent had apologised profusely. 'I am really so sorry,' she said. 'I needed to speak to him and that seemed like a good opportunity. I guess I didn't think. But he should have told me that he was engaged. Anyway, I assure you that I have no designs on Mr Johnstone whatsoever. If you want the truth I dislike him intensely and apart from anything else he is not a gentleman.'

'Oh, how dare you?' responded Victoria, who promptly stormed off, but her subsequent dance with Johnstone was clouded by Millicent's words as well as her partner's actions. As a result she sat in the carriage chewing the edge of her handkerchief and throwing the occasional angry glance at her companion. On the one hand she hoped that Johnstone would now be deeply regretting his failure to honour his engagement and would be anxious to make amends at the earliest opportunity, but on the other she had the gnawing suspicion that there might be something in what Millicent Howard had said and that George Johnstone was not all that his appearance suggested.

Sitting beside Victoria in the carriage, Elizabeth Howard kept a thoughtful silence, anxiously reliving the conversations she had held both with Johnstone and then with her daughter. She could well afford to pay off the young man and thus regain possession of her card and letter, but she hated the idea of giving in to what was blackmail pure and simple. Yet one good thing had come out of it all, she mused, and that was the fact that Millicent seemed as anxious as she was to make sure that the documents did not fall into the hands of the Dowager-Duchess of Westerdale. Clearly Millicent had no intention of ruining her chances of securing her place in society and, provided Johnstone was satisfactorily paid off, the ducal alliance was still a distinct possibility.

Tilly Rossdale too was sunk in thought. Unlike some of the young ladies at the ball her dance card had filled up very rapidly and she felt perfectly sure that at least one of her partners was showing more than a passing interest in her. Unfortunately the looks of delight she noticed on the faces of her parents when she floated into their orbit encircled by the arms of Viscount Brenton were enough to dash the young nobleman's chances entirely. Others might welcome the chance of becoming a future Countess of Eversleigh, but not she. Even as she danced her mind, fuelled by the stories supplied by Charles and by Lady Sarah Wilson, was on what she fondly imagined to be the veldt.

'Oh why doesn't he do something about it,' she thought as she danced the *Waltz – Home Sweet Home* with Charles Sedgley in the early hours of the morning. Then later in the carriage as she mused yet again about South Africa, the excitement and the freedom, she wondered whether she had the nerve and the liberated spirit to suggest that he took her with him when he returned to Cape Town, preferably as Mrs Charles Sedgley.

CHAPTER TEN

1.

Thursday 25th November 1999

About three weeks after I met Mrs Clarke and had written to thank her mother for the bound volumes of *Punch* and the doll, both of which as I suspected Mrs Vanstone was delighted to have for the Sedgley Room, a parcel was delivered to me at Drayfield Hall. I unwrapped it as I drank my ten o'clock cup of coffee and discovered a cigar box bearing the label *Drayfield Odds and Ends*, a ten page photocopied essay entitled *An Introduction to the Heraldry at Drayfield Hall by Nicholas Markham*, and a postcard. The postcard had a view of Ludlow Castle on one side and a message on the other.

It read 'Are any of my bits and pieces of use to you for your exhibition? The article by NM could be a useful guide for visitors. You could even sell it in your shop. Nick would have been delighted. Regards, JW.'

'The elusive Mr Markham,' I thought. I had followed up the line of inquiry suggested by my contact at the Worcestershire County Cricket Club but to no avail. I had gone as far as checking the telephone directories and had even rung up all the schools listed in the Winchester area. Unfortunately no one could help. I then had a brainwave. *The Cartophilic News* was still in existence and I was able to find Nicholas Markham's 1986 address. Once again I met a dead end. The address was indeed a school, a prep school, but it had closed down four years later. The headmaster had died, the school buildings had been demolished and the site was now occupied by a row of houses.

I pulled myself together and turned my attention to the matter in hand. The cigar box contained a clay pipe, a dessert spoon in rather poor condition, some assorted Victorian coins and three china drinks labels, all carefully wrapped in tissue paper. The drinks labels were of the type that would have been hung around the necks of large wine bottles. I was uncertain about the pipe, the spoon and the coins, but was sure that the labels would find a place in the second of Mrs Vanstone's glass topped display cabinets. The first was earmarked for the renowned St Boswells letters. The second was to feature a variety of objects including a set of footman's crested livery buttons, some armorial harness fittings, three letters written by Mrs Rutherford to the Parish Council, a selection of Drayfield photographs and a few newspaper cuttings relating to the Sedgley family gleaned from the library archives.

 I carefully put the cigar box on one side for the attention of Mrs Vanstone and then turned to the photocopied sheets. The first acted as the title page, the second contained four paragraphs of text, the last was blank and the penultimate page was taken up by a family tree and a glossary of terms. The six others each contained a coat of arms and what appeared to be a description of the arms in technical language that meant very little to me. The shields I recognised as those that decorated the lobbies between the Sedgley Room and the dining room, and the dining room and the saloon. What I found particularly fascinating was that two were in full colour; in two the colour had been replaced by an arrangement of tiny lines; and in the last two the colours were denoted by arrows leading from words written outside the shields to areas within the shields.

 I wondered whether the whole essay could be reproduced as a booklet to join Mark's catalogue and my *History of Drayfield Hall* and be put on sale in Mrs McGinty's shop. It was certainly something to be brought up at the next committee meeting and in the meantime I carefully filed the article in my newly acquired cabinet. I then selected a postcard – the one featuring the Wouvermans – from the boxes of cards that had recently arrived from the printers.

'Many thanks for the parcel,' I wrote. 'Excellent additions to our collection. This picture used to hang in the library in the days of the Sedgleys. Another homecoming.' I signed the card, addressed it to Jane Ward, and tossed it into my out-tray which, as I had no secretary, I personally would deal with at the end of the day.

2.

Saturday 10th April 1965

'A little light reading for the flight,' said Nick, and he pushed his essay across the table towards her.

Jane had telephoned him twice that spring term. The first call was to tell him that Victor had indeed got the expected promotion and that he would start work in the Milan office that September; by which time it was expected that he and Jane would be in possession of an apartment. The second was to suggest a drink at *The Green Man* one lunch time. Accordingly, the first Saturday after term had ended Nick made the familiar drive to Barcombe. It was a hot sunny day and no sooner had he carried his beer out to a table in the pub garden than Jane drove up.

'How come you are off the leash?' he asked with a smile as he produced a glass of dry white wine and put it in front of her.

'Victor has a cricket committee meeting at the club house, Sam is on an adventure holiday, Bobbie is at a friend's house for the day, and I have just done the weekly shop. The boot is bulging. Cheers!' and she clinked her glass against his tankard.

'*An Introduction to the Heraldry of Drayfield Hall by Nicholas Markham,*' she read, 'and illustrated as well.' She turned the pages. 'Why are only two in colour?' she asked. 'Not that I am complaining,' she added hastily. 'It's a lovely present and I shall read it avidly.'

'It's your heraldic revision sheet as well as being a reminder of Drayfield,' said Nicholas patiently. 'Two of the shields are emblazoned, or coloured; two are hatched, that is to say the colours are denoted by hatching lines; and the other two are tricked – meaning the colours are written in. Look,' he went on. 'That shield shows you blue, the colour; that one shows you blue denoted by little horizontal lines; and that one shows you blue written down as *az*, and as you well know as is short for . . .' and he paused.

Jane thought for a moment. 'Azure,' she cried out triumphantly.

'Precisely,' said Nick. '*Az* short for azure meaning blue. My gosh, no wonder I am seen as such a brilliant teacher.'

Jane's eyes twinkled. 'I believe I may have taught you a thing or two as well.' She stretched out her hand and held his. 'No, seriously,' she said, 'it was a sweet thought and I really will read it and treasure it.'

'Well, don't read it now,' said Nicholas, 'save it for the plane. When do you fly out?'

'Next Wednesday, mid-day,' replied Jane. 'We have given ourselves a week to start with then we come back. We will go out again in May if we don't find anything this time. Victor will go on working in London for another three months, he has August free, then starts in the Milan office the second week in September. By then we should be settled there. Sam will board at his present school over here, and Bobbie starts at a new school in Milan in mid-September. Victor's meeting at the moment is to decide about the cricket team. David has agreed to take over the captaincy, but the question is when. There is also the problem of infidelity in the ranks, marital not cricketing that is, but I am hardly in a position to comment upon that, am I?'

'So this is probably goodbye,' said Nicholas sadly.

'I think so,' replied Jane quietly, and she gave him a quick glance. 'Do you remember *Roman Holiday*, that film with your favourite, Audrey Hepburn, and Gregory Peck?'

Nick nodded.

'I think this has been rather like that. A magic moment, well two or three actually, but ones that could never last. Never mind,' she added quickly, 'it was great fun while it lasted, wasn't it?'

'It was out of this world,' said Nick seriously. 'You know, I've thought about you every day since we first met, nearly a year ago. I can't imagine not being able to look forward to another meeting, not being able to see you again, I really can't. What about when you get your degree. Will you be able to come over then?'

'Possibly,' said Jane lightly. 'Who knows? Now come on, let's change the subject or you will be sobbing into your beer. I think I shall have a ploughman's. They're usually quite good here. What about you? Come on, cheer up, this can be my treat.'

After lunch Nick thought for a moment and then said,

'I don't suppose we can slip back to your place for a bit?'

'No chance,' replied Jane. 'Victor could be back at any time. He might even be there now.'

How about a walk in Drayfield Park then?' said Nick.

Jane nodded. 'OK,' she replied, and after settling their bill they walked down the short stretch of road before reaching the gates to Drayfield Park. Leaving Hamilton Lodge on their left they strolled across the park until they came to the door into the gardens. Nick self-consciously reached out his hand and held hers. Together they walked along the terrace and turned into the Rose Walk. They passed the goldfish pond and Nick said,

'What about the kitchen garden?'

They cautiously tried the door in the wall. It opened to reveal the familiar rows of cold frames but no sign of human occupation.

'That's where I watched you and Victor,' said Nick, and he pointed at the rusting iron tank in the corner of the garden.

'One last time?' asked Nick.

She leant back against the tank and held out her arms. Nick approached her and they clasped one another.

'Goodbye darling,' she whispered, 'and thank you for . . . well, just thank you,' and she buried her face in his chest.

*

Nick stood on the tank and watched as Jane walked back along the Rose Walk. She passed the goldfish pond and carried on to the terrace. She turned right and continued going until she reached the garden door. As he strained to catch a final glimpse she turned and stared back in the direction of the kitchen garden. She waved and blew a kiss then disappeared through the open doorway.

3.

Sunday 6th June 1897

Charles Sedgley was woken by the footman at half past eight next morning.

'Good Morning, Mr Sedgley, Sir,' said William. 'Your bath has been prepared and I have laid out your shaving things.'

'Thank you William,' said Charles, as the footman placed on the table beside his bed a small tray containing tea, toast and biscuits.

Charles, being family had been allocated the Tower Rooms for his accommodation. These were three tiny rooms behind a glass fronted door at the very end of the main landing. When Drayfield was modernised, thanks to Lady Violet's dowry, one of these rooms had been turned into a water closet, one into a small bedroom, and the last into a cross between a dressing room and a large walk in wardrobe. It was in this last that William had filled a hip bath and had placed on a small table a brass can of shaving water, a stick of shaving soap and a razor. The rooms occupied by Charles's fellow officers in the Lower Corridor and the young ladies on the Upper or Chapel Corridor were considerably larger than his and they had the advantage of modern bathrooms, also courtesy of Lady Violet's dowry.

The Chapel Corridor had gained its name because the main window in the suite of rooms occupied in June 1897 by Sir Robert and Lady Carey looked as if it would have been more at home in an ecclesiastical building of some significance. Both corridors linked the main and more modern part of the house to the original building that had become the servants' wing.

Having bathed and shaved Charles returned to his bedroom to find the bed made and that his clothes had been laid out upon it. The window was wide open and as he dressed he was able to look out on to the front drive and beyond it the park that stretched out in the direction of the Southwater road.

Downstairs in the dining room the aroma of the previous evening's port had given way to the smell exuded by the row of spirit lamps that heated the silver dishes laid out on the left hand of the two tables flanking the fireplace. There kedgeree, whiting, devilled kidneys and eggs of various descriptions sizzled contentedly. The right hand table contained a selection of cold meats. A table under the window was taken up with fruits nestling alongside jugs of water and lemonade, and a fourth table was given over to various porridge utensils. Yet another contained pots of coffee and tea. Mrs Ridley, the housekeeper, differentiated between the teas by attaching little yellow ribbons to the pots containing China tea and little red ribbons to those that were for Indian.

'Red for the empire,' explained Archie Rossdale to Millicent Howard, 'and yellow for the Chinese.'

Millicent, despite the fact that she had a lot on her mind and was not feeling in the best of spirits, spluttered delightedly.

The table in the centre of the room had been laid for fourteen, and on this occasion at least informality was the order of the day. Charles helped himself to porridge, accepted a cup of coffee from Anderson who, together with William and Henry, was in attendance, and sat down. Archie and Millie were in conversation at one end of the table, Sir Robert, Lord Rossdale and Frederick Sedgley were eating in silence at the other, and in between them Lady Violet and Lady Carey sipped their cups of tea and nibbled small slices of toast, honey and marmalade.

As he turned his attention from the porridge to the kedgeree Charles was joined by Lance Rutherford; Elizabeth Howard made a gracious entrance and joined the other ladies; and then and at almost the same moment George Johnstone and Violet Sedgley put in an appearance. Finally, and just as the more senior male members of the party rose to make their way to the smoking room, Tilly Rossdale entered the room.

'Mother has got a headache and I doubt whether she will be joining us for church,' she announced to Lady Violet. 'She sends her apologies, but is sure that she will be fine by luncheon. The Badger is sorting her out with some sal volatile,' she added as she helped her self to some scrambled eggs and sat down beside Charles.

'The Badger?' he queried.

'Harriet Badger, her maid,' explained Tilly. 'We've always called her 'the Badger'. It's really a term of affection. She's been with us for ever, well almost ever, and is as old as the hills.'

'Tilly, dear,' protested Lady Violet.

'I thought her name was Henderson,' said Charles, thoughtfully.

'My governess,' said Tilly, shortly. 'She left at about the same time you went to Eton. I'm surprised you don't remember her, 'the Badger', that is.' She turned her attention to her eggs and then continued in a provocative tone, 'but I'm sure you have had more important things on your mind than Felton Park and its inhabitants. Now tell me Charles, precisely what were you saying when I forced you to dance with me last night? When exactly are you returning to Cape Town?'

'Tilly!' replied Charles, 'I am always delighted to dance with you. It's just that you were clearly monopolised by Brenton and his brother and I should hate to step on your toes, and on one occasion when I approached you Rutherford here slipped in between us. Dashed unsporting, I call it.'

'Oh really, Sedgley,' put in an embarrassed Lance Rutherford. 'I shouldn't dream of . . .'

'Pay no attention to him, Mr Rutherford,' said Tilly Rossdale. 'He knows very well that he is in the wrong. Now Africa, Charles. You have fifteen minutes to enlighten me before I have to prepare for church.'

About an hour later members of the house party began to assemble in the hall. There had been some discussion over breakfast and in the smoking room as regards how exactly transport would be arranged, but in the end it had been decided that Lady Violet and Elizabeth Howard would travel in the victoria, Sir Robert and Lady Carey would have the brougham and that Frederick Sedgley and Lord Rossdale would walk. The younger members of the party had argued long and hard over the merits of taking the wagonette, but ultimately it had been decided that they too would walk.

'That is if Charles does not object to escorting me,' said Tilly.

Lady Violet had made it her business to take care of Elizabeth Howard as she was becoming increasingly aware that all was not as it should be between Mrs Howard and young George Johnstone. They had seemed friendly enough during the early stages of the week but for the last two days a certain frostiness seemed to have crept into their relationship. The result was that whereas on Monday and Tuesday Lady Violet had viewed with horror the prospect of Marlborough House behaviour sullying the corridors of Drayfield, on Friday and Saturday she was concerned that Elizabeth Howard would relay a gloomy report of her week to her friends in London. She heartily wished that the possibilities outlined in her letter to her sister on Derby Day had come true and that Johnstone had long since disappeared.

Lady Violet's fears seemed to be confirmed on the ride to church for her companion hardly uttered a word. The return journey was, however, rather different.

Although vehicles and walkers had left the church at exactly the same time, the carriage drive was at least half a mile longer than the route that included footpaths. Consequently it was only when they reached the stretch of road shortly before the Hamilton Lodge gates that the two groups converged.

As the victoria drew level with her husband and Lord Rossdale, who formed the advanced guard of the pedestrians, Lady Violet asked the coachman to stop.

'Can we offer anyone a lift,' she said with a smile.

'Well, why not?' said Frederick Sedgley. 'We've done our walking for the day. The youngsters can manage the park stretch by themselves.'

He stood aside to let Lord Rossdale clamber into the carriage and then followed suit. As he settled into his seat the brougham carrying Sir Robert and Lady Carey passed them and clattered through the park gates. Frederick Sedgley gave its occupants a mock salute.

'I think they are enjoying themselves,' he said. 'I watched Robert admiring the Sedgley hatchment while we listened to that interminable sermon. I shouldn't be at all surprised if he does not turn out to be a free thinker, you know,' he added thoughtfully. 'We have begged a lift, Charles,' he called out to his nephew, who walked past at that moment, seemingly locked in an argument with Tilly Rossdale, 'but I am afraid that we are now full. Drive on Gibbons,' he called out to the coachman, and the victoria neatly avoided George Johnstone and Vicky Sedgley, who were following the other two and who were themselves tracked by the rather forlorn figure of Lancelot Rutherford.

Elizabeth Howard swivelled in her seat to watch the young people then turned to Lady Violet. Keeping her voice down so that she would not be heard by the two gentlemen, who were obviously continuing the conversation that they had been holding on their walk, she reached out and took Lady Violet's hand.

'This may be impertinence,' she said, 'but I hope your daughter is not getting too involved with that young man. I realise that is none of my business, but I would not like to feel that I had neglected to warn you of his character. Please forgive me if I have spoken out of turn.'

'Exactly what do you mean, Mrs Howard?' asked Lady Violet in a tone of surprise.

'I have been very stupid,' said Elizabeth Howard, 'and I have allowed that young man to take liberties with me that I now bitterly regret. He has repaid my friendship with behaviour that back home would result in a horsewhipping to say the least. Believe me when I say that he is not a man to be trusted.' She stared hard at her hostess for a brief moment before leaning forward to speak to Lord Rossdale. 'And what did you think about that sermon?' she asked with a smile. 'Was I alone in thinking that succinctness was not one of the reverend gentleman's strengths?'

The half-hour that usually elapsed between the return from church and the luncheon gong normally allowed the ladies to retire to their rooms, where their maids repaired any damage done to their hair and faces by the wind in winter or the dust in summer. On this occasion a period of only fifteen minutes was allowed before the ladies were asked to join the gentlemen in the library.

'First,' said Lady Violet firmly to the assembled company, 'I must ask you all to sign the Visitors Book,' and she signalled to Anderson, who stepped forward with a handsome red volume. The book was passed to each member of the party, the signatures were duly recorded, and Anderson withdrew with his usual stately bow. 'Now,' went on Lady Violet, 'this afternoon we are to lose four of our number but the rest of us are going to play croquet.'

The missing four turned out to be the Rossdales, who were committed to visit the Duchess of Malborough at the Deepdene near Dorking. Consequently the croquet party was made up of eight players with Frederick Sedgley and Elizabeth Howard volunteering to be joint-umpires. The contestants were divided into four teams of two players each and the ladies, Lady Violet, Lady Carey, Millicent Howard and Victoria Sedgley, were to draw for their partners. These turned out to be Lancelot Rutherford for Lady Violet, George Johnstone for Lady Carey, Sir Robert Carey for Millicent Howard and Charles Sedgley to partner his cousin Victoria.

'A pleasure and a privilege,' said George Johnstone to Lady Carey, as he took her arm to lead her into luncheon.

'I am not very good at croquet,' admitted Lancelot Rutherford, as he escorted Lady Violet.

'Nonsense, Mr Rutherford,' replied Lady Violet briskly, 'Archie Rossdale tells me that you are a dab hand at all games. I shall expect great things,' and disregarding any further protestations, she swept him into the dining room.

Battle commenced at three o'clock, half an hour after the Rossdales set off for the Deepdene. The croquet lawn was laid out to the left of the Rose Walk, and in the shade of a clump of oak trees Anderson had set out a table bearing jugs of iced lemonade and an assortment of glasses. In the first match, Lady Violet and Lance Rutherford played Lady Carey and George Johnstone. It was a surprisingly close contest. Lancelot was a far better player than he had made out, but the shock of the afternoon was Lady Carey, who even outplayed her partner. In the end Lady Carey and George Johnstone were victors by a narrow margin.

'There you are, Mr Rutherford,' said Lady Violet, 'you played extremely well. I hope that we will have other opportunities to share our fortunes.'

Next on to the lawn were Millicent Howard and her partner Sir Robert Carey, who were matched against the Sedgley cousins. Frederick Sedgley tossed a coin, Millicent called heads, and heads it was.

'Shall we take the blue and the black?' asked Millicent.

Sir Robert nodded. 'Excellent,' he said, 'and might I suggest that you lead off with the blue. It will match your dress.'

Millicent gazed at him in surprise. 'Sir Robert,' she said archly, 'I am surprised that you noticed.'

As the two of them walked over to the starting peg her companion went on rather sadly,

'I am afraid that I have been something of a damp squib this weekend. I had not appreciated that young Sedgley was going to be one of the party. Had I known I should have declined my friend's kind invitation. On the other hand I feel that we both have a greater appreciation of each other's views than we did at the start of the week, so all has not been in vain. Now Miss Howard, we must make every effort. I should dearly like to face my wife in the final of our little competition.'

'I shall do my level best to oblige,' replied Millicent, and Sir Robert watched in slight surprise as she carefully lined up her ball and knocked it cleanly through the first hoop. 'Now, who is red?' she called out. 'Mr Sedgley, your move,' and she stood to one side as Charles Sedgley moved up to the peg, took careful aim and missed.

'Oh, bad luck,' said Millicent. 'Sir Robert, if you can get through you can pick me up and we shall soon be two hoops ahead. Miss Sedgley, I am sorry, but this afternoon the Sedgleys will be mincemeat,' and she watched as Victoria's yellow ball also missed the hoop.

'Mincemeat we were,' said Charles, as they drank their lemonade after a game in which Millicent Howard and Sir Robert never relinquished their early lead. 'So we have a final that is Carey dominated. I apologise, partner, for my abject display.'

He smiled at Vicky, who had been in a poor mood throughout the game, and had in fact been the weaker of the two partners. She gave him a brief nod.

'It wasn't our afternoon,' she said, 'and anyway I am never much good at croquet.'

Charles suspected that in part her ill humour was caused by the fact that she was partnering him and not George Johnstone. He accepted another glass of lemonade from William and walked over to where his uncle and aunt were sitting under the shade of the oaks. Victoria followed him and as they approached Lancelot Rutherford, who was lying on the rug that had been laid beside their basket chairs, immediately rose to his feet.

'May I fetch you a chair, Miss Sedgley?' he asked. 'There's one over there.'

Victoria shook her head. 'No thank you,' she replied. 'I am perfectly happy on the rug.' She sat down beside him. 'I played abysmally,' she said to her mother, 'but then I usually do.'

'Loser commiserations,' said Charles to his aunt, and he too stretched himself out on the rug. 'Ten more minutes and then we must all be attentive. It will be a needle final.'

Elizabeth Howard was sitting in another basket chair a few yards away sipping lemonade and reading a magazine. To her right, her fellow umpire was talking to the Careys. She noticed out of the corner of her eye that George Johnstone, who had been hovering around her daughter, was approaching. She sighed deeply as he reached her.

'It is very difficult to talk to you in relative privacy,' he said. 'Do you have anything for me, or am I to look elsewhere for buyers?'

'I suppose there is no point in my asking you again to behave in a seemly manner and simply return my notes? That would of course be an end to it.' Elizabeth Howard looked at him for a moment. 'William,' she called out, 'may I have a little more lemonade?'

As the footman walked over to them George Johnstone smiled. 'I am afraid not,' he said coolly. 'I am tired of this party; I am tired of this country. I have every intention of returning to the Cape and I will need money to help me do this. It will be to your advantage, of course, as I will not be around to bother you.'

'Thank you, William,' said Mrs Howard, as her glass was filled. 'In that case, Mr Johnstone, meet me in the garden by the fish pond after dinner. I will bring you what you require. And I hope you rot in hell,' she added as an afterthought.

George Johnstone looked a little surprised. 'Really!' he said. 'Not very ladylike, I am afraid. A touch of the Midwest perhaps?' He paused, and then went on, 'by the fish pond after dinner. I look forward to our meeting with eager anticipation. And now I must find my partner. Victory and Sir Robert Carey beckon.'

Johnstone walked away, picking up a croquet mallet as he did so. Behind him Elizabeth Howard and the footman stared at his retreating figure; the one with a look of undisguised contempt, the other with a gaze of undiluted hatred.

Victoria Sedgley and Elizabeth Howard were not the only members of the house party to feel aggrieved by the events of the afternoon.

'How could you?' cried Tilly Rossdale angrily. 'How could you, all of you? I feel utterly humiliated and embarrassed. It was a mean and despicable thing to do.'

The carriage bearing the Rossdales back from the Deepdene to Drayfield Hall had barely left the Deepdene drive before Tilly vented her fury upon her family.

'Here, hold hard,' protested Archie. 'I had no idea that it was a garden party, nor had I any idea that the Eversleighs would be there. I was as much in the dark as you were.'

'Hold your tongue, Sir,' barked Lord Rossdale. 'How dare you take your sister's part against your parents? I will not tolerate it, Sir.'

'But I didn't know,' objected Archie, 'and I do think that it was a bit thick to put Tilly in that position without warning her.'

'It was an ambush, pure and simple,' went on Tilly. 'Mrs Howard would have been proud of you. But instead of the Indians I get Lord Brenton. And when that odious Lady Josephine crept up to me and said "a little bird tells me that an engagement is in the air" I could have struck her.'

'Tilly, darling,' began Lady Rossdale unhappily, but her husband cut her off.

'It is for your own good and nothing less,' said Lord Rossdale. 'Brenton would be an excellent match. If you think you are going to be allowed to marry someone like James Wedgbury, without a penny to his name, you have got another thought coming to you. I will not stand for it, you understand, I will not stand for it.'

Tilly stared at him in mounting fury. 'James Wedgbury,' she repeated with amazement. 'What on earth makes you think I want to marry James Wedgbury? And as for Brenton . . .'

'There's not much wrong with Brenton,' put in Archie, anxious to make peace between the warring factions, but it was to no avail.

'Lord Brenton may not have much wrong with him but as far as I am concerned he has very little right for him. I find him as appetising as a cold rice pudding and only marginally more attractive. I would sooner spend the rest of my life in a nunnery than with Lord Brenton.' Tilly paused for breath then went on. 'And I know what you are going to say next, Papa, so I will say it for you. You'll cut me off without a penny. Well do so. I have my legacy from Aunt Grace and …'

'When you are thirty,' put in her father angrily, 'and until then you are dependent upon me and you will behave as I see fit. Eversleigh is an old friend and I don't know how I shall be able to look him in the eye next week. Brenton would make you an ideal husband and you have the arrant stupidity to turn him down. I put it down to the company you have been keeping. Lady Sarah Wilson . . .'

'Lady Sarah has nothing whatever to do with my feelings towards Lord Brenton,' said Tilly quickly.

'The duchess told us that Lady Sarah's behaviour left a lot to be desired and that her brother is very worried about her. I will not have you associating with her. Is that clear?' And Lord Rossdale fixed his daughter with an angry stare.

'You have made yourself perfectly clear, Papa,' replied Tilly, 'perfectly clear. I think we both have made our feelings as clear as crystal.' She turned suddenly and stared out at the Surrey countryside, and the carriage carrying the Rossdales rattled on towards Drayfield.

Charles felt that he must have endured a more dismal dinner party but that for the life of him he could not think when. Everyone, with one or two notable exceptions, appeared to be a foul mood. The Rossdales had clearly not enjoyed their visit to the Deepdene, and when Archie had informed him that the Eversleigh's had also been there, Charles too felt gloom descending upon him.

'I hear you met Lord Brenton this afternoon,' he had said to Tilly, as he took her in to dinner, and she turned to him and said,

'Charlie, I think I am going to cut your throat.'

The fact that she spent the rest of the meal in a pensive silence was only lightened as far as he was concerned by the fact that she had addressed him by the pet name they had employed when he stayed with them in Norfolk, over ten years earlier.

The Howards, mother and daughter, also seemed to have caught the prevailing atmosphere, and Elizabeth Howard, who sat on his other side, made only marginally more conversation than did Tilly, on his left. Victoria

Sedgley seemed to spend most of her time rebuffing the attempts at small talk made by Lance Rutherford while trying to catch the eye of George Johnstone who was sitting opposite her. Lady Violet looked distinctly unhappy at one end of the table, and in fact the only members of the party who seemed to be enjoying themselves were his uncle Frederick, who was discussing heraldic matters with Sir Robert Carey, and Lady Carey, who had emerged victorious at the end of the croquet.

'It has been a long time since I enjoyed a game quite so much,' she had said to Millie Howard at the end of their match.

At nine forty-five exactly Lady Violet led the ladies out of the dining room and in the direction of the small drawing room. The gentlemen moved up to one end of the table and Anderson produced decanters of port and Madeira, followed by a box of cigars. After some minutes had elapsed and Frederick Sedgley and Sir Robert Carey had resumed their heraldic discussion George Johnstone stood up.

'If you will excuse me for a moment, Mr Sedgley,' he said, and walked out of the room into the lobby. Charles watched him go. Archie Rossdale and Lance Rutherford were discussing military matters and Lord Rossdale seemed sunk in the apathy that he had been displaying all evening. After making a brave attempt to draw him into some sort of conversation Charles, whose seat faced the window, noticed Elizabeth Howard walking towards the Rose Walk. About five minutes later George Johnstone too made his way in that direction. Charles thought for a moment then stood up.

'Excuse me, gentlemen,' he said. He opened the door into the corridor and walked into the front hall. Voices came from the small drawing room as he strolled towards the front door, opened it and stepped out into the drive. He had no wish to give the impression of eavesdropping, although he had every intention of finding out exactly what

Elizabeth Howard and George Johnstone were doing in the garden at that time of night, and so he made his way to the garden by walking around the stable block and then through the door in the garden wall. He walked quietly up the path that ran along the garden wall and parallel to the Rose Walk. About half way along was the right angle turn that led to the lily pond. He had almost reached the junction when he was almost bowled over by a running figure.

'What the devil,' he began, then he realised that the running figure was William, the footman, and that his face and the front of his shirt were covered in blood. 'What the devil is going on,' he asked urgently.

'Mr Charles, Sir,' began the footman. 'I have assaulted one of your guests. I think I have broken his nose, but he deserved it, Sir. He was messing around with my Ellen. I tried to . . .'

But William's explanation was cut short first by the sound of voices and then by the sudden crack of a pistol shot, both coming from the direction of the pond. Charles ran towards the sound, closely followed by William, and there by the edge of the water he saw a shadowy form. He pulled up short and then moved forward slowly as he realised that it was Elizabeth Howard. He stared at her for a moment and then noticed with horror that she was clutching her small revolver. His gaze moved in the direction of the pond itself and there, half in and half out of the water, lay the crumpled figure of George Johnstone.

'Well, Mr Sedgley,' said Elizabeth Howard, slowly, 'I guess you are going to have to turn me in.'

CHAPTER ELEVEN

1.

Monday 7th June 1897

Charles was woken by his repeater at exactly six o'clock the next morning. He dressed quickly as there was much to be done. He made his way quietly down the main staircase, turned right at the bottom and walked to the side entrance that led to the loggia. The key, as William had promised, was lying on the small table by the door. Charles unlocked the door, closed it behind him, and strode down the drive towards the Hamilton Lodge. As he had hoped there was no one about, and he was able to make his way to the station without being seen. The milk train arrived punctually at seven o'clock. Charles watched it depart and then walked briskly back to Drayfield Hall. As he passed through the park gates he waved cheerily to Mrs Simpson, the lodgekeeper's wife, whom he saw standing by her kitchen window. He made a short detour to the kitchen garden then, having ascertained that all was in order, returned to the hall via the garden door. He re-entered the house by the same door that he left it, replaced the key, and silently made his way back to his room.

At half past eight there was a knock on the door and William entered, carrying the tray of shaving implements. His face still bore the unmistakable marks of his fight the previous evening.

'Have you seen your uncle yet?' asked Charles.

'Yes, Mr Charles,' came the reply. 'I told him exactly what you said.'

'Good,' said Charles. 'From now on everything must be as normal.'

'Very good, Sir,' replied William. 'I will prepare your bath.'

'First though,' said Charles, 'read this letter,' and he handed William a sheet of paper and an envelope. 'It is a reasonably accurate account of what happened last night though I have cut out Mrs Howard. Anyone who looks at this will assume that I came across the body of Mr Johnstone, who had shot himself, and that I asked you to help me dispose of the body to avoid any scandal. In the unlikely event of anyone discovering him, this letter will leave you in the clear.'

William read the letter carefully then passed it back to Charles who folded it in three and sealed it in the envelope. He handed it back to the footman.

'Keep it safe,' he said. 'You never know what might happen.'

'Thank you, Sir,' said William quietly.

Before going down for breakfast Charles paused half way down the staircase and then made his way along the Bachelors' Corridor. He stopped outside the door that bore the label *Mr Lancelot Rutherford* and tapped lightly before entering.

'Good morning, Rutherford,' he said breezily. 'A quick word with you if I may.'

'Of course, Sedgley,' was the slightly surprised reply.

'George Johnstone has disgraced himself again,' said Charles, 'and he has decided to make himself scarce. I won't go into the details, but as you can imagine it involves a lady, well two to be exact. He has decided to disappear rather than face the music and I have just this minute escorted him to the station. I thought it as well to put you in the picture before I broke the news to my uncle and aunt.'

Lance Rutherford nodded. 'Good of you,' he said. 'What a fool the man is.'

'Quite,' said Charles. 'If my cousin takes Johnstone's absence badly, perhaps you could rally round?' he went on. 'It would probably be appreciated.'

Lance Rutherford brightened perceptibly. 'I'll be glad to,' he said.

'Well, I'll leave you to finish dressing,' said Charles. 'I'll see you at breakfast.' He handed Lance Rutherford his hairbrush and left the room. He paused at the next door then knocked twice.

'Come in,' shouted Archie Rossdale.

Charles opened the door and entered.

'Archie,' he said, 'I've some rather unpleasant news for you . . .'

When he reached the dining room Charles found that the assembled company in a state of something approaching agitation. His uncle, Lord Rossdale and Sir Robert Carey were standing at one end of the room. Lord Rossdale was waving a piece of toast in the air and as he entered Charles caught the words 'infernal blackguard' coming from him. His aunt was sitting at one end of the table absent-mindedly sipping a cup of tea. Elizabeth Howard sat to her right, staring straight ahead of her. Millicent Howard was seated beside her mother and opposite her was Lady Rossdale, an anxious expression on her face. Neither Vicky nor Tilly Rossdale had put in an appearance. Charles decided to take the bull by the horns.

'Aunt Violet,' he began, but he was interrupted.

'Charles,' said Lady Violet, 'we have some distressing news for you. Mr Johnstone, well he is not Mr Johnstone at all. He is an impostor. He must be asked to leave the house immediately.'

Charles stared at her. 'But he has already gone,' he said. 'He sends his apologies and regrets that he will not be able to be with us today. He caught the early train. I walked to the station with him myself. He felt that his behaviour over the past few days was not all that it should have been, and he decided to make himself scarce to avoid any further embarrassment.'

The assembled company stared at him in amazement.

'That's it,' exclaimed Lord Rossdale excitedly. 'The bounder knew that the game was up and now he's bolted.'

'What on earth are you talking about, Charles,' said Frederick Sedgley. 'Why did you take him to the station? He must be still there. There is no early train.'

'Excuse me, uncle,' said Charles, 'but why do you say that he is an impostor?'

'This letter, Sir,' put in Lord Rossdale. 'It arrived this morning. An apology for his son's absence. Apparently the real George Johnstone is still in South Africa and now his father is apologising. We must apprehend this other fellow at the station and have it out with him.'

'I think it would be as well if we discovered what exactly this young man was doing here,' said Sir Robert, quietly. 'We don't want to stir up a hornet's nest unless it is absolutely necessary. You say you left him at the station, Mr Sedgley?'

Charles nodded. 'The milk train,' he explained.

'And did he give any explanation as to why he was leaving the house so precipitately?'

'He felt that he had let himself down while a guest at Drayfield,' said Charles, slowly. 'He said that he would rather leave before breakfast to avoid embarrassment.'

'Charles,' said Lady Violet 'has Mr Johnstone's absence anything to do with the fact that William looks as if he has been in a fight? Have you seen him this morning?'

'Yes,' admitted Charles. 'He did look a little the worse for wear.'

'Worse for wear,' repeated Frederick Sedgley. 'The fellow looked as if he had been kicked by a horse.'

'Perhaps Mr Johnstone, or whoever he is, is even more the worse for wear,' said Lady Rossdale. 'Perhaps that is why he has not shown his face this morning. After all, he was not to know that we would receive that letter today.'

'I think I can explain what the young man was doing here,' said Elizabeth Howard, suddenly. 'He became acquainted with me in London and he wanted to borrow money. He must have engineered his invitation with that in mind.' She looked round the company and then stood up. 'And now I think I will have some kedgeree,' she said, 'good riddance to bad rubbish. I hope I never set eyes on him again.'

'Presumably he failed in his attempt, Mrs Howard?' said Sir Robert.

'Indeed he did,' was the reply.

At that moment a hush fell upon the company as William himself appeared through the corridor entrance bearing a fresh pot of coffee.

'William,' said Frederick Sedgley, sternly. 'Have you been in a fight?'

The footman looked sheepish. 'I regret that I have Sir,' he answered.

Frederick Sedgley was about to follow up his line of questioning when his wife stepped in.

'Thank you William,' she said, 'that will be all.' Then, as the footman bowed and disappeared into the corridor, she turned to her husband.

'I think that it would be as well if we let sleeping dogs lie, my dear,' she said. 'Mr Johnstone, or his counterfeit, has obviously done the right thing in leaving when he did, and I see no reason why we should cross question William any further. He may fight whom he pleases, provided that is it does not interfere with his duties. More coffee, Sir Robert? and she turned to her guest with a smile.

Just then Anderson, who had been standing beside one of the tables in the window, took a step towards his employer.

'Mr Sedgley, Sir,' he said quietly. 'Perhaps I could have a word with you?'

Frederick Sedgley glanced at him for a moment. 'Come into the lobby,' he said.

The butler politely opened the door for his master then followed him out of the dining room. As they disappeared into the lobby the door into the hall corridor opened and Victoria Sedgley stormed into the room followed by Tilly Rossdale, Lance Rutherford and Archie Rossdale. She walked straight up to her mother and said,

'What on earth is going on? Archie tells me that Mr Johnstone has left the house. It's not fair. The moment someone appears whom I like he is driven away. It is just too awful.' And she pulled a handkerchief from her pocket and blew her noise loudly and defiantly.

'Victoria, dear, control yourself,' said Lady Violet, sharply. 'No one has driven Mr Johnstone away. He left of his own volition. Anyway he is not Mr Johnstone, he is an impostor and he was after our money. The real George Johnstone is still in Africa. Now sit down and Henry will bring you some coffee. We are just discussing what next to do.'

Victoria sniffed and then looked around the room. She flushed and then said,

'I am sorry, please forgive me.' She sat down beside Tilly Rossdale. Lancelot Rutherford promptly took the seat on her other side.

'Let me fetch you some breakfast,' he said.

'Archie,' said Lady Violet. 'You knew George Johnstone, did you not?'

'I was introduced to him as George Johnstone,' admitted Archie Rossdale. 'It was at . . . well it was at a function in town. Mr Rutherford was with me. We were told that he had just returned from the Cape.'

'If either of you gentlemen ever set eyes on him in the future,' said Elizabeth Howard, 'I would be greatly obliged if you would ask him to return my revolver. He expressed an interest in it the other night. I very foolishly lent it to him and he never returned it. I should be sorry to lose it as it was a gift from my father,' and she flashed the quickest of glances in the direction of Charles.

'Of course,' said Archie Rossdale, and Lancelot Rutherford followed up with an indistinct 'certainly', through a mouthful of toast.

At that moment the lobby door opened and Frederick Sedgley returned followed by Anderson, who took up his usual position in the window embrasure. Archie Rossdale walked over to the porridge table, and then turned to Millicent Howard.

'Miss Howard,' he said, 'may I fetch you anything?'

'Some kedgeree would be delightful,' replied Millicent, flashing him a dazzling smile. 'I need to build up my strength, what with all these disclosures. I think the man should be dragged back from the station and horsewhipped; only he can't because he caught the milk-train, if Mr Sedgley is correct. I am glad that mother simply lent him her gun and not any money. With any luck he'll shoot himself with it,' and she gave her mother a pointed look.

'I think I understand the precise circumstances that led to our impostor's sudden departure,' said Frederick Sedgley. 'Apparently he was rather free with his attentions towards a member of the staff and paid the penalty. If my information is correct it would certainly have been embarrassing for him to show his face this morning. Am I not correct, Charles?'

Charles, who had been listening to what had been going on with increasing amazement, pulled himself together sharply.

'Yes,' he said. 'It would have been a little tricky. He must have felt that the milk-train would solve one or two problems.'

'So the fellow got a good thrashing for his pains,' said Lord Rossdale with satisfaction. 'Well, if you want my advice, Sedgley, we should let the whole matter drop. No need to rake in the authorities. House party scandals never do anyone any good in my experience.' He gave a short laugh. 'HRH would probably agree with me on that one as well. Now, I could do with a little more breakfast before we set off. What about you, my dear, more toast and tea. I am sure Henry will oblige.'

'I agree,' said Elizabeth Howard determinedly. I see no reason why the activities of a dissolute young man should mar the memory of what has been a most delightful gathering with some excellent entertainment. Mr Sedgley, Lady Violet, this has been a Derby week to remember.'

'Well then,' said Lady Violet, 'that is settled.'

Later that morning Charles sat in a basket tree under the oak trees, the scene of the previous afternoon's croquet. His arms and shoulder still ached from the exertions of shifting half a dozen railways sleepers and then a large iron tank, but apart from that life appeared to be returning to normal. The brougham bearing Sir Robert and Lady Carey to the station had departed just after breakfast and Sir Robert had even shaken hands with him on their departure.

'I hope we understand each other a little better, Mr Sedgley,' he had said, and he favoured Charles with a frosty smile.

The rest of the party had decided to catch the afternoon train, and for the next two hours Charles felt that he had acted as a father confessor to all and sundry.

'I did not lie to you last night, Mr Sedgley' said Elizabeth Howard, when they met on the terrace. 'I was wrong to confront the man with my revolver, but he initiated the struggle and the gun went off when he tightened his grip on my hand. I had no intention of shooting him, although he thoroughly deserved it. I had hoped to frighten him into giving back my notes. I have been very stupid and I am extremely grateful for what you and the footman have done for me.' She paused for a moment. He was certainly in no position to think straight when he grabbed my hand,' she observed. 'His face was covered in blood and I think his nose was broken. That young man certainly defended his lady's honour with a vengeance. I shall make it my business to see that he won't lose by it, that's for sure.'

'Your money,' said Charles, handing her an envelope. 'I won't be requiring it anymore. As we don't know who he is there are no accounts to settle up, and we have no idea where or with whom he lived. His invitation was collected from the Cavalry Club, but I can hardly start making enquiries there.'

'Keep it,' said Elizabeth Howard. 'You will need it when you return to the Cape,' and she returned his bow with a slight inclination of her head as she walked on towards the garden door.

No sooner had she disappeared than Vicky appeared through the lobby door with a faithful Lancelot Rutherford behind her.

'Charles,' she called out. 'The man is not a total scoundrel. Look!'

She showed him what appeared to be a gold pendant containing a cameo.

'Henry brought this to me. It was found on Mr Johnson's dressing table. I lent. . .,' she paused for a moment then went on, 'I lent it to him the other evening.' She coloured before continuing hastily. 'He could easily have stolen it but he obviously wanted me to have it back, so he left it there when he packed his things.'

'That would certainly appear to be the case,' agreed Charles. 'I gather that we are to travel by the ten past three train, Rutherford,' he went on. 'Well, I am going to read the morning paper and catch up with the cricket,' and he strolled across the lawn to where the rugs and basket chairs had been set out. He had only just settled himself when his aunt appeared on the terrace and bore down upon him.

'I have left your uncle and Lord Rossdale in the library,' she said. 'It is going to be another lovely day. Now Charles, I feel that the less said about this unfortunate affair with the spurious Mr Johnstone the better. As far as I can see no one has actually lost anything as a result of his activities. Elizabeth Howard, well I really feel that she was almost as much to blame as the young man. I mean she must have encouraged him. I am afraid that standards in the Prince of Wales's set are not quite what we have all been used to. Anyway, she seems very keen on keeping quiet about the whole sorry episode and I think we should respect her wishes.'

Charles nodded. 'Yes,' he said. 'I think you are probably right.'

'But what we will do if we ever meet him again I dread to think,' went on Lady Violet. 'The Rossdales are in an even worse situation because his father is their neighbour. No, of course he isn't. He is not George Johnstone at all, is he?'

Charles shook his head.

'Yet it is possible that we might meet the imposter somewhere,' said Lady Violet anxiously.

'I doubt it,' said Charles reassuringly. 'I am sure that whoever he is, he will keep well out of your way.'

'Vicky was very cross at breakfast, but she seems to have pulled herself together now. Apparently Mr Rutherford suggested a stroll around the garden, as the whole thing had obviously been such a shock. He is really quite a nice young man, when you get to know him, and by no means a bad croquet player. I think I will make a point of partnering him again if he ever comes to another party.'

'I agree,' said Charles. 'There is not much wrong with Lance Rutherford, and at least we do know that he is Lance Rutherford.'

Indeed,' said Lady Violet. 'So, when will you be returning to the Cape?'

'Pretty soon, I expect,' replied Charles. 'I shall call in again, of course, to say my goodbyes before I sail. It would be nice to be back there by Christmas. It will make a change though, shooting antelope on the veldt rather than rabbits at Drayfield'.

'How romantic,' said his aunt vaguely, and she patted him affectionately on the arm and wandered back towards the terrace.

Charles poured himself a glass of lemonade and picked up the paper, but before he had a chance to open it he received his fourth female visitation.

'Charles,' said Tilly Rossdale. 'I want to speak to you.'

As was always the case when he met Tilly, Charles felt his heart leap into his mouth. The next thing to happen, he thought with resignation, would be that they would start quarrelling. It seemed to be a sequence of events that was set in the stars. He rose politely to his feet and then noticed with alarm that she appeared to have been crying. Her eyes were red and she still twisted a tiny pocket handkerchief in her hands.

'Tilly,' he said with concern. 'What on earth is the matter? Have you been scrapping with your father? Archie told me that you had been arguing about Brenton again. Well, I think you are quite right. Why should you marry someone you don't want to. But you mustn't cry about it.'

Tilly looked at him. 'It's not that,' she said. 'Oh I have been squabbling with Mama and Papa, but it's not that. It's something I heard Archie saying to Mr Rutherford.

Charlie, will you promise to answer me truthfully if I ask you a question.'

Charles felt a sinking sensation in the pit of his stomach. How was it possible that she could know of his involvement in the events of the previous evening? She must have worked it out from something they had said. Yet they knew nothing either. It was beyond his comprehension.

'Well?' she asked.

'If I can,' said Charles with resignation.

'Have you a woman in South Africa?' asked Tilly, 'go on, answer, me, you promised.'

'A woman in South Africa?' repeated Charles in astonishment. 'Of course I haven't. What on earth makes you think I have a woman in South Africa, or anywhere else for that matter? Tilly for goodness sake, what are you crying for now?'

'I overheard Archie say to Lance Rutherford that it must be a woman who was causing you to return to the Cape,' said Tilly, furiously dabbing her eyes with her handkerchief. 'Otherwise why else would you be going?'

'Actually,' said Charles, slowly, 'it is a woman who is causing me to leave, but not in the way you imagine. There has only been one woman for me as long as I can remember, and it's you, Tilly. I have adored you ever since we were in the schoolroom together. I know it's crazy but it's the truth. I know I have no prospects, and that your father would never ever give his consent, but there it is. I could cheerfully murder the Brentons of this world because they have means and I don't. There, you asked for the truth and now you have got it.'

Tilly was momentarily nonplussed. 'Are you saying that you love me?'

'Without a doubt,' replied Charles. 'When I saw you dancing with Brenton at Hensford I felt positively sick. The best parts of this house party have been when we have been walking together and talking together, but then we always seem to end up in quarrelling. I don't understand it, but one thing I do know . . .'

'Charlie,' interrupted Tilly, 'are you going to ask me to marry you or are you not? I really cannot put up with all this prevarication.'

'But your father . . .' began Charles.

'I am not talking about my father I am talking about me, and unless I get a straight answer in the next minute I shall never speak to you again as long as I shall live,' retorted Tilly.

'Tilly Rossdale, will you marry me?' asked Charles, and he dropped down on one knee.

'Charles Sedgley, yes I will,' replied Tilly, 'but it will probably have to be in South Africa and next year, because you are quite right. Papa would never allow it.' She smiled tearfully, tossed her handkerchief to one side, and flung her arms around his neck. 'You stupid, stupid man,' she said, 'why did you have to put me through all this. You must have known that I would marry you. Now get up quickly. We don't want anyone to see us.'

Charles returned to his chair, pulling up another one as he did so. 'Sit down beside me,' he commanded. 'We can plot without anyone suspecting. Tell me about Lady Sarah Wilson and her invitation. Is that how you are going to escape to the Cape?' He poured her a glass of lemonade and sat back to listen.

2.

Tuesday 8th February 2000

It was on Tuesday the 8th February that we received the news of the discovery in the well. The date sticks in my mind because it was exactly a week after I had moved into

Hamilton Lodge and it was two days before the Beckingsale collection was scheduled to be moved. It was a busy day in the gallery. Louise, the young girl who was helping Mrs Vanstone with the books in the Smoking Room – it had been decided that all the rooms would retain their original names and even the Sedgley Room had *Library* in brackets after it on all our handouts – was doing her own thing. A girl called Claire was setting things out in the future shop and we, that is Mark, Tim and myself, were meeting in the Sedgley Room.

We were discussing the security aspects with Sam Kendle and the man from Art Security Systems, the firm which had installed the assortment of beams, pressure alarms, tremblers and other paraphernalia that were to protect the paintings in the three main galleries. A separate system was in operation in the Sedgley Room to watch over the Wouvermans and the Margaret Carpenter. The other three paintings of the Sedgleys looked as if they were guarded but in fact were not. Apparently the powers that be had decided that they were most unlikely to be pinched.

Security cameras had also been installed throughout the ground floor and there were master switches both in my office and in Mark's sanctum up the staircase. Both of these had to be activated before anything could be closed down.

We were in the process of discussing how and when things were going to be switched off and by whom when there was a knock on the door.

'Come in,' I shouted, and Louise, poked her head round the door.

'Excuse me,' she said, 'but there is someone here from Colleymore's and he needs to speak to somebody in authority. Apparently they have found human bones in the old well.'

'What old well?' asked Tim Lewis. 'I didn't know we had an old well.'

'We haven't,' I said, 'but Colleymore's have. It's in the old kitchen garden. If you walked up the Rose Walk and went straight through the wall at the top you'd probably fall into it. That is you would if it hadn't been covered up with all sorts of junk. They must have opened it up as part of the big clear-up operation.'

Colleymore's had taken possession of the one-time kitchen garden early in the new year and were in the process of levelling the ground and putting down the foundations for their garden centre that was due to open in the spring, about the same time as the gallery. Presumably they had started at the end closest to the road, where they built their new main entrance, and were working down towards the wall that separated their premises from the Drayfield gardens. We decided that all four of us were 'in authority' and we asked Louise to tell the Colleymore man to join us. He turned out to be a youngish fellow with close cropped hair and despite the fact that it was early February was wearing a short sleeved blue polo shirt.

'There are just the four of us there this afternoon,' he explained. 'We have got hold of the office on the mobile, but we thought you ought to know about it as well. We'd shifted the tank and the sleepers that covered it up, and when Mick took a look down with his torch we got the shock of our lives. It's not that deep and is perfectly dry and there at the bottom was this skull and a load of bones.' He paused for effect and then said, 'It gave me a right shock and no mistake. I almost fell down the hole and joined them. Then there'd be two of us down there,' he added.

'I suppose someone ought to ring the police,' said Tim. 'Look, why don't the three of you go on up there. I will do the telephoning and wait here until someone arrives, then I'll join you.'

I nodded. 'Good idea,' I said. 'Louise, would you keep an eye on the room for us?' and without more ado we closed our meeting. We, that is Mark, myself and the security man, who was quite clearly more than anxious to be a party to any exciting discoveries, left the house by the lobby door and followed our guide up the Rose Walk in the direction of the old kitchen garden.

After about twenty minutes Tim reappeared with a solitary policeman, who gingerly made his way to the edge of the well and directed his flashlight down the aperture. It was a far more powerful beam than had been produced by the Colleymore torch and it clearly picked out the bones at the foot of the shaft. The skull, which the torch had barely located, was now perfectly visible.

The policeman stared down the well and sighed deeply. 'Right,' he said. 'I'll get somebody to have a look at it, but I think it's the museum service and not the police you'll be needing.' He paused for a moment. 'Now that's interesting,' he went on. 'Take a look at that.'

I walked around the side of the well to stand beside him and looked along the shaft of light that was directed to a point slightly to the left of the skull. There, amidst a jumble of stones and bits of bone, lay a small silver pistol.

The saga of the skeleton in the well was not allowed to dominate our meeting the following week, but it came a well placed third after Councillor Barnes's update on the royal visit and Mark Paddon-Browne's guided tour of the gallery, now that the paintings were hanging proudly in their allocated places. He was particularly pleased about a group of pictures by one or more members of the Van Mieris family.

'We have one of the finest collections of niche paintings outside London,' he announced to his captive audience, as we stood in front of a group of pictures surrounding the fireplace in the *Small Drawing Room*.

'Niche paintings?' asked Mrs McGinty nervously.

'The use of a stone window or archway to frame the composition,' said Mark patiently. Often the scenes represent cooks, servant girls or shop-keepers. This one, *The Greengrocer's Shop*, is typical,' and he pointed to a picture of an old man and a girl framed within a curtained arch. Below them was a ledge decorated with a sculpted relief while on the ledge was an array of baskets, metal containers and dishes containing a wide variety of vegetables. I was particularly taken with a rat, invisible to the figures in the shop, which was on the ground below the ledge, happily munching away at what I took to be an apple.

We moved from the *Small Drawing Room* through the Saloon, which now bore the legend *Large Drawing Room* on its door and via the *Ante-Room* to the *Dining Room*. As we went we dutifully consulted our Gallery Guides and made the occasional note. We then returned to the *Sedgley Room* or *Library* via the *Lobby*.

'I think your choice of paintings for the Lobby and the Ante Room is spot on, Mark,' said Councillor Barnes.

'I liked the *Group of Cavalrymen talking to three Peasants*,' said Edwin Hooper. 'Do we have a postcard of that one?' He looked at Mark, who shook his head sadly.

'Now,' said Councillor Barnes, 'item seven on the agenda is, as our secretary has so colourfully put it, "The Skeleton in the Well".' He paused for the usual titter that greeted his jokes then went on. 'I think that we can confidently say that in terms of publicity what we lost on the ghosts, or lack of them, we have certainly gained on the skeleton. I am told that there has to be an inquest, but that the pathologist has provisionally put a date of about 1900 on the remains and has said that the bones are those of a male in his middle twenties. Moreover from evidence gained from things like buttons and so on that were found amongst the bones, we have been informed that the victim was probably wearing evening dress.'

He stared around the table and the hum of conversation that had greeted his opening words died away.

'I say "victim",' he continued, because people don't normally die in wells, nor do they cover up those wells with heavy railway sleepers.'

'I suppose, Mr Chairman, there is no clue as to who exactly the bones belonged to?' said Desmond Davies.

'I am just coming to that very point,' said Councillor Barnes. 'The revolver that was discovered alongside the remains and that two or three of you were able to see in location, so to speak, is more than likely to be the very same one that was described by,' and he consulted his notes, 'Lady Violet Sedgley in one of the letters written to her sister, that we have here on loan. It belonged to one of the house guests in 1897. That fact, together with the likelihood that the bones are those of a young male, lead the police to suspect that the remains could well be those of Charles Sedgley. He was the nephew of Frederick Sedgley, the then owner of Drayfield Hall. He was a guest at the house party, and as those of you who have read our secretary's history of the family will already be aware, nothing is known of his whereabouts or fate after 1897.'

'Ken Belton will have a field day with all this,' said Tim Lewis. 'The last of the Sedgleys found murdered in a well on the Drayfield estate.'

'I am not sure that we really need that sort of publicity,' said Mark Paddon-Browne doubtfully.

'Nonsence,' said Desmond Davies, 'any publicity is good publicity. A month or so to go before opening and we will on the front pages. Have we got a picture of this Charles Sedgley?'

'We believe that he features in group photographs of the Derby house parties,' said Mrs Vanstone, 'but as we have yet to find the Visitors Book that contains these photographs we cannot be sure.' She stared in my direction.

'I don't think we are any further along the line in that particular hunt, are we?'

I admitted that things had rather ground to a halt with my search for Nicholas Markham, but that I had not given up the chase. At that point Councillor Barnes called us all to order.

'I don't think that there is much more to be said at this stage,' he said. 'We have three more meetings scheduled before the opening. Perhaps we will have been given more details about our skeleton by then and who knows, we may have located the missing Visitors Book. Now, on to item eight, "The Gift Shop". Mrs McGinty, the floor is yours.'

3.

Friday 14th July 1965

That July Nick received a letter from Jane. It was postmarked Milan. In it she told him how she and Victor and found an apartment and that they would be moving in August.

'This really is goodbye,' she went on. 'I must make the best of things from now on – for the children's sake if for no other reason. I will do the best I can to make this marriage work, and so will not be going up in person to the Congregation. I could be tempted. I do hope you understand. My Drayfield memories will remain with me always. Please burn this letter after you have read it. I really mean that and I trust you to do it, darling. And another please. Send me a postcard – I will be back in Barcombe next week – just to let me know that you understand and forgive. A postcard, mind, so be careful what you say. Love as always, Jane.'

Nick thought long and hard. He fetched a box of matches and, after holding it to his lips for a brief moment, carefully burnt the letter. He then rummaged in his desk drawer until he found a picture postcard of Arundel Castle. He wrote out the name and address before sitting back and staring at the ceiling. After a few minutes had elapsed he wrote,

'Do hope you get the expected result for your masterpiece. I will be thinking of you. Drayfield was a memorable experience and I greatly enjoyed my hours of research. Regards to Victor - Yours Nick.'

He opened another drawer and took out a brown folder. In it he found a sheet of paper covered with names and dates. He studied it carefully then added a postscript to his card.

"PS,' he wrote, 'Charles Sedgley married Matilda Rossdale in Cape Town on 28th May 1898. One down, one to go!'

4.

Wednesday 1st March 2000

Three weeks after the discovery of the skeleton I was working in my office. It was about ten thirty in the morning. The previous day had been mildly chaotic as the display cabinets had arrived for the Sedgley Room, and this had necessitated moving the large table into the Smoking Room to join the bookcases that had already been positioned there. It had taken the best part of the afternoon to get things sorted out and the following day I had a mountain of paperwork to get through; largely a backlog from the previous afternoon. I had just opened a letter from the catering company that we had hired for the big day when my internal phone rang. It was Claire from the gift shop.

'There's an Inspector Jarrett here to see you,' she said. 'A policeman,' she added. 'I'll bring him along to your office, shall I?'

'Yes, please do,' I said, as I rapidly ran through in my mind all the possible misdemeanours I had committed in the recent past that could have resulted in such a visitation.

A moment later there was a tap on the door. 'Come in,' I said, and the door opened to reveal Claire and a burly figure carrying a brief case, whom she ushered into the office.

'Good morning, Sir,' said the Inspector. 'You are Mr Richard Tregaskes, the Gallery Administrator, I understand?'

I admitted that this was indeed the case. We shook hands and I indicated the seat facing my desk.

'I have some objects of interest for your exhibition,' he said with a smile as he sat down. He opened his brief case and produced a brown cardboard box, which he handed over to me.

I opened it and there inside was the small revolver that I had last seen in the well alongside the skull and assorted bones, together with some buttons, a cigarette case and what appeared to be a pair of nail clippers. On closer examination it turned out to be a cigar clipper.

'From the pockets of the deceased?' I queried.

'Indeed,' said the inspector

'Very many thanks,' I said. 'Mrs Vanstone will be positively delighted. We are rather short of exhibits for our Sedgley Room display and these will certainly go some way to filling up a gap. Presumably you have no further need of them for your investigation? By the way, do have a cup of coffee.'

The inspector glanced at his watch. 'That's very kind of you,' he replied, and he snapped his case shut while I put the box carefully on the bookcase behind my desk. I picked up the housephone and dialled 3.

'Louise,' I said. 'Any chance of a couple of cups of coffee, well three to be exact, then come and join us? I have something exciting to show you.'

I was rather proud of our internal telephone network. I was number 1. Number 2 took me through to Mark's office. Number 3 was the Smoking Room, where Louise was busy sorting out material that Mrs Vanstone had supplied from the library. Number 4 was Claire in the gift shop, number 5 was the restaurant to be and number 6 took me through to Sam Kendle's flat. All phones were mobiles but were not supposed to be removed from their designated locations, a restriction that seemed to be lost on Mark, who kept leaving his in one of the galleries.

As we drank our coffee and Louise stared in delight at our latest acquisitions the inspector explained.

'A promising start but then everything fizzled out,' he said. 'The pistol shows every sign of being that described in the letter in your collection and the remains appear to date from the same period. Thanks to that thesis and the Visitors Book we know the names of individuals who were around at the same time as the pistol. Two of them disappeared from sight at about the same time as the house party described in the thesis. Then things got even better. Take a look at the cigarette case.'

I opened the box and took out the case.

'That cigarette case has a monogram,' said Inspector Jarrett, 'and although it is pretty indistinct what with the original curls and swirls, and a hundred years worth of corrosion, it looks as if it is **CS**, for Charles Sedgley, one of our missing guests. It could even be **GJ**, in which case it would be George Johnstone, who was the other one. We seemed to have an open and shut case. My money was on Sedgley,' he went on, 'because there is no note of his death in *Burke's Landed Gentry*, and that always struck me as suspicious.'

Both Louise and I studied the case.

'The first letter must be a ***C***,' said Louise. It doesn't curl round enough for a ***G***. I am not at all sure about the second. The wiggly bit at the bottom could be either from a ***J*** or an ***S*** and the top bit is so messy it could be anything. I think I would go for ***CS***.'

'Funnily enough our expert thought it was more likely to be ***CJ***,' said the inspector, 'but as things turned out it didn't matter anyway.'

'Why,' I asked, 'what went wrong?'

'We ascertained that both our potential victims were around long after the house party took place. No question about that. So we decided to look at every other house party listed in the Visitors Book after 1897. There were seventeen altogether. One of our trainees spent a couple of days checking out every single young man who visited Drayfield during those years. There were over nineteen altogether and we have accounted for every one.'

'Only nineteen?' said Louise.

'Several came more than once,' said the inspector, 'and the parties got more and more middle aged as the years went by. What was depressing was the number of youngsters who were killed in the war,' he added, pensively. 'There you have it. No obvious victim. Of course it could have been someone who visited the house and did not sign the Visitors Book, but they seem to have been pretty meticulous about it. It wasn't just a Derby party book for there were other occasions as well. They seemed to go in for an autumn rabbit shoot party most years. Though there weren't as many guests for those. We even checked the staff in case the buttons and fabric came from a footman's livery. No joy there either.'

'There was a footman called William and one called Henry, wasn't there?' I put in.

The inspector nodded. He consulted his notebook. 'William Bridgewater and Henry Hawkins. William left in 1899 to take up an appointment in Norfolk. Henry was promoted and was joined by another chap called Timothy Batterham. They both stayed there until the war so neither was down the well. We even wondered whether the bones dated from after 1914 because the house was used as a hospital during the war and the place was absolutely crammed with officers, but we have been assured that the bones are either late Victorian or Edwardian.' He sighed deeply. 'So we have decided to call a halt. There seems certain to have been foul play but it was a long time ago and everyone connected with it will have been dead for fifty years plus. I am afraid we have more pressing things on our hands.'

He made to get up.

'Hang on a second,' I said. 'You spoke as if you had seen the original Visitors Book, not just the bits quoted in the thesis?'

The inspector looked slightly surprised. 'Of course,' he said, 'it's at the station.'

'But how on earth did you find it?' I asked.

'We rang up the chap who owns it and he lent it to us,' he replied, as if it were the easiest thing in the world. 'Nicholas Markham is his name. He's the fellow who sorted out the heraldry for the lady who wrote the thesis. We thought that he was likely to belong to the Heraldry Society in London. We were right and they gave us the address.'

I stared at him open mouthed. 'Do you think you could hang on to the book a little longer?' I asked. 'I would like to write and ask him whether we could at least borrow it for our exhibition.'

'I don't see why not,' replied the inspector. 'He's a very obliging chap and I shouldn't be at all surprised if he doesn't lend it to you. He was most helpful to us in our enquiries. In fact it was Markham who told us about George Johnstone and Charles Sedgley, our two potential victims.'

'Go on,' I said.

'He's a bit of an historian,' said Inspector Jarrett, 'and he had done some work on the Boer War. He had come across Johnstone's name in a magazine called *The Black and White Budget*. It was a popular periodical that covered the story of the war and Johnstone cropped up amongst a list of officers who had survived Spion Kop. That was a battle there,' he explained. Apparently he was a major at the time, but I have forgotten the details of his regiment or whatever. We checked it out of course and Markham was absolutely right.'

'And Charles Sedgley?' I asked.

'That was even easier,' replied the inspector. 'He was related to him. Mr Nicholas Markham is Charles Sedgley's grandson.'

CHAPTER TWELVE

1.

Saturday 15th April 2000

The week before the grand opening I met Tim Lewis and Mark Paddon-Browne for a pub supper at *The Green Man*. It was a chance to celebrate my moving in to Hamilton Lodge and to welcome Louise to the Drayfield team. The council had decided that she was to be based at Drayfield with special responsibilities for the Sedgley Room and the Smoking Room. In order to balance things up Tim brought his wife Helen and I asked Judy Fredericks.

'We've done great things since you gave me the Sam Emburey lead,' I said, 'so the least I can do is to buy you supper.'

I explained about Jane Ward, Bobbie Clarke and Nicholas Markham.

'He's a bookseller in Berwick,' I said. 'He's happy for us to hang on to the Visitors Book and he said that he would bring *The Drayfield Tray* down with him when he comes to the great event. We are hoping that he will donate it,' I went on, 'but that may be something of a forlorn hope as it's probably worth a bob or two.'

'What tray?' queried Judy.

'It's a piece of family silver that we've been searching for,' I said. 'We call it *The Drayfield Tray* and Mrs Vanstone has been after it for the display. We thought that it had been swallowed up by an antique shop in Edinburgh, but it seems that Nicholas Markham must have bought it.'

'So he's been invited as a thank-you?' said Judy.

'Partly,' replied Louise, 'but Mrs Vanstone suggested to Councillor Barnes that we should try and find a few descendants of the house party guests of 1897 and have a grand reunion, so to speak. I've suggested that we have a little 1897 exhibition case with a few pictures in either the Sedgley Room or in the Smoking Room and Councillor Barnes went along with it. The local press thought the idea of descendants being present was a marvellous idea as well. I thought we might be swamped but as it turned out there were surprisingly few candidates. Well, three to be exact, and one of those lives in Australia.'

'Why so few?' asked Helen Lewis.

'They'd all married each other,' explained Louise. 'So we were left with Nicholas Markham and the present Lord Rossdale. He has other relatives, but we only wanted one per family.'

'And Nicholas Markham?' asked Helen, 'is he descended from an 1897 guest?'

'Yes,' I said. 'I got that from the local constabulary. He is Charles Sedgley's grandson. That's probably why Jane Ward, Jane Emburey, that was, got him to help her with her thesis. The police thought that it was probably Charles Sedgley down the well, but when Nicholas Markham turned up that rather scotched the idea.'

'So as far as Sedgley guests are concerned we have Lord Rossdale and his wife, Nicholas Markham and Jane Ward, who wrote the thesis upon which your great work is based,' said Tim.

At that moment we were informed that our table was ready and so we adjourned to the restaurant. When I indulged at *The Green Man* with Tim and Mark we usually had our meal in the bar area, but on this occasion, with ladies present, we decided to push the boat out.

'Who was it who lived in Australia?' asked Judy as we got going with our starters.

'A lady who was descended from Sir Robert and Lady Carey,' answered Louise, 'and as she wasn't a Carey and lived in Queensland Mrs Vanstone rather lost interest. She couldn't see Councillor Barnes forking out an air fare.'

'Are you putting up your other guests?' asked Helen. 'I mean your Sedgley Room guests. Presumably the others will be off to the palace or somewhere equally grand.'

'Good gracious, no,' said Louise. 'We sent them a list of local hotels, but I understand that the Rossdales are staying with friends in London and Jane Ward is being brought by her daughter who lives in Bromley. I have no idea what Nicholas Markham will be doing but I am sure he will manage.'

'It's a pity that you haven't got a genuine Sedgley to come,' said Judy. 'Couldn't you find anyone?'

'There are no direct descendants at all,' I replied. 'At least in the male line. Frederick Sedgley, the last Sedgley to live at Drayfield if you don't count his daughter, Mrs Rutherford, had younger brothers and one had descendants. There are some males there, but we know nothing about them and they are not descended from anyone at the party. No, I think we will have to make do with Nicholas Markham. At least his mother was a Sedgley.'

With our main course, and most of us went for a chicken and mushroom pie that appeared to be the speciality of the house, the conversation changed.

'So no one has any idea about the bones in the well?' said Judy.

'Trail's gone dead,' I said indistinctly through my chicken. 'All we know is that the bones date from round about the turn of the century and the gun appears to be that owned by Elizabeth Howard, a guest in 1897. Every single one of those present has been accounted for, including Charles Sedgley and George Johnstone. Of course, Elizabeth Howard could have left her gun behind her and it could have been used a year or so later by someone else. That, I suspect, we will never know. More wine for anyone?' I asked, and waved around a bottle of rather pleasant Pinot Grigio.

'I think that Elizabeth Howard had a secret lover,' said Louise, thoughtfully. 'He probably jilted her so she met him at the ball they all went to on that Saturday. She lured him back to Drayfield Hall then shot him and put his body down the well.'

'With a team of assistants to move the railway sleepers and the tank,' said Mark scornfully. He held out his glass in my direction and I obligingly topped it up. 'The problem with all this is that the Beltons of this world lap up all the gruesome details and use it to sell copies of their newspapers. We should be feeding them facts and figures about the collection. Colleymores will be cashing in on all this free publicity. All those idiots who will be going along to see what was once a well and is now a site for selling garden compost will stagger away loaded down with pot plants and lengths of hose pipe without realising that a short walk away is the best collection of Dutch masters this side of Dulwich. It's a bloody disgrace,' and he stared mournfully at his empty plate.

'Cheer up Mark,' said Judy, sympathetically. 'He gave you a massive spread last week. Royalty orientated, but massive none the less. Mark my words, Mark,' she giggled, 'in a few weeks time you will be packing them in.'

After we had all gorged ourselves on liqueur ice-creams I suggested that we adjourned to Hamilton Lodge for coffee. The idea went down well and, having settled the bill, we walked the two hundred yards or so down the road to Hamilton Lodge.

'Welcome to my humble home,' I said, as I turned on the porch light and ushered them into my sitting room.

'Loo straight up the stairs and turn left,' I continued, as I headed for the kitchen. 'How many for coffee and how many for tea? We have Earl Grey, Darjeeling and peppermint.'

When I returned a few minutes later with a tray, I found Louise holding forth to Judy and Helen, Mark was obviously upstairs, and Tim was sitting on the window seat staring out into the garden.

'This must date from about the same time as the hall,' he said.

'Exactly,' I replied. 'Six months ago it was an utter shambles, but they have really done a decent job on it. Apparently before the war a married couple and three children lived here. Cosy must have been the order of the day.'

'We are going to hang James Hignett's plans in the Smoking Room,' said Louise, 'plus some rather good photographs we have had made. There are blow-ups of the six Edwardian picture postcards we were given, and enlargements of the pictures in the Visitors Book. They are being framed at the moment. And the other day we had another find. It's a postcard, but not one of the set of six. It must have been published locally and it is a photograph of Victoria Sedgley coming out of the church after her wedding to Colonel Rutherford. You can just make her out amongst a sea of top hats.'

'How do you know it's her?' asked Helen.

'It says *St Peter's Church, Barcombe* on the bottom,' replied Louise. 'And on the back the message reads *Miss Sedgley's wedding 14th May 1899, Love Florrie.* I wonder who Florrie was,' she added.

'You've got to hand it to her,' Tim said quietly to me, 'Louise, I mean, not Florrie. She's keen. Did you know she's trying to track down another sale catalogue at the moment? Chapmans did the sale, but they have no records from before the 1950s and Drayfield was sold in 1938 when the old lady died. At the moment we've only got Sir Denzil's copy that gives details about the pictures – prices they fetched and who bought them – but no extra information about furniture and fittings. Poor old Mark's a bit miffed,' he said as he sipped his coffee. 'He feels that everyone is talking about the Sedgleys and his pictures are not getting the attention they deserve. He was edgy in the pub when they were on about the skeleton, and when I asked him about the ghost he almost bit my head off.'

'Ghost,' I queried, 'what ghost? Tea and coffee up,' I called. 'The mug with cricketers on is the peppermint one, Helen.'

Tim looked a trifle embarrassed. 'The other day,' he started rather sheepishly, 'when I called in with the books for the Smoking Room I . . . I had a rather strange experience and that prompted me to ask Mark whether he had come across anything unusual since he had been living up at the hall. You remember that conversation we all had about Anne Boleyn and Emma Hamilton and things that go bump in the night.' He paused.

'Go on,' I said.

'Well, I thought I saw someone sitting in the corner of the room. I was in a rush so I plonked the books down on that central table and went back into the corridor. I then thought that I had better check up to make sure that whoever it was should have been there. So I went back in, and the room was empty. The chair that I thought the bloke had been sitting in was there, but there was no one in it. It was a bit creepy and I felt the hairs prickling on the back of my neck. Hang on,' he said suddenly, changing the subject. 'Here's Mark. I'll tell you more later.'

In the kitchen, about quarter of an hour later, Tim went on with his story.

'Of course whoever it was could have gone out into the corridor then either down past your office or in the other direction towards the shop and the door to the loggia. Either way he could have left the building, but it was all very strange. The more I thought about it the more odd it seemed. He wasn't dressed correctly either. It only registered later, as these things usually do, but I am almost sure that he was wearing an evening suit.'

2.

Monday 7th June 1897

Lady Violet Sedgley felt that the luncheon on the terrace was perhaps the most successful of the meals that she had organised for her guests in June 1897. The pall of gloom that had appeared to hang over the party the previous evening and the agitation that had attended the breakfast next morning had both disappeared. The young people seemed to be cheerful, Tilly Rossdale was no longer quarrelling with Charles and even Vicky had calmed down. The Rossdales exuded bonhomie and only Elizabeth Howard gave the impression of being slightly preoccupied. Lady Violet put it down to the absence of Sir Robert Carey.

'But then I always felt that he should not be invited to such a gathering,' she said to herself. 'Frederick really should keep friends of that sort for the Athenaeum.'

After luncheon the reason for some of the good spirits became clearer.

'Violet, my dear,' said Lady Rossdale, conspiratorially, 'I want a word with you.'

The two ladies walked over to where the rugs and basket chairs were still laid out under the oak trees. They sat down, accepted cups of coffee from Anderson, who was then waved away with gracious smiles, and Lady Rossdale began.

'I am telling you this in the strictest confidence. Not even Frederick must know. You will never guess, but Archie and Millicent Howard have formed an attachment. He spoke to Elizabeth Howard about it before luncheon, and he told us both while we had our jelly. Edward was positively flabbergasted. What with all the troubles we have been having with Tilly it was like a ray of sunshine. Of course Edward, being Edward, was initially annoyed that it had all happened without his knowledge, but he soon pulled himself together. There is no question of them announcing an engagement just yet of course, but they both seem very determined. I know one shouldn't think in such terms but she is an extremely wealthy young woman. The future of Felton will be assured and of course she is also very beautiful. Archie really is an exceptionally lucky young man.'

'Millicent Howard?' said Lady Violet in amazement. 'Surely, I mean we were all led to believe that she was on the point of announcing an engagement to young Giles Westerdale.'

'Apparently that was all her mother's doing,' said Lady Rossdale. 'As a result Elizabeth Howard has a slight problem. She has accepted an invitation on behalf of herself and Millicent to join the shoot at Westerdale in August. Millicent told her not to, but she wouldn't listen. Now she is going to have to withdraw with all the grace that she can muster. I don't think she is very happy about that, because the Prince of Wales will be there, but they can hardly arrive at Westerdale to greet a host who is also a broken hearted lover, can they? The silly woman has been telling too many people that her daughter will marry a duke, and now she is to marry Archie. The announcement will be made next week when we are all back in London. It really is most exciting.'

'Well, well,' said Lady Violet. 'Wonders will never cease. At least as far as Edward is concerned that will soften the blow of Tilly's rejection of Lord Brenton.'

'And do you know what Elizabeth Howard said when Archie admitted that he was in love with her daughter and Millicent assured her that she was determined to marry him? "Casca il mondo", that's what she said, "Casca il mondo". That's Italian, you know, for "the world is collapsing". What a funny thing to say. Millicent told me that it was said by Pope Pius when he heard the news that the Austrians had been defeated by the Prussians in that war back in the sixties. She's a very clever young lady, you know. One mustn't be fooled by her good looks,' and Lady Rossdale looked across to the terrace where her future daughter-in-law was drinking coffee and chatting to Victoria Sedgley.

Lady Violet followed her gaze. 'Oh I do wish Vicky would find someone soon,' she said, 'but at least we have been spared the horrors of that dreadful Johnstone man.'

3.

Friday 21st April 2000

Nick sipped a glass of dry white wine appreciatively and then turned his attention to his scampi. *The Green Man* had changed considerably since his last visit some thirty-five years earlier. There certainly had been no restaurant in those days nor had they offered accommodation. The invitation to the opening ceremony had been accompanied by a list of hotels and pubs in the area, and he had plumped for *The Green Man*, partly for old time's sake and partly because it was so close to Drayfield Hall. The write-up on its web site seemed satisfactory as well.

He had broken his journey south from Berwick at Birmingham, where he was able to visit a couple of shops on business, and thus had a fairly leisurely drive down to

Drayfield that morning. After booking in at *The Green Man*, he had revisited the church, then made his way to the hall as he had arranged. He was greeted by the Gallery Administrator, a youngish man whose boundless enthusiasm for the job in hand was immediately apparent. Nick was amused to see that he wore a waistcoat and sported a large pocket watch on a chain. For all the world he could have stepped out of *Alice in Wonderland* as the White Rabbit. With him was the Borough Librarian, a Mrs Vanstone, and their delight when he unwrapped what they referred to as *The Drayfield Tray* knew no bounds.

'The Visitors Book belongs here, so as I said over the phone, please regard that as an outright gift,' Nick said. 'At this stage the tray better be considered as a loan,' he went on, but I certainly won't be requiring it in the foreseeable future.'

He was then invited to sign a deed of gift, to cover the book, and a similar document that related to the tray. 'Insurance,' said Mrs Vanstone vaguely. Nick then followed them into the Sedgley Room and admired the work that had already been carried out.

'A most impressive display,' he said. 'I see you have left a space for the tray,' he continued, pointing to a cabinet beneath the portrait of Lady Violet Sedgley. He stared at the card headed *The Drayfield Tray*, which announced the fact that the tray was a wedding present to Frederick and Lady Violet Sedgley in 1874.

'The description of the heraldry must be correct,' said Mrs Vanstone with a smile, 'as my assistant took it from the Emburey thesis, and I understand that you were responsible for the heraldic input.'

'Guilty as charged,' replied Nick, 'and yes, the blazon is perfectly correct.'

'We must leave you to your own devices now,' said the White Rabbit, 'as we are up to our eyes in things to do before tomorrow. If you could get here by about two o'clock we will have plenty of time to run through the order of events before royalty arrives and I will introduce you to other members of the Fine Arts Committee and so on. We are planning to have a more informal drinks session here in the Sedgley Room at about six o'clock. The great and the good have to leave Drayfield by five at the latest. They're probably scheduled to have supper at Windsor Castle or something similar. Anyway, if they are the guests of honour from two thirty until five, you, Mrs Ward and Lord and Lady Rossdale will have our undivided attention from six onwards.'

'Lord and Lady Rossdale?'

'Yes,' replied the White Rabbit. 'We thought it would be appropriate if we asked the descendants of our 1897 houseparty to be guests at the re-opening of Drayfield in 2000, plus Mrs Ward, of course. You are descended from four of those present in 1897 and Lord Rossdale is descended from five.'

Nick nodded and thought for a moment. 'The future Colonel and Mrs Rutherford had no descendants, so that knocks them out as well as Frederick and Lady Violet. George Johnstone never married as far as anybody knows. What about the Careys. Did you draw a blank with them?'

'The line died out, at least as far as the males are concerned,' said Mrs Vanstone. 'Sir Robert and Lady Carey had a son and two daughters. The daughters never married, the son did, but his only son was killed in the Second World War. He had a daughter as well, but she married an Australian and as far as we know she is still living in Brisbane. It would have been a very long journey,' she mused, 'so we never sent her an invitation.'

The following morning Nick had an early and very light lunch then made his way across the park to Drayfield Hall. He entered the gardens by the door in the Tudor wall and there ahead of him he saw a middle aged lady in conversation with another woman and a young couple. He paused for a moment then carried on with his arm outstretched.

'Hullo, Jane,' he said. 'It has been a very long time.'

Jane turned, stared and with a broad smile on her face took a step towards him. She shook his hand and as she did so she leant forward and kissed him on the cheek.

'Nick, how lovely to see you,' she said. 'Bobbie, darling,' this is Nick Markham. Nick, you know Bobbie of course from years ago, but you probably don't know Lord and Lady Rossdale.'

Nick shook hands with all three.

'I remember you from thirty-five years ago,' he said to Bobbie, 'but you've changed a bit since then. Lord and Lady Rossdale, it is a great pleasure. We are distant relatives, you know,' he said to Lord Rossdale, who was a youngish man in his early twenties.

'John and Celia,' said Lord Rossdale with a sweep of his arm that included his wife. 'So I understand. Jane was telling me that we share a common ancestor in the fourth Lord Rossdale.'

Nick nodded. 'Yes,' he said. 'He was my great-grandfather and your great-great-grandfather. That makes us second cousins once removed.'

'Wow,' said Celia Rossdale. 'I can never understand all these relationships, but I'll take your word for it. And I'm so glad that you are wearing a blazer. I told John that a suit was far too formal for a summer afternoon function. Not that we've attended any art gallery openings before, still less one featuring royalty.' She motioned in the direction of her husband. 'I gather that you and John are going to have a starring role because you are family so to speak.'

'Nick is also the heraldic expert,' put in Jane. She turned in his direction. 'And why, may I ask, did you fail to inform me thirty-five years ago that you were a Sedgley? No wonder you could let me know that Charles Sedgley married Matilda Rossdale. I was so impressed at the time, as well. And that young man who appears to be organising everything. He told us that you also cleared up the mystery of the other missing guest, the elusive George Johnstone.'

'Ah,' said Nick, but he was interrupted by the arrival of tall, balding man in his early thirties, who was carrying a sheaf of papers in his right hand.

'Do excuse me,' he said apologetically, 'but Councillor Barnes asked me to catch up with you. I am Tim Lewis, a member of the Fine Arts Committee. Can I give you all a name-tag. Mrs Ward and Mrs Clarke, these are for you. Presumably you are Mr Nicholas Markham. This one is yours, and . . . Lord and Lady Rossdale?'

He looked inquiringly at John and Celia, who both nodded.

'Yours to command,' said John Rossdale. He took the proffered tags, pinned one to his lapel and was about to pin the other to his wife, when she prevented him.

'No darling, I had better do it,' she said, 'you'll only put it in an inappropriate place.' She took the tag and carefully fixed it to her dress.

'Now,' said Tim Lewis, 'if we could make our way round to the front of the house. They will arrive at about two-thirty when there will be introductions. Councillor Barnes wanted to break things up a bit, so he will welcome them and introduce them to the Mayor and his wife, the trustees and to Mark Paddon-Browne, the gallery curator. The countess will then say a few words and unveil the plaque, and Mark will then take the party inside and conduct them through the first three rooms. Meanwhile,' he went on carefully, 'Mrs Ward, Mr Markham and Lord Rossdale will come with me through the side door and we will make our way to the Sedgley Room. Richard Tregaskes, the Gallery

Administrator will have been introduced to them by Mark once he has completed his bit of the tour, and he will bring them all into the Sedgley Room and that's when the three of you will be introduced. Is that all OK?'

'What about my daughter and Lady Rossdale,' asked Jane.

'Oh, we'll mingle with the throng,' said Bobbie Clarke hastily. 'If that suits you?' she added, looking at Celia Rossdale for confirmation.

'Absolutely,' came the swift reply. 'We'll mingle.'

'Splendid,' said Tim Lewis. 'The idea is that the royal party will be followed by other guests, mainly councillors and one or two art experts, as they do their tour of inspection. Once it's over they will leave the house from the lobby door just behind us and there will be tea and cakes in the marquee over there. I understand that they will be pushing off between four-thirty and five, so then we can all relax, and we've got drinks in the Sedgley Room at six.'

'Synchronise all watches,' whispered John Rossdale to Nick as they all followed Tim Lewis along the terrace and around the side of the house to the front entrance.

'And don't forget, Nick,' said Jane. 'I want an answer to my question. Why exactly did you not tell me of your connection with the house. You've had thirty-five years to think up an answer, so it had better be a good one.'

4.

Saturday 22nd April 2000

All things considered I felt that the Saturday Grand Opening had been a great success. About two hundred people were there to watch the plaque being unveiled, about twenty, including our royal guests, did the Mark tour, and between forty and fifty had tea in the marquee. I even managed to make sure that every single one of the Fine Arts Committee was introduced. Councillors Barnes, Collet and Lathom together with Mrs Fitter before the ceremony started. Mark had his turn just after the ceremony finished. Mrs McGinty when the party reached the shop, Mrs Vanstone when it reached the Sedgley Room, and Messrs Davies, Hooper, Lewis and Sam Kendle in the marquee. Tim Lewis stage managed the movements of our other guests and I managed to keep the main party on the move.

Mark was slightly miffed that HRH seemed to spend as much time studying our macabre skeleton display in the Sedgley Room as she had the Van Mieris's in the Saloon.

'And you say that this pistol was owned by your great-great grandmother, who visited the house in 1897,' she asked Lord Rossdale.

'So I have been informed, ma'am,' he replied.

'How absolutely fascinating,' she answered. 'And nobody knows who this poor man is, or rather was?' and she studied the various photographs of the skeleton that had been supplied by *The Barcombe News* and *The County Times*.

'They have accounted for every single member of the house party at which Lord Rossdale's great-great-grandmother was a guest,' put in Jane Ward.

'At one stage we thought that it was Charles Sedgley, a nephew of the then owner of the house,' I explained, 'but when Mr Markham explained that he was Charles Sedgley's grandson, that rather exploded the theory.'

'Well it would, wouldn't it,' laughed her royal highness. 'And here we have all their signatures,' she said, as she moved to the cabinet containing the Visitors Book. 'This really is most interesting. I do congratulate you on a first class display,' she said to Mrs Vanstone, who looked suitably gratified. 'It would have to be good, though, to match up to those marvellous pictures. Mr Paddon-

Browne,' she continued, turning to Mark. 'Do let me know if you ever decide to sell the Metsu. If you do I will force my husband to make you an offer.'

We all laughed sycophantically, none more so than Councillor Barnes, who knew a thing or two about stage-managed applause.

Tea in the marquee rounded off a most satisfactory afternoon. Our royal guests, or rather the male half, seemed very taken with the young and extremely attractive Lady Rossdale.

'I gather that the Rossdales have something of a reputation for marrying beautiful women, or so I am informed by that lady over there,' he said. 'If that is the case then your husband has certainly kept up the tradition. Do tell me,' he went on, 'the daughter of the lady who owned the gun, the one who had a reputation for being a stunner, she was your husband's great-grandmother?'

'I think so,' replied Celia Rossdale, 'but I am afraid that until we arrived here a few hours ago we knew next to nothing about the family's forbears, dubious or lovely as the case may be. Our distant relation over there,' and she pointed to Nicholas Markham, 'is the expert, and this gentlemen', and she turned to me, 'wrote the Sedgley family booklet and knows all about the links.'

I acknowledged that this was indeed the case, but admitted that my work had largely been based on Jane Ward's thesis.

'Well, well,' said our interlocutor, but he was clearly far more interested in talking to Celia Rossdale than in cross-questioning either me or Mrs Ward, and so I eased myself into the background once again.

At five-fifteen, having spent at least half an hour more than had originally planned, our guests departed, assuring us that their visit had been well worth while.

'I think we can safely say that we have done our bit in putting the council on the map,' said Councillor Barnes to the mayor, as the royal car moved off down the front drive. 'Now, a short break to gather ourselves together and then I think we can treat ourselves to a drink or two in the Sedgley Room. It will be just the members of the Fine Arts Committee and half or dozen or so invited guests,' and the two men retraced their steps to the front hall.

5.

Saturday 22nd April 2000

'So,' said Jane, 'what is your excuse for never letting on that you were a Sedgley? And how exactly are you a Sedgley?'

'My mother was a Miss Julia Sedgley,' replied Nick. 'She was Charles Sedgley's only child. I was born in 1943 but both my grandparents died before the war so I never knew them. When I was introduced to you I was well and truly smitten. I thought that I would be able to feed you snippets of information, which would mean that I would always have an excuse to keep in touch. Then when it became unnecessary to spin tales the moment never seemed right. You didn't seem to want to know. I almost told you when we were in the Borders, but I didn't, and after that it became rather irrelevant.'

Jane smiled sympathetically. 'It's a long time ago now, isn't it?' she said. 'Presumably you bought the tray because of the family connections, and all that talk about Edinburgh antique shops was a load of hooey?'

'I'm afraid so,' admitted Nick. 'But tell me. Mrs Ward? Presumably you came back to England after your Italian jaunts and then married David? I suppose that it was David and not another Ward?'

Jane nodded. 'I am afraid that I am not very good with husbands,' she said. 'Victor ran off with an Italian signora and then David died on me shortly after we moved to Ludlow. That's twenty years ago. I'm better with children. I'm staying with Bobbie and her husband at the moment and I see a lot of Sam and his family. Incidentally, when he knew that we were likely to meet he told me to ask you whether or not you still supported Brighton and Hove Albion.'

Nick shook his head. 'It's Berwick Rangers now,' he said.

Jane laughed. 'From my limited knowledge of the Football League I doubt whether Sam will think that an improvement,' she said. 'Why on earth Berwick Rangers?'

'That's where I live,' explained Nick. 'I gave up teaching about ten years ago and moved back up north. My marriage had cracked up and I thought I would make a fresh start. I run a little topography and family history book shop. Well, it's more of a mail order business than a shop, but it keeps me out of mischief and I always was very fond of that part of the world.' He rummaged in his wallet and produced a small card.

Jane took it. 'Bluebird Books,' she read. 'Nicholas Markham, Quayside House, Berwick on Tweed.' She stared at the card more closely. 'That bluebird,' she said. 'That's the Sedgley bird, isn't it? *Argent a chevron between three sedge-warblers azure*,' she quoted.

'Excellent,' said Nick. 'I am glad that all my efforts were not wasted.'

'May I hang on to this?' asked Jane. 'You never know, I might even send you a Christmas card.'

'Do,' replied Nick. 'I am rather proud of them. You will have noted that the sedge-warbler is perched on a torse in the correct heraldic fashion. Perhaps I could have your address in exchange.'

Jane rummaged in her handbag and produced some little gold address stickers. She handed one to Nick who carefully peeled it off its backing and stuck it on to another of his cards, which he replaced in his wallet. Jane watched him, then said,

'Nick, prepare to be shocked. You know that skeleton that everyone has been talking about?'

'What about it?' replied Nick.

'Do you know where it was found? I mean precisely where?' asked Jane. 'Because if you don't I shall tell you. It was in a corner of the kitchen garden that is now being developed, and the well was covered over by railway sleepers and a large metal tank.'

'I don't believe you,' said Nick, and he started laughing. 'You do realise, don't you,' he continued. 'We might have fallen down that well and joined whoever he is, or rather was.'

'Give or take a few railway sleepers,' replied Jane, and she too began to laugh.'

'What on earth are you cackling about, mother?' said Bobbie Clarke as she joined them from across the room. 'Have you been overdoing the wine?'

'Old time jokes, dear,' replied her mother. 'Just talking over old times.'

'Who is that rather ancient individual over there,' asked Bobbie, pointing to a figure who was deeply involved in conversation with Mrs Fitter.

'James Hignett,' answered Jane. 'He helped me with my diagrams and plans, and he also did the family tree and the plans that are hanging in there,' and she pointed to the door leading into the Smoking Room. 'He seemed on very good form when we spoke to him earlier, wasn't he? Now Nick,' she went on. 'That young man over there, the one who is whizzing around like a demented bluebottle, he told me that you had cleared up the mystery of George

Johnstone, which is why he is no longer a candidate for the man in the well. Is that another secret you kept from me?'

Nick shook his head. 'No,' he said. 'I decided to sort out George Johnstone after you left me for sunnier climes.'

'Left her,' interrupted Bobbie. 'Was Nick an ex-boyfriend then?'

'Mind your own business, dear,' said Jane. 'Go on, Nick, we are all ears.'

'I checked the family out in Kelly's *Directory for Norfolk*, because one of those letters mentioned that he was a neighbour of the Rossdales, and sure enough a George Johnstone was listed as living at Nuttall Priory near Aylsham. That must have been our man's father. He rented the property from 1892 until 1899.'

'Celia,' called out Jane to Lady Rossdale, who was standing close by in conversation with Tim Lewis. 'When you have a second, come and tell us about Nuttall Priory.'

Celia Rossdale and Tim Lewis both turned round. 'Nuttall Priory?' said Celia. 'It's a school about twelve miles away from us. Why do you ask?'

'It's where one of the 1897 guests lived,' explained Jane. 'Nick is telling us how he discovered that this man couldn't have been the mystery figure in the well.'

'It's a ghastly Victorian building,' said Celia, 'so he certainly hadn't much taste. The school has quite a good reputation, though,' she added.

'Do you still live at Felton Park?' asked Nick with interest.

'Felton Park!' said Celia. 'Good gracious no. We live in The Dower House on the edge of the park. The house was sold by John's grandfather just before the war. It's now a rather plush hotel. We go there occasionally for dinner. In fact John proposed to me there. It was very romantic.' She blushed slightly, before going on rapidly. 'They still have some of our portraits on loan and long may they keep them there. They are quite awful.' She paused and looked round. 'Sorry,' she said, I'm changing the subject. What were you saying about Nuttall Priory?' and she turned to look at Nick.

'Oh yes,' he said. 'I came across a little booklet called *Nuttall and its Neighbourhood* that came out just after the war and it listed the various houses in the area and gave a potted history. Apparently the Priory was built by a London tea merchant in the 1860s and on his death it was let to various tenants. The Johnstones had it during the 1890s and they built the billiard room. There was the father, who made his money dealing in guano, and two sons, Clive and George.'

'What's guano?' asked Celia.

'Bird poo,' said Jane briefly. 'Go on, Nick.'

'George was commissioned into the Royal Welch Regiment, but had to resign his commission at about the same time as my grandfather, perhaps for the same reason, I don't know. Then the trail went cold. Until . . .' Nick looked around expectantly.

'Yes,' said Bobbie, 'until?'

'I discovered a magazine called *The Black and White Budget* that came out at the time of the Boer War. George Johnstone is listed as an officer who fought in the battle of Spion Kop. He was mentioned in dispatches and all that sort of thing. Then during the First World War he cropped up again, this time serving in East Africa. He died in 1916 on leave in London. Apparently he picked up some disease overseas that carried him off. He even merits three lines in *The Times*, which mentions his father as well, so there's no doubt that he's our man.'

'So he's definitely not down the well,' said Celia with finality.

'No,' said Nick. He's definitely not down the well. He's actually in Kensal Green Cemetery alongside his father. Interestingly enough the paper refers to his "somewhat chequered early career" so he was probably a bit of a bad lad back in the 1890s. That would explain Lady Violet's caustic comments in one of her letters. But as I say, bad lad or not, he was certainly alive and kicking long after the 1897 house party.'

'You are looking very thoughtful, mother,' said Bobbie. What's on your mind?'

'I've suddenly realised,' said Jane, with a tone of slight excitement in her voice. 'He must be my ghost, the man in the well, I mean. Do you remember that I said the house was haunted when we did our heraldic tour?' She looked at Nick. 'Well I realise now that it was a man in an evening suit that was doing the haunting. I didn't exactly see him but I was aware of him. Yes, that makes perfect sense, he must have been the man in the well and he had come back to haunt the house in which he had died.'

The others looked at her sceptically.

'I was once told that you were most likely to see a ghost when the balance of your mind was slightly upset,' said Bobbie. 'You know, drink, drugs, fear, love, that sort of thing. Well, I think that mother was so bowled over by Nick's proximity that she was fair game for wandering ghosts. Love was playing tricks on her.' She grinned wickedly at her mother.

'Bobbie, please,' Jane said weakly.

'I think we should change the subject,' said Nick. 'This is becoming extremely embarrassing.'

'I saw a television programme once,' said Celia. 'There were ghosts in it and they remained to haunt the place of their death as long as their bones were there. They were American airmen, you see. They had crashed during the war,' she explained. 'Once their bones had been removed the ghosts went away.'

'So our mystery man will be haunting the police morgue if he's haunting anywhere,' put in Tim Lewis, who had been following the exchange with interest. 'That's an absorbing thought, isn't it?'

'Nick,' said Celia, 'I must ask you. How on earth do you make money by dealing in bird poo?'

6.

Saturday 22nd April 2000

'I've suddenly realised,' said Mrs Ward, 'he must be my ghost, the man in the well, I mean.'

I pricked up my ears. I was talking, or rather listening to Councillor Barnes, who was involved in an animated discussion with Mark Paddon-Browne and Roger Collet. We were standing in reasonably close proximity to our guests, and I had been torn between listening to Councillor Barnes's views on the royal family and picking up snippets about Nuttall Priory and the Johnstone family. A moment later my attention switched one hundred per cent to our guests.

'A man in an evening suit,' said Mrs Ward.

I thought back to my experience at Drayfield that night in September. My ghost was a man in an evening suit as well. And so was the man seen in the Smoking Room by Tim Lewis. I was on the point of making my excuses to Councillor Barnes and joining the other group when I realised that he too had overheard the other conversation.

'I see that ghosts are replacing skeletons in conversational terms now that the wine is flowing,' he commented dryly.

'In my opinion,' said Mark firmly, 'when we hand in our copy for the papers we should play down the more melodramatic elements and stick to the pictures. Unless we are careful we are going to come across as a theme park with a speciality for the macabre and not an art gallery with an unusually fine collection.'

'I agree,' said Roger Collet. 'Poor Denzil would not wish to be upstaged by this Johnstone fellow, whoever he is or rather was.'

Councillor Barnes tapped the edge of his glass with his finger. 'We certainly don't want to come across a rival to Chessington Zoo, that's for sure,' he said. 'Image these days is everything and it is important that we get the right message across from the word go. It's a pity that Belton is so keen on the so-called popular side of things. He was banging on about a story with a human touch when he disappeared.'

'What do you think?' said Mark, looking at me.

I thought long and hard. I had suggested to Tim that we kept quiet about our spectre at least until after the opening. I rather agreed with Mark about the publicity, and Tim like me did not want to be saddled with a reputation as a man who was prone to seeing peculiar things. Besides, our gentleman in the evening suit seemed harmless enough and at least he didn't throw things. I made up my mind.

'Yes,' I said at last. 'We need a story about the pictures that will give Ken Belton his human touch, and I think I have just the one. You remember when we were laughing at the thought of Mark selling the Metsu to our exalted guests?'

My audience nodded.

'She liked it, but he was not quite so taken with it. His favourite was . . .'

'The Wouvermans,' put in Mark. 'He said that he liked pictures with a bit more action to them. He said that the Wouvermans was the one he would pinch, and he was quite taken with the idea that it happened to be the one that had originally hung in the library in the old days. In fact he said "in that case I won't send the van round tonight" or words to that effect. Yes, we could make something of that, I am sure.'

'Prince covets picture that came home,' I suggested.

'Royalty admires Dutch Old Masters,' said Roger Collet. 'A Metsu for her and a Wouvermans for him.'

Councillor Barnes thought for a moment. 'Well, I am sure that Mr Belton will produce a suitable caption, but we must certainly give him the story. Perhaps you could come up with a piece?' and he looked at me inquiringly.

'Certainly,' I said. 'I will write something down first thing tomorrow. Mark can double-check it and we can get it to Ken Belton by lunch-time.'

7.

Wednesday 25th May 1898
The Countess of St Boswells,
Ashurst Lodge,
Bridgenorth,
Shropshire
Derby Day 1898

My dearest Kitty,

It is indeed fortunate that your birthday falls at such a propitious time for I can hardly forget to send to you our usual greetings, although this year's Derby date means that I anticipate by nearly a week. Last year, as I recall, I was late. We will not mention anything as vulgar as age but suffice it to say that Frederick, Vicky and I wish you very many happy returns of the day in question.

This year's Derby gathering promises to be very different from that of 1897, with all its attendant problems. The younger generation are represented by Frederick's nephews, Freddie and Charles James, who stand in for Charles and that odious individual who caused us so much trouble last year. Charles is of course back in Africa and goodness only knows where Johnstone is. I neither know nor care, as long as it is nowhere near Drayfield. Mr and Mrs Archie Rossdale, she looks as lovely as ever, are here. Apart from the racing they are celebrating the anniversary of their first meeting. Then there is Lancelot Rutherford, who I may say seems to be getting along exceedingly well with Vicky, and who makes up the quartet of young gentlemen. As far as the ladies are concerned, Vicky and Millicent Rossdale have been joined by Clarissa King-Montagu and Lucy Fitzhenry.

Our, that is to say Frederick's and my, half of the party is made up as ever by the Rossdales, who are joined by George and Mildred Hunter, whom you will remember from Doncaster. I suspect that politics will not play such a large part in this year's conversations. Africa is no longer news, well not in the national sense, Sir Robert Carey and Charles are not with us and George Hunter lost all interest in politics when Lord Beaconsfield passed away.

The name of Tilly Rossdale has yet to be mentioned, but I mean to quiz Sybil Rossdale most severely on the subject after dinner tonight. I will add a postscript to this letter if I learn anything of note. All I know so far is that she too is in South Africa, but under whose protection goodness only knows. In my opinion Lady Sarah Wilson has much to answer for.

There will be no ball at Hensford House this year as Lady Clonkerry is not well. Instead we have been invited to Brenton Towers, where Lord and Lady Eversleigh are entertaining a large party. Croquet will as usual be played on Sunday afternoon and I will arrange that I am drawn to play with young Rutherford.

Today's racing was very exciting and this year Mr Rutherford drew the winner, Jeddah. When I spoke to Mr Rutherford after the race I said to him that it was his lucky year. He replied "I do hope so, Lady Violet". Now what do you think he meant by that?

We did not join HRH's party this year, but then we had no Elizabeth Howard with us. She apparently is back in New York and very much in the thick of things there, as Millicent Rossdale puts it.

I see that it is now time for me to prepare myself for dinner. Unless there is more news of Tilly R., I will send kind remembrances to all at Ashurst and sign off as,

Your affectionate sister,
Violet.

8.

Thursday 18th May 2000

A few weeks later Nick received a letter from Celia Rossdale.

Dear Nick, she wrote. *I recently visited Nuttall Priory. As I told you it is hideous and very appropriate for a man who made his money in bird droppings. I took the opportunity to call into the village church and met the vicar. He showed me a most interesting wall tablet which, he said, had been put up by a Miss Mabell Johnstone. According to him she was a Miss Marple like character who had lived in the village for centuries in a cottage covered in roses. Anyway, this tablet commemorated her father George, our bird poo merchant, and her two brothers Clive and George.*

George died in London in 1916 aged 41 of a fever he picked up while on active service in East Africa. I think you probably knew that. But what I am sure will be new to you concerns Clive. Apparently he went missing in Matabeleland in 1897, the year of the party. How about that? A great pity that Mabell died in 1958 (another wall tablet). Had she lived for another few years you could have cross-questioned her.

What a lovely time we had at Drayfield. Do pass on our best wishes to Jane, when you next see her, and we must keep in touch.
Best regards from John,
Love, Celia.'